The Rose of Rhodes

by

Lita-Luise Chappell

Published by
Templar Media
24881 Alicia Parkway #E-144
Laguna Hills, California 92653
www.templar-media.com

First Edition

ISBN 979-8-9869848-1-0

Front cover art by J. C. Johnson

Printed in the United States of America

Visit the author at www.LitaChappell.com

Dedication

This book is dedicated in loving memory of Vere and Sheryl Chappell, parents of my husband, with whom we traveled to Rhodes in 2005.

Vere Chappell was a Distinguished Professor Emeritus of Philosophy at the University of Massachusetts, Amherst. He enjoyed a long and successful career as a scholar, teacher and administrator, earning him many awards for his academic work, most notably for his studies of early modern philosophy on Descartes and Locke. Sheryl was an avid museum interpreter for twenty years at Historic Deerfield Village, a superlative cook and great companion on their many world travels. They were married forty-seven years.

Acknowledgments

There are several special people who supported me in this endeavor, and I am very thankful for their help publishing this book.

I would like to first acknowledge and thank my dear and long-time friend Sharon Sheinker, who is my webmaster, social media manager, first reader and copy editor. She is the star on my team and I will always be indebted to her for her constant support.

My thanks also go to my new neighbor Tyler Konishi, for sharing his knowledge about the cargo shipping business.

With all my heart, I am sincerely thankful for my husband, Vere Chappell, who did the final review and layout of this book. His continuing attention to detail, his ongoing encouragement, and his constant support have helped me become a better writer. And his unfailing love has graced my life with continual joy.

And last but not least, my sincere thanks to the many readers who have enjoyed the books I have written over the years—especially those who have written glowing reviews! I promise to keep creating works that both inform and entertain.

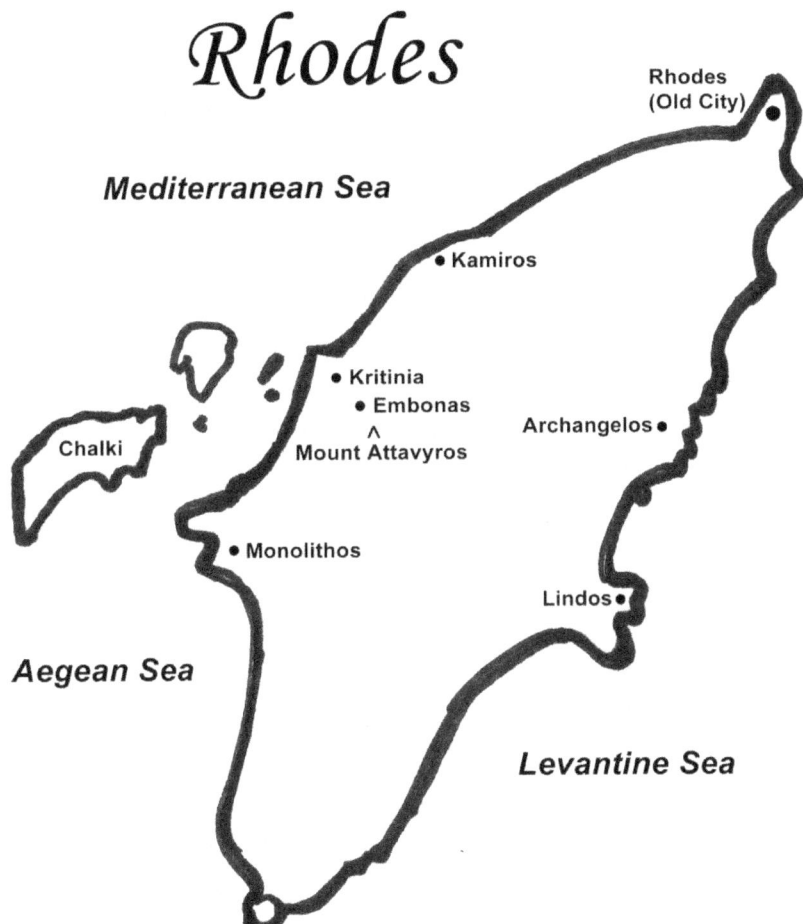

Rhodes

Rhodes
(Old City) ●

Mediterranean Sea

● Kamiros

● Kritinia
● Embonas
^
Mount Attavyros

Archangelos ●

Chalki

● Monolithos

Lindos ●

Aegean Sea

Levantine Sea

The Rose of Rhodes

Prologue

Port Town of Kirra, near Delphi, Greece
355 BCE

Amaltheia stood at the back door of her home in the village of Kirra, staring out over the small vineyard which had been planted three years before, and beyond where loomed Mount Parnassus. Her slender body leaned against the doorframe, while breezes ruffled her sleeveless long chiton at her ankles and her long black curls draped over her shoulders and shapely breasts. Her outward beauty, youthful looks, and partial smile were not what they appeared to be. She fondly watched her fifteen-year-old son Egan as he walked between the rows of vines examining the small clusters that were forming for the first time since their planting. Ordinarily, she would be feeling joy in anticipation of the coming harvest, but her heart was in turmoil. She was troubled by doubts about her relationship with her lover, the temple she prayed in, and the unrest within her country, all of which left her with deep dark feelings for what might be coming in the near future.

Kirra was a largely pastoral town on the coast of the Phocian region in central Greece. It was located on the Gulf of Corinth and stretched up to a singular point at the Malian Gulf. The area had a long history of invaders including the Persians, Spartans, Athenians, Boeotians, and Thebans. The region had become more important and valuable ever since the oracle at the shrine of Delphi had been established in the seventh century BCE, and that was the reason why the region was now involved in another war.

The house and vineyard where Amaltheia and Egan lived had been a gift from her lover soon after they met. Phayllus was a well-known general in the Phocian army. He had been promoted from the ranks by his brother Onomarchus to serve in the Third Sacred War against Thebes. The fighting had begun with Philip II of Macedon, the commander-in-chief of the federation of Greek city-states. Philip was angry with the leaders of Phocis because they were quickly gaining power and wealth due to the increased popularity of the Delphic oracle, and the area was strategic due to its commercial growth. But the reason the Theban ruler used for the fight was the newly-instituted rule that sacred land could not be cultivated. The Phocians had long settled and farmed the region, stretching from the Gulf of Corinth in the west all the way to the east where Mount Parnassus towered above Delphi. The entire countryside was dedicated to the Dionysian Mysteries.

When Amaltheia first met Phayllus, he swept her off her feet with kindness and generosity. He was from Amfissa, less than ten miles north of Kirra, and he had originally come to town to seek wisdom at the Temple at Delphi. He first saw Amaltheia on the street walking past him. He was immediately taken with her lovely face, aristocratic profile, slender hips, and long legs. His desire drove him to follow her and he would not let up until she told him her name. He finally learned that it was Amaltheia, which he rolled around on his tongue like a fine wine. She kept putting him off, for her heart was still filled with the memory of her deceased husband, but Phayllus endured.

When he returned to Kirra, he decided to rob the temple to fund his army. Among the items taken from the Temple of Delphi was a necklace of such splendor that he knew it would be the perfect gift to win her over, and it did. They became lovers, and he soon bought a house with some land and had the vineyard planted. But it all came with a price. She could have no other lover and she must wear the necklace whenever he was in town, but never when she left the house. It was for his eyes only. At the time, it seemed a small price to pay.

Phayllus, like his brother Onomarchus, was corrupt. Phayllus had forcefully taken the temple's donated treasures and then sold them in order to pay high wages for a mercenary army. Most of the shopkeepers in Kirra had experienced his unkindness, but they knew little of how much worse he had come to treat Amaltheia. Before meeting Phayllus, she had been a well-loved and respected widow in town. Her son came from her marriage to a man who had perished in the regional wars when Egan was only six. But things had changed between her and Phayllus.

Each time Phayllus came to Kirra that first year, it was entrancing for them both. All of his gifts seemed to seal the promise of him one day leaving his wife and moving full-time to Kirra to be with Amaltheia. But as time went by and he lost more battles than he won, his disappointment and frustration turned into aggravation and depression. With these feelings of inadequacy, he became jealous of lovers whom he imagined she must be having while he was away or on the battlefield. He was mistaken, for Amaltheia stayed true to her word. Consequently they began to argue, his temperament became spiteful, and their lovemaking became unpleasantly rough.

Egan was aware of all of this. He heard them arguing and her crying when she did not think anyone was listening. At first, Egan was thankful for his mother's happiness and their nice home. As time went on he began to dislike the way Phayllus was treating his mother, to the point that he tried to avoid him whenever the man was in town. They did not get along. He soon learned from his friends that Phayllus was the man who had raided the temple of goods, and was thought of as the tyrant of the town. When Phayllus would arrive at the house, Egan would leave out the back door, often hiking up the hillside behind their house.

Since Phayllus spent a great deal of time away on military campaigns, Amaltheia and Egan were often left alone. When Phayllus was gone, she would make her way to the Temple of Apollo at Delphi, bringing offerings of cloth and food to the priestesses, and donations of money for the temple whenever she could afford it. She was not oblivious to the knowledge that it was Phayllus who had robbed the temple. In the only way she knew how, her offerings were an attempt to try and set things right. On her many visits to the temple, she got to know one of the Priestesses of Pythia, named Myrine, and they became close friends.

Myrine was the oldest of the three Pythia priestesses who worked at the temple. She worked only two days a week, but the hours were long, from sunrise to sunset. When not at the temple, Myrine lived at the north end of Kirra, only a ten-minute walk from Amaltheia's home. The temple was a steep three-hour walk up from the town. Even though Myrine was just forty and married, she still had to dress in maiden whites when she worked at the temple. She also had to live separately from her husband, Timon, a merchant seaman who traveled from island to island in the Aegean Sea, so he was rarely in town anyway.

On one of Amaltheia's visits to Myrine at her home, Amaltheia confessed that Phayllus had won her over by giving her expensive gifts. Myrine was honest enough to tell her that any gift she received had probably come from the temple. It was then that Amaltheia realized the reason she had been told not to wear the necklace outside of their home. Amaltheia knew she could not return the necklace to the temple. If she did, at the very least, Phayllus would simply take it back, and then turn her and Egan out onto the street. No, she must always wear it at home to pacify him. She had no choice.

One night in 353 BCE, Phayllus was in town about to march with his army north. After the evening meal, Egan had gone to his room from where he overheard Phayllus and his mother arguing. Phayllus had been there for two days and was leaving the next day for Thessaly to fight in what would become known as the Battle of Thermopylae. Egan heard Phayllus threatening his mother, saying that she better stay true to him while he was gone or he would hear of it and make her life miserable. She tried to tell him that if he were there more often, he would see that she was always true to him. This angered Phayllus and he called her a liar.

Then Egan heard his mother being slapped. But Phayllus' anger did not end there. He began to violently rape her. Egan heard his mother's muffled cries through the ordeal, and winced at her pain, while a growing anger for Phayllus rose up within him. He wanted to run to his mother's aid, but Phayllus was a big man who could throw him across the room with one arm. When Phayllus was done, Egan heard his mother whimper, but then tell him with a pleading voice that she was immediately going to the Apollo Temple to pray all night for Phayllus' safe return. Good, he responded. He'd gotten what he wanted, and he needed a good night's sleep before leaving in the morning.

Egan was beside himself with anger. When he heard his mother leave, Egan ran through the vineyard and up the hill to get away. As he sat on a rock which overlooked the house, he hatched a plan. He would set fire to the house and vineyard and finally put an end to Phayllus as he slept.

Amaltheia had no intention of going to the temple to pray, for as she lay feeling weak from the fresh abuse, she began to form a plan of her own. When she left, she took with her the one thing that might save her and Egan's lives, and went directly to Myrine's home. Amaltheia told Myrine what had happened to her that night, and how she had suffered long under Phayllus' treatment. Myrine was appalled. Slowly, Amaltheia regained control of herself, and made known to Myrine her decision that she would no longer remain Phayllus' lover. After what had just happened, she was afraid for her life and feared that if the relationship did not end, she might also lose Egan. He had told her he hated Phayllus so much that he threatened to run away. Amaltheia shared her concern that before Phayllus made his departure in the morning he might take the one thing she had of any value, the necklace. He might want to take it from her and sell it to further fund his war efforts. After receiving it as a gift and wearing it for several years, she had grown too fond of it. She shared her plan that after Phayllus left, she was going to pack up her things and move with Egan to where Phayllus could not find them. As Phayllus owned the house and property, all she had of any value was the necklace.

With her plan revealed, Amaltheia took the necklace out of her bag and showed it to Myrine. Myrine knew exactly what it was. She explained that it was no ordinary necklace. It had a long history of giving the one who wore it youthful beauty and a life of luxury, but it would also cause the wearer harm and tragedy. That is why, after centuries of tribulation for many previous owners, it had been donated to the temple for safe-keeping. Amalthea acknowledged how it had affected her, for every morning she seemed to stay young, and her house was beautiful, but the necklace had also brought her a cruel and violent man. Still, she begged Myrine to hold on to it and hide it, so that after Phayllus left, she could sell it and that money would fund her move for a new life.

Reluctantly, Myrine took the necklace and promised to hide it in her home. Amaltheia begged to stay with Myrine through the night, but Myrine convinced Amaltheia that she should return home before the night was over. It might be more important to be home in bed when he left. For if he was killed in battle, could she ever forgive herself for abandoning him in their last hour together? Through her tears Amaltheia agreed, but it took several hours before she could steel herself to return home. She was still so upset that Myrine gave her a draft to calm her and help her sleep. Amaltheia drank the draft, returned home and fell immediately to sleep next to Phayllus.

Phayllus had heard her return very early and while it was still dark. He was racked with conflicted feelings. He was fearful that she would go to another man when he was gone. But he also loved her dearly, and because she had returned and was asleep next to him, she must still love him, and wanted to be near him on their last night together before he went off to war. But he could not get back to sleep, so when he heard her slumbering, he got up and dressed. He did not want to face her in the morning or endure her tears, so with his things already packed, he left. He wanted to go to his men who were camped just north of town. That way they could depart early on their march to Thessaly.

Believing that Phayllus was still inside, Egan finally worked up enough courage to set fire to the back of the house. Then he ran back up the hill to watch the flames take hold and leap to the vineyard. He was elated with his decision to set his mother free of the man. Once rid of the tyrant, he consoled himself that he and his mother would have a fresh start together, without the man he had long hated. Because he had been wandering the night in the hillside seething with anger, Egan didn't know that Amaltheia had returned and that Phayllus had already left.

Myrine woke before first light, still greatly concerned for Amaltheia, and decided to go to her in order to support her friend after Phayllus' departure. As soon as she left her house, she saw smoke spreading over the town. When she got closer, she was appalled to see that flames were engulfing Amaltheia's house. The townspeople had also seen the smoke and had come to help. Myrine convinced two men to run in and find Amaltheia and the boy. They managed to find Amaltheia through the thick smoke and flames in her bedroom and carried her out to Myrine, but the boy was not to be found. Myrine sat cradling Amaltheia in her arms, who seemed to still be drugged from the draft she had given her. But as the sun began to rise and the house was collapsing, Myrine realized that Amaltheia had passed away. At first, she wondered if Phayllus had caused her death before he left, because bruises were still present from his assault the night before. But then she realized it could have been the sleeping draft she had given her, which might have kept Amaltheia from being awakened by the smell of smoke and the sound of the flames. Racked with guilt, Myrine wept, believing that she had contributed to her friend's death.

As Myrine sat sobbing with tears, still holding Amaltheia, Egan, who had heard the townspeople calling his name, came running to see his mother lying lifeless in Myrine's arms. But what about Phayllus, he asked? Where was he? Myrine asked the same question of one of the townspeople, and found out that Phayllus had left with his men before daybreak. When Egan realized that his plan had failed and that his mother lay dead by his own hand instead of Phayllus, he ran away, mad with grief. A townsperson saw him throw himself into the sea. He must have drowned, for later that morning, his body washed up on shore.

Two days later, after Amaltheia and Egan were buried, Timon returned to see his wife and Myrine told him what had happened. Timon informed Myrine that he had heard Phillip was marching south to sack the area. He had hurried home to take her away. At first she said that she could not leave the temple, but he begged her to leave and she finally relented. So she gathered her things and safely packed the necklace to go with her. They traveled from Kirra to Athens by land, and then got on Timon's waiting ship and sailed to the island of Rhodes. Myrine decided that she would rededicate herself as a new priestess at the Temple of Apollo on the Acropolis of Rhodes and placed the necklace there for safe-keeping.

Chapter One

Chante stood at the sliding glass door to her backyard and couldn't help but laugh, watching Lucien dance across the patio with Melodia balanced on top of his tennis shoes. Time had gone by so quickly watching their little girl grow. Her baby fat was gone and she gained two inches in the last year. She had turned six years old in mid-February, and even now her personality was developing along with an exceptionally organized and inquisitive mind. Lucien and Chante had discussed whether they wanted to have another child, but they decided that they didn't want to be distracted from every precious moment of their daughter's development. Melodia displayed a wide range of emotions and wasn't afraid to speak about what she thought or how she felt. She seemed already half grown up and was easily able to occupy herself for hours on her own without getting bored.

They had witnessed her examine a problem, think about it, and then methodically arrive at an answer. For instance, a week before, Chante had watched Melodia arrange and rearrange her stuffed animals all in a row, calling out the sounds in conversations that each animal would have made. At last Melodia appeared to be satisfied with her final placement. The first item was a big red fish, then a small white rabbit, a tiny gray mouse, a medium brown beaver, a large orange cat, a medium yellow frog, a small brown horse, a large black dog, a small green parrot, a medium tan lion, and a small blue whale. She hadn't placed them according to her most favorite, or by their color or their size. When Chante asked Melodia why she had put them in that order, she said she put them that way because of the sound they made, from those that made no sound to those that made a big sound. Chante was astounded and could only fathom that she must have learned that from a children's television show.

For the last two and a half years the world had suffered through the pandemic. Because Melodia was a young child, it was an opportune time for Chante and Lucien to remain at home and raise their daughter. Lucien took very few jobs during that time to keep his family safe. Instead, he used the time to increase his knowledge of investigative work by studying many cold cases and taking special courses. By then, his father Gervais had retired from teaching at the university, but was still writing books. In order to better support one another emotionally, Gervais had moved out of his small house and into their larger home just outside Perpignan in southern France. With his retirement pay from the university and the royalties from his books, he was able to greatly contribute to the household so they could all live together comfortably and safely. With three adults who adored Melodia, her language and reasoning skills had developed quickly. They taught her both French and English at the same time, knowing both would be to her advantage when she grew older. She could also count to twenty and write those numbers. She knew the letters of her name and could print her name, Chante's, Lucien's and Gervais', but she preferred to call them Mama, Papa, and Grand-père. Melodia's vocabulary was growing quickly and she talked a lot.

By late July of 2022, the pandemic seemed to have waned, and Lucien was aching to get back to work. That's when he got a call from Monsieur Teniet, from UNESCO's

Paris office, asking if he was ready and willing to take on a new assignment. Teniet had previously directed him to work on Cyprus, and his accomplishment brought him recognition within the department of that venerable organization. Now there was a problem on Rhodes. An archaeologist working on a large dig site had unearthed many revealing artifacts, only to have some of them stolen. Lucien's assignment was to investigate the theft, find out why the items were stolen, who stole them, and if at all possible, have them returned. So the Reynard family decided to accept the opportunity and take the time to finally get away together, this time taking Melodia with them, for her first grand adventure.

There was much talk around the dining table about the possibilities of a trip to a place they had never been before. Melodia sat next to them drawing a picture. Chante had regained her figure quickly after giving birth, and as a busy mom, her long brown soft curls were more often now clipped up, though shorter wisps still hung around her lovely face and light brown eyes. Lucien had commented that she seemed more relaxed and happier as a mother, with a gentle and patient nature. Chante replied that it was because her love for Lucien had grown, and having Melodia had brought her so much delight. It was impossible not to be happier.

Lucien was as handsome as ever. His lean hard jaw, usually clean-shaven, had gained a small amount of stubble since he did not need to report to anyone. He also had a small but neat pyramid mustache that was new in the last year. He had gained a couple of pounds from eating many home-cooked meals, but he went jogging in the neighborhood to stay in shape. He was still tall, his hair still dark, and his eyes still had that sharp blue clarity. Chante was still captivated by him, and just looking at him could produce a gentle flurry of elation within her.

Gervais was much the same man he had been six years before, only his hair was grayer and the prescription of his glasses was stronger. He looked every bit the retired professor in his still-preferred corduroy pants, plain shirt and cardigan sweater with a shawl collar. His English had improved as well. In fact, he often preferred to speak it so Melodia would learn it by listening to him. He still spoke French to Lucien when they were alone and when he got excited or frustrated, but he spoke more English when Chante was around.

As usual, they each had their laptops in front of them, prepared to discuss all aspects of the upcoming trip.

"I hope to see something of a Templar past on Rhodes," began Lucien. "They were there, weren't they?" His love for these past warriors had not waned.

Gervais had to enlighten him. "Very few Templars went to Rhodes, son. After the fall of Acre in Jerusalem in 1291, a handful of Templar Knights went more directly to Cyprus. Then, with the call to arrest all Templars by order of King Philip IV of France in 1307, any Templars who had escaped capture were scattered across Europe. In 1310, it was the Order of Knights of the Hospital of Saint John of Jerusalem that went to Rhodes. They were commonly referred to as the Hospitallers, because they built hospitals. With the official dissolution of the Templars in 1312, any Templar who wanted to elude capture but continue God's work shifted to healing the sick. They would have gone to Rhodes and joined the Knights of Saint John, and became known as the Knights of Rhodes."

"All the more curious," mused Lucien. "Then I will want to learn about the Hospitallers, explore their building sites, and examine their history."

"Then you will find them of interest, as will I. Just don't get too carried away when you have a primary task of an investigation."

"Don't you worry. Believe me, that is much on my mind."

Chante was more concerned with where they would stay. "I don't particularly want to stay in a big hotel this time. I would prefer something on a smaller scale, maybe even a place that has a private enclosed garden or yard where Melodia can play outside." Chante had already done a search and shifted her computer toward them to show what she had found. "Something like this. It's a B&B in the old town where I can walk to a grocery. There are nearby restaurants and I won't need a car."

They were impressed. It was very pleasant, with a medieval wall backing a private garden, no busy streets nearby, and breakfast was included. They nodded their approval and Gervais got the phone number and promptly called them. The preliminary questions were asked: when would they be arriving, what kind of room did they want, and how long would they be staying?

With the phone on speaker, Gervais looked to Lucien to answer that one. "Would it be possible to book two rooms for one month?"

"Let me check the bookings," the woman said. "So that would be from August 1st to August 31st?"

"Yes, please. I'm not sure if my work will require me to be there that long, but I can let you know as soon as possible."

The woman was pleased to have them as guests for so long, and asked if they had any specific requirements besides a small bed added to the master, and asked about their breakfast food preferences.

After they hung up, Lucien booked their flights. His would be reimbursed by the culture department, and the others, they would cover. Then they got busy planning what they would pack, so they would be ready to go in four days. Before they knew it, the day had come.

When the family arrived in Rhodes, they were met by their B&B host, Nils Lindgren, and he took them directly to the B&B to meet his wife, Gala. Nils and Gala were a middle-aged Swedish couple who had come to Rhodes in 2001, bought the place, fixed it up, and had been open for business since 2002. Gala was in her late forties, Nils was older by twelve years, and they had been happily married for twenty-two years. Both were blond with short hair, but Nils had some streaks of white. They had reconstructed the old ruins of a house with modern conveniences, and decorated it appropriately with medieval touches. It felt very comfortable and was nice and quiet, off the main streets.

Gala showed the Reynards their rooms, while Nils carried up their suitcases. There were four upstairs bedrooms and two bathrooms. The Reynards shared a bathroom between two rooms at one side of the stairs, which was fine as they were used to doing so at home. The other two rooms, open to additional guests, shared a bathroom in the hall. The owners had their private living space downstairs, facing the backyard. Chante, Lucien and Melodia had the largest room at the end of the hall which faced both the backyard garden and the narrow street in front. A small sitting area had been curtained off with a twin bed for Melodia, whose window overlooked the front of the building. When she ran to her bed and looked out the window, she was very happy to see a cat across the lane in the upstairs window of another home. Gervais' room was next door and his overlooked the backyard. They were all very happy with their accommodations.

They were told to come downstairs once they got settled in, to see the rest of the B&B. On the way downstairs, Gervais commented on how nicely the house had a blend of the old with the new. Gala heard them coming and called for them to come through the building to the main sitting room. The room had a dark plank ceiling with carved wooden posts that held up heavy crossbeams. A large stone fireplace was at one side of the room, and several dark maroon stuffed chairs were comfortably arranged. Adjacent to that room was a more modern room for dining, with a bank of windows that let in lots of light, and several square tables that were covered with white cloths for breakfast service. Then Gala led them out a back door to a flagstone patio where more small tables were set up. They had their option of dining inside or out on the patio for breakfast. Potted plants separated the tables, and all along the edge of the high medieval stone wall were plots full of flowers. A bougainvillea had been trained up the wall in the far corner and overflowed with a profusion of fuchsia-colored blooms. Along the beds were planted a mixture of pink hydrangeas, lavender-striped clematis, sprays of white jasmine, and ground-level pink impatiens lined the edges. There were also bushes of the Rhodian Rose. Filling in between were plumes of pinkish feather grass. It was positively a perfect hidden jewel of a garden.

"Your garden is so beautiful," commented Chante.

At that, Melodia went to the rose bush to smell the flowers.

"Be careful," Gala said, "don't prick your fingers. The roses have thorns."

Since it was such a pleasant afternoon, Gala bid them to sit and enjoy the garden while she brought some refreshment. A few minutes later, she reemerged with two round plates piled with sweet things, and Nils followed with a tray of drinks. He offered milk to Melodia and coffee to the adults.

Melodia was the first to notice and pointed to the pastries covered with honey. "What are these?"

"Those," explained Gala, "are called *katimeria*. They are like a donut, and have been soaking in honey all morning." She looked at Melodia. "Would you like one?"

"Yes, please," said Melodia, bouncing her head in several nods.

"And these," said Gala, indicating the second plate, "are called *takakia*. They are filled with a ground nut mixture with cinnamon, clove and nutmeg. Please, everyone, help yourself."

With their mouths full, the Reynards gave Nils the opportunity to speak. "So welcome to Rhodes! Have any of you been here before?" They shook their heads. "Well, it is a place filled with history, and still has some mystery to it. You surely noticed the old part of the original building inside, but that high back garden wall of bricks is part of the old Byzantine wall that encircled this lower part of the old city. It was one of the reasons we were most attracted to this property."

"Was there anything original in the kitchen?" asked Chante.

"No, not at all, that had to be completely gutted and rebuilt, but interestingly enough, we did find an ancient iron griddle buried in the floor. We cleaned it up and it hangs on the wall in the kitchen. It was probably used to cook flat cakes on."

There was a pause and then Gala suggested they pick up a city map from the front room, and there were other fliers there with information on what else to see in Rhodes.

Nils added, "A month is a long time to visit Rhodes. You mentioned on the phone that you are here for work. May I ask what that is?"

Lucien smiled and swallowed the last of his honey cake. "Yes, I'm a detective who specializes in investigations of stolen archaeological items and the illegal moving of those items across international borders. I work under the direction of UNESCO, and have been assigned to investigate some artifacts stolen from the Rhodes acropolis site."

"If there is anything I can assist you with in Rhodes I would be happy to help. We speak Greek if you need an interpreter. The local dialect is a little different from the Greek on the mainland. It has a somewhat sing-song rhythm with heavy Italian and Turkish overtones."

"We understand that English is widely spoken. But thank you for offering. Your assistance may come in handy. I'll let you know. I've promised Chante that we would divide our time between work and play. After being largely cooped up at home during the pandemic, we wanted to once again travel as a family, this time with Melodia."

"You're in a good and safe place to begin, here on the oldest part of the island. Most pandemic restrictions have been lifted. Most of the sites, museums, and restaurants are within a two-mile walking distance and we have lots of recommendations for dining. But feel free to wear masks in crowded places."

Gervais finally spoke up. "Since we will be here for some time, one of the things we would like is to get to know your island. What we could use is a private guide."

"Of course. I know a wonderful tour guide. She's a history teacher during the year, but also works as a guide during the summer. I'll give her a call and see when she is available. When would you like to have me book her?"

Gervais looked at Lucien, as he knew his work came first.

"Perhaps the day after tomorrow. I'll need to meet tomorrow with the other people involved with my case."

"Very well. I would recommend first a walking tour, and then she can take you on a driving tour outside the city to anywhere on the island that you would like."

"Sounds good, thank you," responded Lucien. "I think we will want to relax a bit, and then we'll go out for an early dinner."

"Very well. And again, welcome to Rhodes."

They all rose and bid good afternoon.

Chapter Two

The next day was a clear Monday and a lovely morning on the back patio. Breakfast was presented with a full accompaniment of fragrant baked bread, sweet butter, three jams to choose from, soft-boiled eggs in their shell, some smoked ham, fresh-squeezed orange juice, and coffee. The Reynards were delighted.

As soon as breakfast was over, Nils was happy to drive them over to the acropolis, going along the same way one would walk, up the steep path from the city. By foot it would take twenty minutes, but by car, half that time through busy traffic. He dropped them off at the public parking lot near the top on the east side, and they walked along a fenced-in area until they found a gate where they could enter. The path continued further down the slope heading north, where the rest of the tourists entered through the lower site. The plateau where they now stood was large, but they could see a few people working on the site, obviously part of an archaeological team.

At the gate, Lucien waved over the guard on duty. With bulging muscular arms, he looked more like a club bouncer. He wore a tan-colored uniform and matching tan cap. The man's face was wide and suntanned, with a dark beard.

"*Kaliméra*. I'm looking for Professor Sander Ekonomos. Can you direct me to him?"

"May I ask what business you have with him? He is very busy."

"I'm detective Lucien Reynard. I'm here to meet with him about the stolen artifacts."

The guard took a few seconds to stare at him and the others in his party, and then responded. "Only you can enter. No children or families allowed."

Chante stepped forward to protest, but Lucien held her back and responded. "That's fine. Just let me speak to him." Then he turned to Chante. "I'll be right back."

Reluctantly, the man unlocked the gate and let Lucien through. "Be careful where you step and follow me." He relocked the gate once Lucien was through.

Lucien followed him up to the top of the hill where the team was working. A man was bent over with his back to them. "Professor, someone is here to see you."

Professor Ekonomos was kneeling on the ground wearing long olive green pants, a white shirt and a tan bucket hat. Lucien saw that he was in his mid-fifties, with brown hair and a thick mixed brown chevron mustache. A white kerchief was tied around his upper forehead under his hat, and his eyes were honey brown.

"*Kaliméra*, Professor Ekonomos. I'm Detective Lucien Reynard from the culture department at UNESCO."

All of a sudden, the professor was on his feet and pumping Lucien's hand. "Hello, *Kaliméra*. It's very nice to meet you. Thank you for coming."

The guard walked away, a little perturbed by the professor's happiness upon seeing his visitor.

"Not at all. Happy to help." Lucien looked at the guard walking away. "I think your guard was put out a little by my coming. He seemed a bit curt."

"Oh, never mind him. That's Daikonos. He has to put up with tourists trying to sneak in all the time."

"Sir, if you don't mind, my wife and father are at the gate. They are actually part of my research team. My father is a European researcher and discovered the identity of the

Byzantine princess in Mystras, and my wife is also a researcher, and our project writer. I need them to come in as well, so I won't forget anything important. We need to look at the site and the location where the items were found. Mister Lykaios stopped them from entering."

"Yes, yes, of course. I'll walk over with you to let them in."

When Gervais saw the professor and Lucien coming toward them, he bent down, picked up Melodia and held her in his arms. He said to Chante, "I'll carry her while you take notes."

"Mama, why does Grand-père need to carry me?" asked Melodia.

"Because children aren't allowed unless they are held," she explained. Then Chante pulled out her notepad and pen from her bag.

The guard watched the professor unlock the gate and admit them, then he turned and walked in the other direction down the hill.

Lucien introduced the professor to his family, and the professor slowly walked them across the field to where he had been working.

"This entire acropolis dates back to at least the third century BCE, and quite possibly before. Even in its early days, Rhodes had a large population that flowed over these eastern slopes, now called Aghios Stephanos after Saint Stephen. Originally, there were stepped terraces and retaining walls that were filled with fields of grain and groves of trees. The name of the hill was changed to Mount Smith, after Sir Sidney Smith, an admiral in the English navy. In 1802, he built an outpost on the eastern edge in order to keep an eye out for any ships of the Napoleonic fleet entering the harbor. But this area was not fortified, because there were too many ancient public buildings, underground areas, sanctuaries, and temples.

"There were two previous archaeological digs. The first excavations were organized in 1912 by the Italians and their Archaeological School, and the second in 1946 by the Greek Archaeological Services. A lot of information was gleaned from both excavations. They found a mixture of Byzantine, Christian, and village remains, but they only scratched the surface of what lay beyond their few dig pits and trenches. After the Greek team ran out of money, an archaeological area of just over three square acres bordering the upper west edge was set aside. Building and construction were prohibited, allowing any future archaeological teams access to the untouched ground, which was fortunate for us."

Now they stood under the three large columns and tumbled walls of the Pythian Temple of Apollo. At the far side they could look over the city to the west harbor far below. With the sky clear, the view was expansive and they could see all the way to Turkey.

"The Temple of Pythian Apollo was once considered the guardian of the city, with a single row of pillars on all sides. The remains were much smaller in size when compared to other temples found on the rest of the site. The northeastern part of the temple suffered quite a lot of damage during the Second World War, due to artillery gun emplacements and bombing of the island. Extensive restoration work was needed, and in 1996 further restoration work was done. Originally, four columns held up a carved lintel that rested on capitals."

Professor Ekonomos then walked them to a further leveled side of the hill to the southeast, where the remains of a long narrow horseshoe stadium was open to the north. He pointed out the curved outline of the structure.

"This is the old stadium. It was excavated by the Italians and found to be one *stadion* long, a measure of length equal to six hundred feet, and the origin of the

English word 'stadium.' What survives is the curved end of the stadium, called the *sphendone,* as well as the starting blocks for the athletes, the seats where the officials sat, called *proedries,* and some lower seats. It was here that athletic competitions once took place."

He pointed to the east where there was a very large area of ruins. "Next to the stadium was the gymnasium where all the athletes trained and prepared for the Pythian Games held here, or they went to Delphi for the Pythian Games held there."

The professor then led them to the west side of the ruins. "In this area a refreshment pavilion was discovered, measuring a little longer than the length of the stadium, in order to service the hundreds of people who came to the acropolis, and it was an important area where works of art were put on display."

He continued to lead them to an area just northwest of the stadium. "Here you can see part of the restored *odeon.*"

When Lucien took on a questioning look, Gervais explained. "An odeon was a small theater structure where the ancient Greeks would have listened to poetry competitions and singing performances. The word 'ode' is the same in many European languages, meaning 'singing place'."

"Yes, that is true," added Professor Ekonomos. "It was also where rhetoric lessons were given, and famous orators came to speak. It held up to eight hundred attendees." They walked to the north of the stadium, where the hillside began to slope down, and he continued. "A library once stood here, containing many of the works spoken at the odeon, and documents of the events were stored."

Further down the slope of the hill, heading toward the north of the acropolis area and overlooking the water to the west, was another partial temple.

"Here is what remains of the Temple of Athena Polias, and further is the Zeus Polieus Temple, meaning that both gods belonged to the city-state of Rhodes. Both are oriented east-west and had double Doric porticoes on all four sides. Some of those columns and their capitals with partial lintels can still be seen. It's where treaties were kept, as they were thought to be as sacred as the gods."

As he was explaining this, he walked to the eastern edge of the temple layout and pointed to the four ruined squares of stone to the northeast.

"In this direction is what remains of four separate Nymphaeums. They had an entry one level above ground, which opened to a central courtyard. And one floor down there was a planted garden. These stone-cut steps descend down into cave-like structures with many passages, where water cisterns flowed for bathing and relaxation. Ancient historians say that there were niches in the walls holding statues for artistic decoration and worship.

"Reconstruction work was also done to them in the 1960s and 70s, and again in 1996. Then to the west of the two most northern Nymphaeums, a very long building running north and south was discovered, which was an ancient Hellenistic *stoa*. This was an ancient covered walkway that would have adjoined a large building. It was held up by two rows of columns that supported a roof, but was open to one side. It was a place where locals had offices, shops and markets. At the farthest northeast terrace was an *Artemision*, where a small ruined temple was dedicated to the worship of Artemis."

At this point, he turned back to the southern area of the Temple of Athena, where long troughs of a dig were surrounded by a flimsy plastic orange fence. Two archaeologists were working there.

"This is all that is left of the Temple of Athena, just a few column bases. It is my theory that these are the remains of what was once a formal colonnade linking the Temple of Athena to the Temple of Apollo on the hill. This walkway between the two temples, as you can see, is where we are digging a long pit." He walked to a particular area and pointed to the ground. "It is along this trench where the bulk of the artifacts we discovered were found."

Lucien was glad to finally get to the point of their tour. "When you unearth items, where do you clean, document and store them?"

"We are required to house all finds onsite in a secure locked building, which is near the Temple of Apollo where we began. Guards patrol the site day and night."

"Do you have photographs of the missing items?"

"Yes, I have copies, and our photographer also has a set."

"How soon were the items taken after they were put into the secure building?"

"Less than thirty days after they were found."

"How would anyone even find out about anything discovered at the site?"

"That's the most surprising thing of all. The information is not publicized."

"What kinds of items were found?"

"There was a small bronze statue of the Colossus of Rhodes, two bronze spearheads, a broken sword handle, a ring, an earring, remnants of a gold chain, a bracelet, and seven coins. The first set of items seems unlikely to have been taken for the small amount of metal, but numismatic collectors would have found the coins of value. I'm afraid that is about all I can tell you."

The professor walked them back to the gate and unlocked it for them to exit.

Lucien pulled a card from his wallet. "Here is my card with my phone number and email. Can I also have your contact information so I can reach you?"

Chante noted his cell number in her notes.

"Thank you, Professor Ekonomos," put in Chante. "We very much enjoyed your tour and look forward to discovering what happened to your items."

The professor shook their hands and then lightly touched Melodia's nose. "And you, young lady, were the perfect little princess. Are you always this quiet?"

Chante answered for her. "Oh no, she talks up a storm when given a chance. I think she is just overwhelmed by all that you have showed us."

"Thanks again," Lucien chimed in, "I think we should get Melodia out of the sun and have some lunch."

They waved their goodbyes and turned to walk down the street to the old medieval city and their B&B.

That evening, the three of them began their online research. Chante and Gervais delved into the history of Rhodes and the Pythian Games, how each of the ruined buildings were once used, and the value of ancient Greek coins. The professor had emailed them a list of the items that had been taken. The key question Lucien had was, who exactly were the few people that knew about the finds? He sent back an email asking for a list of the people working at the site, along with their CVs.

Chapter Three

Nils let the Reynards know that their tour guide was available and would be arriving at 9:00 a.m. the next morning to take them on a walking tour of the old city. Lucien and Gervais decided that they would head to the Archaeological Museum later that afternoon.

On Tuesday morning, Chloe Selinofoto arrived at the B&B. The Reynards were still having their breakfast on the patio, so Nils took her back to meet them. She appeared to be in her late thirties. Her long straight black hair was partially swept up from her face and secured with a barrette at the back of her head. She had a genial smile and dark chocolate brown eyes. A simple dark blue dress fit her slim body and she wore blue flat shoes. Her neatness and small pearl earrings lent professionalism to her appearance. Introductions were made and she sat with them to discuss what they would like to see and do on the island. Lucien told her they were interested in history, the Hospitallers, and museums, but they also wanted to balance the intellectual with fun things to do for their daughter, Melodia.

Chloe turned to Melodia. "What do you want to see?"

Melodia got excited. "I want to see birds and cats, ponies, deer and turtles. Are there any elephants here?"

"No, but I can show you all those other animals, and more."

That seemed to please Melodia. They could split the day. In the mornings they were up for being tourists, but in the afternoons Lucien needed to focus on his investigation. Although that might need to be reversed depending upon what came up in his work.

"Well, you make my work easy," Chloe responded. "I'm a history teacher at the local high school, and in the summer I enjoy sharing the island with visitors. If you are up for it, since it is a nice day and still cool this morning, I would recommend a walking tour of the old city. On other days, I can take you on half-day driving tours to other parts of the island."

They briefly discussed her fee and her schedule.

"All of that sounds great, Chloe," said Chante. "If you just give us a few minutes, we'll be ready to leave."

When everyone had assembled in the living room, Chloe led them out the side door and down the small street. Since their hotel was in the southwest portion of the old city, she led them north two blocks to their first stop, the old municipal Turkish baths. She paused and indicated the pink and tan building before them.

"I know the building from this side isn't much to look at, but it is one of the last standing Turkish baths in Rhodes, called the Great Hammam. It is quite large inside and was built in 1558 when the city was under Ottoman rule. Originally it was open only to men, but it has since been converted with an additional entrance for women and other genders. The baths were added on to by different Muslim rulers and consequently took on different names, such as the Mustafa Baths, the Yeni Hammam, and the Baths of Suleiman. Inside, the floors and walls are of marble, and there are graceful fountains. There are skylights that allow light to flow down, highlighting bathing and resting areas, and domes soar up several stories high. One can enjoy being washed by special attendants, undergo exfoliation, or have a massage. Let me know, Chante, if you want to go, and I will go with you.

Now let's go to a place where you can enter and actually look around."

She walked them down a couple of blocks to the Palace of the Grand Master of the Knights of Rhodes. When they reached the towering main gates at its entrance, Chloe paused to give them a bit of history.

"On the original site of this palace stood a temple to the god Helios, the Greek deity of the sun, who raced with his horses…"

Melodia interrupted. "Are there horses inside?"

"Shush, Melodia," said Chante. "She's telling a story."

Chloe continued with large arm motions. "No, no horses, Melodia. Helios rode his chariot every morning from the east and ended his ride every day on the other side of the sky. Then he sailed around the ocean in a huge cup, back to the other side of the earth to begin a new day. Helios was designated the primary deity by Emperor Julian, sometime in the mid-fourth century. Eventually Helios became known as Apollo, although Apollo is more the god of light.

"By the seventh century, the temple had fallen into ruins, and the Byzantine Empire constructed a citadel in its place. In 1096, while still in Jerusalem, the Knights Hospitaller of Saint John of Jerusalem, a Catholic order devoted to taking care of the sick and protecting pilgrims, were forced out of the Holy Land by Islamic forces. When the First Crusade was begun in the same year, many also became fighting knights. The Hospitallers first went to Cyprus, which had its own set of political challenges. With the need to establish their own domain, their Grand Master, Guillaume de Villaret, decided to look at Rhodes. In 1310, they gained not only the island of Rhodes but several others. When the pope dissolved the Order of the Knights Templar two years later, their property was turned over to the Hospitallers. With this influx of wealth, the Hospitallers turned the citadel into their new headquarters and made it a palace for their Grand Master and a place of administration. In the fourteenth century, the Knights Hospitaller built the Hospital of Saint John of Jerusalem, along with other fortifications on the island. In 1481, the island had a strong earthquake, which killed 30,000 people and afterward many parts of the palace had to be rebuilt.

"In 1522, Turkish troops of the Ottoman Empire besieged the palace and captured Rhodes. They used the palace as their fortress, and part of it became a prison. They held the island for almost four hundred years. In 1856, a fire started when lightning hit an ammunition depot, causing a huge explosion that left the palace in ruins. The palace remained that way until the Italians came and occupied the island during the Italian and Turkish war, between 1937 and 1940. The Italian architect Vittorio Mesturino was hired to reconstruct the palace. After the building was completed, the Italian king Victor Emmanuel III made it his holiday residence for a few years. And for a very short time, the fascist dictator Benito Mussolini came here, but once he was dismissed by the king, he never returned. In 1948, after the Second World War, Rhodes was ceded to the Greek government, and the palace became a museum. This palace and the city's entire medieval old town have been designated as a UNESCO World Heritage site since 1988. Now let's go inside."

Once they obtained tickets and entered under an archway between two huge round towers, Chloe had more to say. "You are now standing in the castle's interior courtyard, which holds many Greek and Roman statues. Surrounding this courtyard runs a shady arcade with stairs that lead to the rooms. The palace itself is over six and a half thousand square meters. That sounds large, but not all of it is open for viewing. It must be remembered that this is still a stronghold, surrounded by three separate walls of stone, and to protect it a bastion still stands on the west side lined with canons.

"There are many remarkable rooms that you can now visit: the Chamber of Colonnades, the Chamber of the Nine Muses, the Grand Reception Hall, the Music Room, a chapel, and the private chambers of the Grand Master. There are collections of books, costumes, furniture, jewels, and tapestries, along with an exceptional collection of art, especially some ancient mosaics from the Greek island of Kos."

Chloe let them wander while she waited for them to take their time and explore the palace. It took over an hour to see everything. When they returned to the arcade, she led them down the block to the Street of the Knights.

"This lovely long street runs over six hundred meters long, straight to the Hospital of the Knights of Saint John at the sea. Behind each arched doorway that you will see on both sides, a Hospitaller knight once trained, prayed and lived. We will also pass seven separate large inns, built between 1492 and 1503. Upon each of the inn's doors will be an emblem from one of the seven countries that the knights were from. Since most of the Grand Masters were from France, that inn door has an especially fine décor, which we will come to. Now all of these doors lead into offices for cultural institutions and departments of government."

At the end of the street they turned left and walked north about three hundred feet to come first to the Temple of Athena, and then to the Temple of Aphrodite at Symi Square.

"As you can see, both temples are in ruins from approximately the third century BCE, but this one is my favorite of the two. This ruin was once a temple dedicated to the goddess of love and beauty, Aphrodite. We cannot enter the temple grounds, but it is easy to see past this metal fence to view all the tumbled columns and building blocks from what must have been an impressive temple. It is here that the Aphrodite Pudica statue comes from, which is now held in the Archaeological Museum. That is the pose where her right hand partially covers her left breast and her left hand covers her pudenda."

After a few minutes walking along the fence, Chloe had them take a short stone path to the main street and then head north to the Municipal Gardens.

"Within this area is held the Sound and Light Show in the Municipal Gardens. I suggest you call for reservations and see this show in your language at the designated time. The history is dramatized with lights and music.

"Now you are welcome to further walk the city at your leisure and find a place for lunch. I can give you some recommendations."

They invited her to lunch and she accepted. They followed her suggestion and ended up at a nearby place for a delicious meal. During lunch, she learned that Chante would be heading back to the B&B for Melodia's nap. She offered to walk with her to make sure she knew the way. And because she learned that Gervais and Lucien would be heading to the Archaeological Museum afterward, Chloe gave them a short rundown on its history, which had begun as a Roman building.

"Construction for a hospital began in 1440, under the Grand Master Jean de Lastic, and it was enlarged by Grand Master d'Aubusson in 1476. It was constructed with medieval architecture and was surrounded by a double portico with a colonnade in the Gothic style. The ground level was a courtyard where visitors could arrive on horseback, so there were lots of stables…"

"And horses," added Melodia.

"Yes, and lots of horses. Also on that level, to make deliveries easier to unload, multiple warehouses were set up for storage of the hospital's needs. All the wards for the sick were located upstairs. In 1480, the Turks attempted to seize the island, but failed. But in 1522 they were successful and used the building both as a hospital and barracks. Finally, in 1913, after the Italians took control of the island, they converted the old hospital into the Archaeological Museum."

Thankful for the additional history, after lunch the two parties separated, and Gervais and Lucien walked to the museum. The front of the museum was made of the same tan stone used for the entire town, with a series of recessed archways for doors all across the front. They entered the center one through a pointed Gothic door. Inside, they stepped into a large courtyard surrounded by the portico which Chloe had mentioned. There were cannon balls placed into pyramidal piles, and stone fragments lined the outer edge of the interior. Opposite the entry, a reclining lion held between its front paws the head of Taurus the bull, as described by a nearby plaque.

"I don't understand the symbolism here," said Lucien. "I know that the lion symbolizes power and strength, and I know that Taurus was a bull, also a sign of strength, but what is this statue saying?"

Gervais had an idea. "I believe it is based on the Greek story of Europa, a woman Zeus fell in love with. He appeared to her as a white bull and she was so enamored of his beauty that she got on his back, and then he kidnapped her and took her to Crete. There he turned into an eagle and enraptured her. It was Zeus who placed a group of stars called the Hyades in the heavens and they make up the head of Taurus. They are both astrological signs, of course, and although I only occasionally read the horoscope in the newspaper, I know that Taurus is an earth sign and people born under this sign are said to be stubborn, materialistic, and possessive, but they like being cared for. Leo is a fire sign that is associated with being ambitious, generous and protective of those they care about. They are also leaders and they honor the brave in battle. I think the statue is saying that even the strong need protection and healing."

They walked the ground level along the portico, which was noticeably cooler in contrast to the hot sun reflecting off of the stone courtyard. The downstairs rooms held guns and artillery of the Rhodians and Ottomans, sarcophagi, stone altars, Greek statues and steles from different sites on Rhodes and from other Dodecanese islands. When they had finished visiting the rooms on the lower level, they climbed an inner stairway to the second level. On that level were more important archaeological artifacts: various famous mosaics, a perfectly preserved clay pyxis jar decorated with painted partridges, a marble head of Helios, a headless statue of Artemis, a drunk Dionysus, statues of Venus, and the famous Statue of the Crouching Aphrodite from the first century BCE.

Thoroughly enchanted with this look at ancient Greek works, they spent more time in the rooms that had coins to see the variety of monetary units, as well as the styles of jewelry worn, including displays of rings, earrings, bracelets and necklaces. Lucien took a lot of pictures of each display to hopefully match the museum finds to the items that were stolen, and to get an idea of their age and value. That night, Chante, Lucien and Gervais researched those Greek artifacts.

Chapter Four

When Lucien and Gervais were back at the B&B later that afternoon, Lucien saw that Professor Ekonomos had emailed him a list of the archaeologists who worked at the site, and had attached their CVs. His email read as follows:

Detective Reynard,

Please find included a list of those persons on my primary dig crew. I've included their CVs and their work assignments. Each person was thoroughly screened and was well-qualified to be here. There is an unwritten understanding that finds are not to be discussed outside of the team, but no one signed a non-disclosure agreement. After the theft, I asked each one of them if they had told any person outside of the dig about what had been discovered. Every one of them said they had not and would not have, and I believe them. They are all experienced and knew of the real risk of thieves after artifacts, especially at night and particularly in Greece.

What is curious about this theft is that someone got access to the secure area through the outer fence, even with a night watchman on the grounds. They were able to cut the lock on the warehouse without being heard. There are bright lights on the building at night, but there are no cameras in that area, so there is no way to see who got in. What is even more interesting is that there were more valuable items in the building that were not taken, which makes it look as if they either didn't know what they were taking, or they took items that must hold a special meaning for them.

I must tell you that two major teams have worked at the site, one professional and one amateur. From April 1st to May 31st, the first team consisted of only my core professional workers with credentials. From June 1st to July 31 we were joined by a summer crew of archaeological students from the University of Thessaloniki. This team was on site until the end of July, but our professional team was given an extension to work until August 15th. I have a list of only the names of the twelve students and know little about them. Their work was overseen by their professor, but my core team was also there to make sure the students worked correctly. I had no problems with any of them. Their professor can be contacted if you want to know more.

In the meantime, I have been working with the local police, as I reported the theft to them. I spoke with Inspector Lex Nomikos. I mentioned that you would be coming to Rhodes and would make contact. I have included contact information for both the university professor and the inspector below. I'm sure I will speak more with you soon.

I sincerely thank you for your assistance in this matter and hope you will be able to find the culprit or culprits and the missing artifacts.

Sincerely,
Sander Ekonomos

Lucien shared the email with Chante and Gervais.

"Beginning tomorrow, Chante, perhaps you can contact the professor at the university to get more information about the students who were part of the dig. Ask him if any of his students did any boasting about what was found. Then you and Papa can divide up the CVs and look into each one. I'm going to pay this inspector a visit tomorrow and see what he's discovered, if anything. I want to find out who specifically wrote up the details of the artifacts and who reads those reports, as it seems someone was fairly particular about what was taken. In regards to what Ekonomos said about the culprit not knowing what to take, to me it seems like the theft was precise and well-timed. It feels like an inside job, but it's way too early to make a judgment. If I can get in to see the detective in the morning then we can plan something to do in the afternoon with Melodia. If I can't get in until the afternoon, then let's call Chloe and see if she has ideas for a morning driving tour."

After they returned from an early dinner and Melodia went to bed, the three decided to use the large table desk in Gervais' room to set up their computers and get to work. It would serve as their office while they were in town.

Lucien began with a comment. "I know that each archaeological dig operates differently depending on who is funding it. With little money, it can be one man who does the work, or if funding is good, then a whole team of experts, like we have here, can be working together. This dig seems to have a good number of people working on it, despite the pandemic, and a lot of money must be behind it." Then he gave them some time for preliminary searches on how archaeological sites operate. After about an hour, Lucien asked what they had found.

Gervais began. "I found out how archaeological digs are approved in Greece, as outlined by the Hellenic Society for Law and Archaeology. All excavations must be approved by the Archaeological Service in the Ministry of Culture. Applications can be submitted by Greek research teams or any domestic educational institution that specializes in archaeology. Foreign schools can do so as well, but in this case, it was a domestic university. The application is given a thorough review, and must include a degree of professionalism. The director must certainly have scientific authority and a minimum of three years of excavation experience. They are required to include in their application why the work needs to be done, what their proposed mode of excavation will be, and the expected contributions the dig will bring to the country's knowledge of the site. A budget must be included for the time frame, and how the site will be conserved and protected must be described as well. As part of the application, a list of each proposed team member and their designated titles and specialties must be added. Applications are to be submitted by October 1st each year, in order to begin on April 1st of the following year."

"Wow, it takes that long for an application to get reviewed?" asked Chante.

"Apparently. The usual run for an approved dig is eight weeks. It seems that enough was discovered in the first eight weeks by the opening dig team to warrant a continuation of the dig, as they were granted another eight weeks, and the professor from the University of Thessaloniki also got approval to bring his students to work the site. And now, it seems they have been allowed a further extension."

"So how is a dig financed, and more specifically, how was this one financed?" asked Lucien.

"That is not very clear. Normally the owner of the site is responsible for the financing, but it can be pretty costly, especially if they have a dozen specialists working for them. I suspect they query private parties for financial support. It could be an archaeological research corporation, a special monuments organization, a particular museum which wants to take on the holdings of whatever is found, or perhaps a wealthy collector with a specific interest in the area. One of those may be how the first team was supported, but for the second dig with the university students, the university probably paid a good portion.

"One more thing," added Gervais. "The primary director of the excavations must submit periodic reports about what was discovered, and by April of the following year, he must submit a complete formal report listing all of the items with photographs and detailed drawings showing where each item was found."

Lucien tilted his head in thought at what his father just said. "But some person or some committee is looking at the earlier periodic reports."

"I would assume so, but who or what group of people are seeing the reports, we'll have to find out."

Chante also had information to tell them. "Although we have been to many archaeological sites and even worked with archaeologists, we've never really been involved in the specifics of how they work. Since we are investigating the possibility of a theft by a member of the team, I thought it might be best to find out exactly how these specialists work together."

Lucien smiled at his wife. "Yes, of course, that would help us immeasurably."

"All right, then here you go. First of all, even specialists get dirty in the field, and seldom work from an office. They usually carry their office with them, in the form of tablets, laptops, and cameras. Everything depends upon the quality of the input to establish a dependable database of information from the site. Once the items are found and documented in situ, and are then removed, that information is valuable to the team. There are certain procedures that must be followed and the excavation leader is responsible for making sure each member follows it and adds to the data pool, so the work can be focused in the direction it needs to go. They are also responsible for the safety, care, and protection of the team, as well as making sure all the needed equipment is available and working properly."

"That makes complete sense," commented Gervais.

"And what *are* the usual titles and their jobs?" Lucien asked.

"There is usually a project officer who works between the client and the site supervisor. They may be the one in charge of the finances and all the required paperwork throughout the dig period. They also coordinate with subcontractors, like those who are needed to put up fences around a dig, companies that bring in sifting machinery, and security for protection of the site.

"Then there is the site supervisor, who directly works with the staff in the field. They check on the documentation of the finds and make sure everything is running on schedule. On some digs, this person is also the project manager. If there is a project officer for this dig, we don't know who that person is yet, but we do know that Professor Ekonomos is the site supervisor. He may be both. There may also be a trench supervisor, who may also be the site supervisor.

"Diggers are the next category, though this can be on several levels. Some are students without any experience. Others are experienced site diggers who have various degrees in archaeology. They use a shovel and trowel, filter soil, bag and tag items, wash and clean them, code and record, draw maps, take pictures, and document the general area. There may also be specialized diggers on site. Some of these people might be archivists, anthropologists, biologists, conservators, geologists, illustrators, paleontologists, photographers, surveyors, and topographers, depending on the site's needs."

Lucien nodded. "That was helpful. So what specialized people do we have working on this site, aside from the students?"

They took a few minutes to look through the CVs and made a list.

Chante had the totals. "We have one site supervisor, five general experienced archaeologists, a conservator, a geologist, an illustrator, a photographer and an archivist."

"Okay, now we know what we are working with. Let's take a good look at each of their backgrounds, and see if any raise a red flag. Of course, we will also need to speak to them individually in person."

Lucien's computer dinged. "Ah, I sent an email to the inspector and I have an appointment with the guy at nine-thirty tomorrow morning at the Old Town precinct next to the port terminal. I hope he has some additional information for us."

Chapter Five

Lucien followed the address to the police station on the card and was surprised to learn that it was not at the port, but inside the old city walls on Ethelonton Dodekanision Street. At the front desk he produced his own card and said he had an appointment with Inspector Lex Nomikos. After the attendant made a brief call to the inspector's office, Lucien was told to wait and the inspector would be out to meet him. A few minutes later, a woman in her forties, wearing dress blues in a skirt with a white shirt and black tie, approached him. She had white stripes on her lapels, white insignias on her shoulders, and a Greek police patch on her left arm. Her blond hair was pulled back into a bun with long front bangs, but that was the only thing that softened her otherwise pale attractive face. Her lips were thin and her eyes were ice-cold blue.

"Detective Reynard?" she asked.

"Inspector Lex Nomikos?" he asked in return, visibly surprised.

"You did not expect me to be a woman. I get that all the time. Lex stands for Alexia. But rest assured detective, I am qualified, thorough, and tough as an old pair of boots."

"And I can assure you inspector, you look nothing like an old pair of boots."

That, at least, made her smile.

"Come, we'll go to my office to speak." She led him down a corridor and into a small but well-appointed room with a large wooden desk. "Have a seat."

Lucien noticed that there were no photographs of family, but a nice one of her on the wall, shaking an older officer's hand, and there were several well-taken photographs from around the old city.

"So you are here on behalf of the culture department of the UNESCO offices. You are not Greek, what nationality are you?"

"I'm French, and I am here with my father and my wife who act as my assistants and researchers, and we also brought our daughter so she could have a small holiday."

"Then it is a family business."

"I can assure you, it is always a team effort."

"Do you speak Greek?"

"No, but I have the assistance of an interpreter, if I need one."

"Very good. Now that the niceties are out of the way, how can I best assist you with what I am calling the Acropolis theft?"

"I understand that Professor Ekonomos reported the theft about two weeks ago. If you share what you have done and discovered so far on the case, then I won't be repeating what you have already accomplished. I would also be grateful if you would let me know if any of the dig team's background checks revealed criminal activity. Do you have any leads?"

Inspector Nomikos leaned back in her chair, paused, and then responded.

"None of the dig members have criminal records, aside from one caught painting graffiti on a city wall in Athens when he was sixteen and a few with parking tickets. They all checked out. We also spoke with the professor who brought the students for the second dig, but all had their luggage thoroughly checked when they departed, and nothing but tourist tokens were found. We've put out a bulletin to the neighboring post offices around the university to contact us if any packages come in from the island. So far nothing. We fingerprinted the door area of the building from which the items were taken, but only the team's fingerprints were found, and any heavy-duty bolt cutter could have cut the lock. We interviewed the dig team members and the private security men, but no one saw or heard anything on the night of the theft. We've put out the word to our local undercover agents who monitor the sales that take place in secondhand and pawn shops, in case someone tries to sell any of the stolen items. But so far, I'm sorry, we don't have any leads."

Lucien was somewhat surprised and disappointed. He'd hoped for something. "I see, well perhaps you can help me with one thing. Do you know who or what organization has been financing the digs?"

That made Inspector Nomikos slowly sit up. "No, I don't. I assume it was a private institution, like most digs. Do you consider this an important element of your investigation?"

Lucien had a slight smile. "Maybe yes, maybe no. I don't know. Still, it is an element of the case that I'd like to have an answer to."

"I'll see what I can find out for you." Then she stood. "If I can help you with anything else, just let me know. As far as our end is concerned, we are at a standstill unless more information comes to us or a package shows up in Thessaloniki. We will let you know, of course, if anything is discovered. I trust you will do the same."

She reached out her hand to shake and gave him a pleasant smile.

"Yes, I will. Thank you for your time, Inspector Nomikos."

Lucien left a little down-hearted. He had nothing to go on and the basic steps had already been followed. But by the time he returned to the B&B, Chloe was there, and the family was waiting to depart for their afternoon adventure. Lucien had a minute or so to speak with Chante while he was changing his clothes.

"Were you able to reach the professor?"

"Yes, but he hadn't heard from any student and had nothing new to share."

When they went downstairs Chloe said that they were headed for a park and Melodia would get to see some animals. Then Melodia ran to Lucien and hugged his legs. "Papa, we are going to see ducks, fish, turtles and peacocks."

As they were walking out to Chloe's car, Gervais had a moment to ask. "So did you find out anything from the inspector? Was he forthcoming?"

"First of all, he is a she, and a tough gal at that, but she's already covered the basics and found nothing. I'll give you the details tonight when we return."

Heading south out of the city, Chloe told them about the park they were going to. "Rodini Park is documented as being one the earliest parks in existence, and the first park to be landscaped. It dates to 330 BCE, when the Romans built an aqueduct to provide water for the city of Rhodes, along with a large water tower. Later, a language school was founded there. If you walk to the end, there is an ancient Ptolemaic tomb from 300 BCE and a couple of small devotional caves."

After Chloe parked the car, she reached into the glovebox and retrieved a small white plastic bag.

Melodia saw it. "What's in the bag?"

"It's a surprise. Wait and see."

Melodia's eyes got big with anticipation. She loved surprises.

Just inside the entrance, there was a large pond where ducks quacked, turtles were half out of the water sunning themselves on rocks, and large orange and red carp were swimming. Melodia got excited and leaned over the rocks to get a closer look. Water flowed out over the end of the pond to continue into a stream, and a path went along on both sides. Melodia chose which side to follow, racing across a wooden bridge which spanned to the right, so they followed her run of enthusiasm.

Once they crossed the bridge, they began to weave under the shade of pine and cypress trees. All of a sudden, they heard a wild cry of an animal, and turned to see two peacocks across the stream, one with its dazzling feathers spread wide, parading around a peahen. Then, from their right, three cats came through the bushes and began to meow. Here Chloe pulled out the bag she had brought and opened it for Melodia to see. Chloe said it was cat food. She told Melodia to reach in with both hands and toss the dry food to them. Melodia bounced for joy at the sight of the cats going for the food. Before the cats had finished their flurry of feasting, Chloe led the family on. Soon some butterflies came floating along above the stream, and Melodia cried out, pointing to them.

Further still, they came to a flower stand displaying bunches of verbena, white and pink dahlias, raspberry pulmonaria, red Rhodian roses, and white tuberose that could be smelled all the way to the bench where they sat to rest. Blooming along the stream were cherry black-eyed Susans, yellow heliopsis, and orange lantana.

Next to the display of flowers was a stand that sold cold drinks, pre-packaged sandwiches, and dried snacks. Lucien bought them all drinks, and Melodia said she was hungry. She mewed like a cat so Chante would feed her, which made everyone laugh. Since it was almost noon, they opted for sandwiches. While they sat and ate, a peacock came strolling up the path and eyed their food. Chloe pulled out the bag of dried food again and asked Melodia if she wanted to throw some to the peacock.

"Peacocks eat cat food?" she asked in astonishment.

"Yes, they do. And it is better to throw them food, rather than having them come over and try to take your sandwich from you."

With that, Melodia gave Chante her partly-eaten half sandwich and got up to feed the peacock. While they watched her feed the bird and giggle as it pecked at the ground, Chloe had one more bit of information about the park.

"In 1317 the Hospitaller Knight, Grand Master Foulques de Villaret, had an attempt on his life near the palace. Somewhere along this waterway he had a retreat, though nothing remains of it now, so I cannot even point out where it might have been. Part of the woods which used to surround this area had deer, but it is rare to see deer here anymore."

When they finished eating and the peacock was looking for more, they walked on for a short time. Chloe explained that the path went on for about twenty more minutes of walking time, and at the end were the tomb and a small waterfall. But Melodia was disappointed because there were no other animals on the path. She said she was tired and wanted to go back to the pond. Lucien was relieved, as he thought he should get back to the B&B and start doing some research. So they ambled their way back, paused for Melodia to enjoy the fish and turtles, and then drove back to the B&B.

Once Melodia was taking her nap, they met in the downstairs living room with glasses of wine, which were offered by Gala. When Gala left the room, Lucien filled them in on how his meeting with Inspector Nomikos had gone.

"So where do we go from here?" asked Gervais. "We haven't got much to go on."

"The only thing I can think to do is to conduct our own interviews with the team members and see if they have remembered anything since the theft. I'll text Professor Ekonomos and find out when we can come to the site, or where we can meet his team for the interviews. Sometimes people are more willing to speak out when they are not intimidated by an officer sitting in a police station. I'm going to suggest that they come here, if it is all right with Gala and Nils. It has a more relaxing atmosphere. Perhaps sitting in the garden will calm them enough to open up and provide additional information."

"What about the security guards?" asked Chante. "Do you think they will be willing to come here?"

"That may be a little different. I'm willing to bet that since their jobs have been called into question, they would feel more secure being interviewed on the job. They are in uniform, and while there, they might retain some self-confidence and respect."

Chante had something else on her mind. "I'm assuming that the majority of the team will want to work during the day, and might be more open to coming here in the evening. Perhaps you can question the guard on duty tomorrow first thing in the morning, and that would leave time for the driving tour which Chloe recommended for midday."

"That might work," said Lucien. "I would like to see more of the city."

An hour later, Lucien got a response from Professor Ekonomos saying that he was welcome to come to the site and speak with Dimitri, the guard in the morning, between eight and nine. He had also spoken to three of the team members who were willing to come to the B&B that evening, beginning at 6:30. Would it work to have the next one at 7:00 and the third at 7:30? Lucien responded that those times were good.

Chapter Six

Lucien was up early on Wednesday morning, and this time he walked to the east entry to meet the guard on duty. He had checked the list of workers and knew the man's full name. The guard was standing at the gate, wearing tan pants and a tan cap with a company logo on the shirt, *Fýlakes tis Ródou* (Guards of Rhodes). He was young, maybe only in his late twenties, and had a bit of a scruffy chin, but his black hair was very short. His face was tanned with light brown eyes and he had the look of a student about him.

Lucien approached. "*Kaliméra*. Dimitri Kouris?"

Dimitri nodded, "Yes sir, Detective Reynard. *Kaliméra*. Do I need to unlock the gate and let you in?"

"No, that's not necessary. I can see and hear you well enough. We can just talk through the fence. Professor Ekonomos said that you would be willing to answer a few questions."

"Yes, sir. What would you like to know? I already spoke to the police."

"I know, but they didn't tell me what they asked you, or what you replied. What did they ask you?"

"They asked me if I was on duty on the night of the theft, but I wasn't. I didn't come on until the next afternoon, but by then the theft had already occurred and it was news to me."

"How does the schedule work between the three of you?"

"We rotate every twelve hours. Daikonos came in at six on the evening of the theft and worked until six the next morning. Calix Kalogeras came in at six the next morning, and that's how they trade off. I'm the third guard with whom they switch on and off with, and so on. If one of us gets sick, the company sends a stand-in, but that hasn't happened for months."

"I see, and where do you go if you need to sit, rest, eat, or use the toilet?"

"We have a guard shack." He pointed to a tiny building with windows on three sides and its back against the fence. "If it's raining we hole up in there, and we can sit, drink and eat inside. The windows allow us to keep an eye on things. We are required to walk the perimeter every hour or so, even if it's raining. There are public washrooms down by the Nymphaeums. We use the same ones as the tourists."

"Would you say it might be possible for someone to cut through the border fence, cut the lock on the storage room and get back out, in the time it would take one of you to go to the washroom and back?"

"Yes, it's possible, and the three of us came to that conclusion. Daikonos said he used the facilities at around four that morning. Then he came back to the shack and had some coffee before going on his next perimeter walk. That's when he noticed the storage facility lock was broken."

"On the days previous to the break in, did you see anyone hanging out for a time, watching you? Did the other two guards make any comment as such?"

"No, I didn't, and they didn't say. Sorry, but we move around too much during the day when tourists are here. I don't recall the police asking that question, so you might ask Daikonos and Calix."

"Do any of the archaeologists come at night?"

"Not that I've seen."

"Just one more thing. It seems like a large area for just one man to watch. How do you manage that?"

"If there is a problem at the other end of the site, we might hear about it from the tour guides. Near the bathrooms there is a small first aid room with a walkie-talkie they can use to call us, wherever we may be on the grounds. If there is a problem, we run to where we are needed."

"All right, Dimitri, you've been very helpful. If you think of anything else, here's my card. Feel free to call me any time."

Dimitri took the card, glanced at it and then put it in his chest pocket. "Yes, sir. I hope you catch the person who did this. It's such a problem in Greece." He stood a bit taller when he added, "That's why I'm working this job, so I can afford the classes to become a police officer."

The young man was either proudly boasting or overdoing it to show innocence, which made Lucien reflect nonetheless. "That's commendable. Well, good luck with your studies. Thank you."

The young man beamed. "Thank you, sir. Have a good day."

Chloe arrived at ten o'clock to pick up the family for their city driving tour. They would go around the old city following the Byzantine walls and see the eleven gates. She explained that the medieval old town of Rhodes had been guarded by different knights according to the language or tongues they spoke, called the *Langue* of the Knights. There was the Langue of France and Auvergne, the Langue of Spain and Portugal, the Langue of Germany, the Langue of England, and the Langue of Italy. Each langue was responsible for certain towers, as well as bastions, which were projections from the fortification built out at an angle to defend it from enemy fire, and terrepleins, which were raised level spaces where a battery of guns had once been mounted.

They began by heading east. On the south side of the medieval wall was the terreplein of England. Chloe described the area.

"This is where the Knights of England guarded this portion of the wall. And this is the first gate, the Gate of Saint John, built by the Grand Master d'Aubusson. It is also known as the red gate, because of all the blood that was spilled here during the siege of 1522.

"And here along the edge of the southern wall was a moat, which is now filled in. The moat kept any enemy approaching by land away from the walls. Near the end of this grassy area was the Bastion of Italy. It had tall walls and a circular tower for the knights from Italy. Before the bastion was built, a smaller tower had been there, but in 1480 it was closed off and the Grand Master Pierre d'Aubusson had it converted to a bastion. He also built a vaulted corridor with openings for artillery and cannons to fire at any enemy that might reach the moat. Unfortunately, during the 1481 Siege it was breached by Mehmed II, a Turkish sultan of the Ottoman Empire. Afterward, the bastion was reinforced by Grand Master Fabrizio del Carretto."

They came to the southeast corner of the old city. "Here is the Acandia Gate. It was opened in 1935 by the Italians to link the bastion to the harbor for commercial use."

Chloe now turned left and was heading north. "Along this side is the Gate of Saint Catherine, also known as the Windmills Gate. Commercial grain mills once located along the harbor were more easily accessed from town through this gate. Just across that narrow watery inlet is the Tower of France of the Windmills."

They passed near the central police station where Lucien had been the day before, but they were one block east of it. At the end of the street, along the eastern docks, Chloe turned west in a northerly curve. "This is Kolona Harbor and that gate is called the Gate of the Virgin. Its name comes from the Virgin of the Burgh church, nearby. This is the area where the respectable middle class lived, as opposed to the Knights. It was open for vehicle traffic in 1955."

Further on, she pointed out the next gate. "This is the Marine Gate, also known as the Sea Gate, as it was the main passage from the harbor into town. Grand Master Pierre d'Aubusson had it built in 1478. It has two crenelated towers on both sides of its arched entry, and the Virgin Mary, Saint Peter, and John the Baptist are carved in stone relief above. It was bombed during the Second World War, but restored in 1951. We're coming to the small Arnaldo Gate, which was built to access the New Hospital of Saint John, where the Archaeological Museum of Rhodes is housed."

At the northeast corner of the city she pointed again. "This is the Gate of the Arsenal. It was originally a smaller gate built by the Grand Master Juan Fernández de Heredia. He was a Spanish Knight from Aragon in the early 1380s, and his coat of arms can still be seen over that gate. The Ottomans widened it in 1908 for better access to Kolona Harbor.

"And here is Saint Paul's Gate, built in the second half of the 1400s by the Grand Master d'Aubusson. It gave access to the harbor used by the Knights' navy, and was the end point of the road that came from villages on the east coast. There is a low wall that surrounds the towers with a stone relief of Saint Paul at the gate, and between this one and Saint Catherine's Gate, the Knights had their arsenal.

"Next to Saint Catherine's Gate is Naillac Tower, formerly known as the Tower of Saint Michael. It was built by the Grand Master Philibert de Naillac sometime in the early 1400s. The tower was approximately 150 feet high with four small round turrets, and a smaller octagonal tower rose in the center. Unfortunately, two earthquakes, one in 1481 and the second in 1856, caused severe cracks in the structure. Due to the danger it presented by possibly collapsing on ships in the harbor, it was dismantled; but the bridge leading to the tower, which was built by Pierre d'Aubusson, still stands."

They turned to the west. "This is the Liberty Gate, the main entry to the harbor, offering a connection between Kolona Harbor with Mandraki Harbor. It was built in 1924 by the Italians in the same medieval architectural style as the older gates."

She drove out through the gate to a large parking area and turned the car to face the harbor.

"Linking the two sides of the harbor once stood one of the Seven Wonders of the Ancient World. It was the Colossus of Rhodes, a statue of the Greek sun-god Helios that stood over thirty meters high. It was thought to have been built in 280 BCE by Chares of Lindos. It stood for only fifty-five years. It collapsed due to an earthquake in 226 BCE. There are several theories as to where the Colossus of Rhodes really stood, and many modern projects to rebuild it have been proposed, but none have been accepted. In the meantime, sculptures of the Rhodian Deer stand on either side guarding the harbor, one a stag and the other a doe."

At this point Chloe suggested that they get out of the car and take a short walk along the boardwalk to get as close as possible to enjoy the stately deer statues. She would wait for them.

Melodia loved seeing the deer with their golden backs sparkling in the sun, and learned that the stag deer was named Elafos and the doe Elafina. When the family returned, they got back in the car and continued with the tour.

After the Tower of Saint Paul, which oversees Mandraki Harbor, they came to the northwest corner of the old city. "Here is the Grand Master's Palace, which you have already visited, and just below the palace is the most grand gate, the Gate d'Amboise. The entrance has a covering over it, and below, the ancient studded wooden doors can still be seen. It has triple defensive walkways and two large round towers to either side of the entry."

Then, turning south, they passed another filled-in moat along the side of the coast. "The moat goes around this pentagonal-shaped Bastion of Saint George and the tower of Spain. The bastion was built in the late 1400s. It was laid siege to, and then rebuilt in 1522. Above its entrance is the coat of arms of the Grand Master Philippe Villiers de L'Isle-Adam.

"Here is another terreplein, this one of Spain, which was erected down the center of the moat after the siege of 1480. This thick-walled structure protected the inner wall from cannon fire. In 1522, the Ottomans tunneled under the moat to gain access. And at the end is the Tower of the Virgin. In the southwest corner is the Gate of Saint Athanasios, also known as the Saint Francis Gate, as the Saint Francis of Assisi church is just outside the wall. The gate was built in 1441 by the Grand Master Jean de Lastic. The Turks claim that it was through this gate that Suleiman the Magnificent entered the city, but the sultan had it closed in case another conqueror chose to enter through the same gate. It was re-opened by the Italians in 1922, on the 400th anniversary of the Ottoman conquest."

Now, having made the complete circle of the town's gates, towers and bastions, and ending up near their accommodations, Chloe dropped them back at the B&B.

Before she departed, Chloe mentioned to Chante that since Melodia liked the butterflies in Rondini Park, there was a place that had nothing but butterflies where she could take them to visit. Chante thought that was a great idea and they would consider it for the next day. She thanked her and said goodbye.

At six thirty that evening, the first person from the dig team arrived. Lucien had asked Nils and Gala if it would be all right with them if he invited a couple people into the garden to talk. They were completely fine with it. Gala wanted to play hostess and asked if they would want refreshments, but Lucien declined. Chante and Lucien sat in the front living room, waiting for the archaeologists to arrive. Chante would greet them if Lucien was still questioning the one before.

Lucien opened the front door. "Lydia Karas?" he asked. She nodded. "Please come in. I'm Detective Lucien Reynard. I've been hired by UNESCO to assist Inspector Lex Nomikos of the Rhodes police, to uncover the theft." He shook her hand. "Thank you for coming. Let's go chat in the back patio as it is such a nice evening."

When they reached the back, he motioned for her to have a seat. The jasmine was sending out a sweet scent and soon the garden underbrush lights would be on, which set a relaxed atmosphere. This was just what Lucien was hoping for.

"I understand you are one of the archaeologists on the team. When did you first hear about the theft?"

Lydia was middle-aged with short curly brown hair. She immediately shifted in her seat while remembering. "I didn't hear about it until I arrived that morning just after eight o'clock."

"Do all of you get there that early?"

"Sometimes earlier. That way we have at least a full hour before the site is opened, and it gives us a head start on the day before it gets too warm."

"Did you notice anything different with anyone on your team or the guards, or perhaps any tourists, on the days leading up to that morning?"

She gave it careful thought before answering. "I do remember seeing something I thought was odd when I arrived. The guard who was on duty that night was Daikonos. When I got there, I noticed that he was sweating profusely, even though that morning it was overcast and cool before the fog burned off. I thought he may have been nervous and upset because the theft happened on his watch. He also might have feared for his job. He had probably rushed through another round before we arrived. When we did, we all assembled at the storage building to see what had been taken. Professor Ekonomos had already completed an inventory, and made a list of the missing items for the police."

"Do you trust all of your coworkers not to have been a part of the theft?"

"Absolutely."

"Good. If there is anything else that comes to mind, no matter how small, please call me." He gave her his card and escorted her out.

The next person, Dru Cirillo, arrived. Lucien greeted him and escorted him also to the patio. He was in his early forties with dark hair, a dark beard, and glasses. He was the illustrator for the site.

Lucien asked the same questions and Dru gave similar answers as Lydia had, knowing nothing more than she did, but promised to call if he thought of anything.

The third person, Gregory Andino, was the archivist. Gregory was a short man in his late forties with longish dark hair that was pulled back into a pony tail, and he wore glasses.

"Forgive me for asking, but what does an archivist do on site? Don't you spend more time searching for information in archives?"

"A lot of people think that, and believe me I do a lot of research, but I am in the field as much as the others. It's my job to help identify artifacts as they get unearthed, based on the research I have already done on the area, and I collate the information that the others write up on a find. The information I have may be based on previous archaeological or anthropological finds, or on the social history and cultural changes of the people who once lived there. But particularly for this site, knowledge of their religion."

"That's fascinating, thank you. Is there anything you can tell me that might aid us in our investigation? Anything you heard, or saw, about any of the other members, the guards, or tourists whom had visited?"

"Hmm, not the people, per se, but I did find a few of the finds of particular interest. Some of the coins were especially nice, and the small bronze statue."

"Was the statue particularly old?"

"I'm not sure. It still needs to be properly dated."

"Well thank you very much for coming and enlightening me on what an archivist does. If you can think of anything else, please let me know." Lucien gave him his card and walked him out.

Chapter Seven

That night, a man known as *"to Liontári,"* the Lion, stood on his terrace overlooking the lights of Embonas, a village located halfway down the western side of the island. This old village rested at the foot of Mount Attavyros, the island's highest peak. The man's home was built on three levels, three hundred feet above the village and almost nine hundred feet below the ancient ruins of the Temple of Zeus, which crowned Mount Attavyros.

His home was only thirty-three miles from Rhodes' ancient city, but it suited his desire for separation from the village below, and made him feel closer to the ancient god above. Nestled in his lion's den perched on the side of the mountain, he could look down and see the terraced land of grapevines and olive groves that graced his tongue, lined his pockets, and soothed his sensibilities. Like the carnivore he was named for, he most enjoyed the meat of goat. His private chef was preparing his dinner, while the carcass of a kid goat was sizzling on the rotisserie.

He had not garnered the moniker "the Lion" for nothing. In his younger years he had longer and thicker blond hair, but now that he was seventy-two his hair was shorter and whiter with small waves that rippled back across the top of his head. His eyes were green with brown edges, like a dense jungle in shade, but his eyelids were downturned and slightly reddened by years of stress and lack of sleep. The Lion had a large drooping nose over a white chevron moustache, and thin lips which were more often pursed than upturned. He was round-chested, but slender in the waist, and fairly short at five-six. Like the wild feline, he was more active at night, and he liked to roam his house and grounds, thinking and planning, musing and brooding. He continually focused on the strategic maneuvers and conceived arrangements required by his many business operations, and he was always plotting a way forward.

He had begun working in his late teens as a deckhand at the harbor. Many stories were told by the other men about the Mediterranean countries and island ports which made him eager to see them all. One day he met a man thirty years older than him, well-respected in the cargo business, who took a liking to him. The older man eventually took him under his wing and became his mentor, teaching him all about the shipping business. It was this mentor who nicknamed him the Lion, because his long blond hair blew wild working at the docks.

By the time the Lion was thirty-three, with help from his mentor, he had purchased his first small cargo vessel and gone into the shipping business. He shipped out products from the island: Rhodian wine, small amounts of the grape distillate called Souma, and fresh pressed virgin olive oil from small local farmers. He brought back wine and distillates from other Mediterranean countries. By the time he was thirty-five he was a millionaire, and each year after that his millions multiplied. When he had his choice where to live, he chose the island he had been born on.

While sipping his Souma, looking out into the night sky, his cell rang. The evening's business had begun. He saw that it was a man who worked for him.

"*Naí*," which was 'yes' in Greek, though the Lion spoke several languages.

"Sir, three things. Your shipment of Mandilaria wine arrived safely in Athens, and Austria is requesting a quote for shipments of the extra virgin oil."

"And the third?"

"I've heard from my man near the site that UNESCO has sent a detective to investigate the items taken from the acropolis."

The lion took a deep breath. "Make sure he doesn't find out anything."

"Yes, sir," he said, and rang off.

The Lion knew he had at least ten minutes before the goat was ready. He made his way down smooth marble stairs and entered his office. Swinging open a small framed painting on the wall, a code panel was revealed. He punched in secret symbols which made a door silently draw into the wall, and he stepped through. The door silently closed behind him. The lights automatically went on inside, and the room was pleasantly cool as it was climate controlled. Within was a collection of Greek art that he had amassed over a lifetime.

Since the Lion and his mentor had become close friends, when the older man's father died in 1980 at ninety years old, the Lion spent a long weekend with his friend to help him get through the loss. His mentor drank a lot in his sadness, but the Lion was glad that he was not drunk when his friend shared something that he would never forget. The man told him that somewhere his father kept a handwritten note that had been passed down from his father's great grandfather, telling a story that had been handed down through the family before that. The man said he had heard the story many times growing up. It was about a distant ancestor who came to Rhodes with a godly treasure, but it was yet to be found. He told the young Lion that *that* was the reason he had funded an entity to dig at the acropolis site, so he could closely follow any discoveries. He didn't tell the Lion that a piece of that treasure had already been found, and he was just waiting for more of it to be unearthed.

The Lion's mentor passed away in 1984 from a heart attack, just four years after the man's father had died. He had been only sixty-nine. Having never married and with no living relatives, he named the Lion to inherit all of his worldly goods. When the Lion got into the man's house, it wasn't the paperwork for his mentor's four ships, or the shares in the shipping empire that the Lion searched for, it was the handwritten story that he had been told about. When the Lion finally got access to the man's private vault at his bank, he found the story and surprisingly, a piece of the treasure that had been described in the letter. Then he knew there must be more waiting to be found.

Now, sitting in his over-stuffed, dark emerald velvet chair, the lion unlocked and opened a hidden drawer in the desk before him. He pulled out the story, which had been preserved and encased between two thin sheets of clear plexiglass. Once more, he read through the story. Then he focused all of his attention on the small black velvet jewel case next to it. He slowly opened it to stare at not only the first fragment, but now a second piece that he had recently obtained. It was an excellent beginning toward finding the entire object. Of all the things in his entire collection, what he coveted the most was what he now lovingly stared at. He was now certain at long last that more of the treasure might be closer at hand than ever before. It was just a matter of time. That's why he had authorized a two week extension on the acropolis dig, and would consider a third season if need be.

The chef, having perfected the roast, announced that dinner was ready by ringing a four inch steel and copper-coated goat bell. The chef had gifted the bell to the Lion, who highly approved of the gift, and requested that it be rung upon completion of every roast. His mouth had long been watering.

Chapter Eight

Thursday morning, Lucien was up early to meet with Calix Kalogeras, the second security guard at the acropolis site. He approached as he had before, only this time, he had obtained cell numbers for everyone on site and had let Calix know he was on his way. Calix waved and met Lucien at the gate.

Calix Kalogeras was in his early sixties, of average height, had a squarish tanned face, a pleasant smile and friendly eyes framed by bushy eyebrows. His hair, eyes and eyebrows, moustache and beard were gray. Kalogeras had already unlocked the gate and stood at the entry.

"Mr. Kalogeras? I'm Detective Reynard. Thank you for seeing me."

"Of course, sir, how can I help you?"

"How long have you been a security guard?"

"Eight years for this security company." He indicated the name on his hat. "Before that I was warehouse manager for my brother's business for ten years."

"Then you've heard about thefts and probably seen what can happen at sites like this. What's your best guess as to who took the artifacts?"

Calix could not help but grin. He'd seen plenty, but he'd held his job because of one thing, his honesty. Asked a straight question, he would speak straight out. He looked at the detective and then looked down. "I know this is going to sound funny coming from a possible suspect, but

I think someone on the inside had something to do with it."

This perked Lucien right up. "You mean one of the team members? What makes you think that?"

"Only the three of us and our boss know our schedule. It had to be someone who knows our routine, how long it takes to make a round, where all the lights are, and what kind of cutters would make quick work of the storage building lock."

"So you don't think a thief could watch the site with binoculars from a hotel across the way and walk the site as a tourist to discover all that?"

They turned to the block of tall buildings to the east. The Vista Hotel had five floors.

Calix squinted his eyes. "Maybe."

"If it was someone on the inside working alone, with or for someone else, who do you think it could be?"

Calix raised his shoulders. "I have no idea. It's just how it feels."

"What's to keep me from thinking that you might be saying that to throw me off looking closer at you?"

"I'm getting too old to turn dishonest now. No detective, I don't know anything about the theft or who could have done it. It could have been a group effort, for all I know."

Anything was possible, but it gave Lucien pause.

"All right, Mister Kalogeras. I believe you. But I have to keep digging."

They both winced at the pun.

"I understand, detective. If I discover anything, I'll be sure to let you know."

Lucien thanked him, handed him his card, and Calix left on his next round. As Lucien was turning to go, two more members of the site team were crossing the street arriving for work. It was Amara Sideris and Julien Ganas, an archaeologist and the geologist, both carrying their digging kits.

As they reached him, he began. "Missus Sideris and Mister Ganas, *Kaliméra*. I'm detective Lucien Reynard. I don't suppose one or both of you could give me just a couple of minutes to ask a few questions?"

Amara and Julien looked at each other, and then back to Lucien. It was Amara who responded. She tucked her short graying brown hair behind one ear.

"Of course, detective, we were asked to cooperate and we will."

"Thank you. I appreciate that. First a little background. How long have both of you been working with Professor Ekonomos? How do you know him? Had you worked together before?"

Amara put down the metal box that held her field kit. "I've known the professor for a long time. I think we met probably twenty years ago at a conference. I liked the jobs he was getting, so I applied to work with him."

Lucien looked at Julien. "I'm the opposite. This is my first time working with him. I had just finished a small dig in Thessaloniki and met Professor Philemon at the university there. He told me he had applied to take a group of his students to work on a dig in Rhodes and that I should apply for work on the team."

"I see. Did you know Professor Philemon very well?"

"No, not really. I was doing research at the university and someone in the library recommended I speak with him in the archaeology department. I had some questions about where a specialized pot clay came from. He was helpful and we ended up having lunch together. I communicated with Professor Ekonomos a couple of times, and at last he told me I had been accepted to join the team. It wasn't until we all arrived here that Professor Ekonomos and I met in person."

"Thank you." Then Lucien looked at Amara. "You've known the professor for a long time. Have you been on one of his teams before when there was a theft?"

She didn't seem to like the way he put the question. "Professor Ekonomos is exceedingly honest and would never be party to anything untoward."

"I'm sorry. It was not meant as an accusation. I'm just trying to explore all possibilities. But you didn't answer my question."

"I'm sorry, too, detective. You can probably tell that I admire and respect Sander Ekonomos. To answer your question, there was a theft about eight years ago, but the young man who took the items confessed and went to jail. Professor Ekonomos was very upset because he had hired him. But that is way in the past."

"I understand. Thank you for being honest with me. Did either of you see anyone suspicious around the site before the theft?"

They looked at each other again. This time Julien replied. "Not me."

"Nor me," she responded.

Julien added. "We go right to work and our heads are down most of the time. We make it our task to ignore all the tourists beyond the fencing, and concentrate on what we've been hired to do."

Lucien reached into his pocket and handed each of them his card. "Please don't take offense, but I have to ask. Do either of you have any doubt as to the reliability or honesty of any of your team members?"

Both stood quiet, but shook their heads no.

"Well, if anyone says something odd referring to the theft, or if you see anyone suspicious, please call me and let me know."

"Does this mean we don't need to come for the interview?" she asked.

"Yes, no need now. Thank you both for your time." He shook both of their hands in order to leave on a friendly and thankful note.

Amara picked up her kit and they both walked into the site.

Lucien had an appointment with Inspector Nomikos, so he took a taxi to the police headquarters. After waiting for a few minutes, she came out to get him, they shook hands hello and she walked him back to her office, as before.

Once they were seated, Lucien was curious. "So inspector, you have discovered something for me?"

"Yes. The last time we spoke you had some questions, and one of them I couldn't answer. But now I have a partial answer."

"I'm sorry, which question was that?"

"You wanted to know who financed the digs. I found out from the Hellenic Ministry of Culture that before the Second World War, digs were financed by an investment company, but after the war, a different organization took over all digs."

"What is the name of this company and who owns it?"

"That's what I don't know. I was told that a board of directors deals through a middle man who submitted the applications and the money, and they gladly accepted. They were not open to saying who the board members are, or the name of the attorney who the board deals with."

"That's interesting. So no one knows who is on the board? Doesn't that bring up a red flag for the Ministry of Culture? I would think they would want to know exactly who was supporting the archaeological endeavor."

"They didn't seem concerned. Perhaps they know and were requested not to disclose that information? Maybe as long as the money came in year after year, it was enough? Does it really matter who is financing it? The Greek ministry, I'm sure, is happy to have the money to continue its searches into the past. Perhaps you should try another avenue in the case? I don't see how this will help you."

Lucien wasn't sure what he was sensing, but something didn't sit well with him. Money always mattered, and the greater the amount of money involved, the more it mattered. If there was an endless supply, then whoever was controlling the money was someone he needed to know about. Knowing there was no more he could learn from Inspector Nomikos, he thanked her and left.

When Lucien returned that afternoon, the family was met again by Chloe, who had promised Melodia a surprise visit to the Valley of the Butterflies. While Chloe drove the fifteen miles south of the city, she described a little about the place.

"We call the place Petaloudes, which means butterflies, but the name came from a man, a slave named Pelekanos, who took his own life in this valley a long time ago, in 1728. Subsequently, the river that runs through the area also took on the name. Then a German entomologist, Rheinhard Bger, came to study the butterflies that settle in this valley each summer and then leave in September. You see, the area is known for its forest of Oriental Sweetgum trees that we call Zitia. The trees have a strongly scented sap that attracts a particular type of moth called the Panaxia Quadripunctaria."

Chante had to interrupt. "I'm sorry, but why do they call it the Valley of the Butterflies if it's a moth that made the place known? I confess, I'm not sure of the difference between a moth and a butterfly. I believe one flies during the day and the other at night."

"That is an excellent question, and I will explain the differences. First, there are butterflies that come to the valley, but it was this particular insect that made the valley popular. It is the day-flying moth of the family of Erebidae. The common name for this moth is the Jersey Tiger.

"There are many differences between a moth and butterfly. The first is the way they rest their wings. Moths rest with their wings open, but butterflies rest with their wings closed, unless they are purposefully sunning themselves. Most moths are nocturnal and active at night and most butterflies are diurnal and are more active during the day. The antennae on a moth is usually more leaf- or feather-shaped, whereas butterfly antennae are usually long and thin with a bulb at the end. Moths have what is called a frenulum, which is sort of like a strong muscle that couples and strengthens the wings, helping it to fly, but butterflies don't have one. A butterfly caterpillar will spin a pupa made of protein called a chrysalis. A moth caterpillar will also form a silk pupa, but it is called a cocoon. Moths are usually stockier and have a furry coat, but butterfly bodies are smooth. Also, their eyes are different. Moths have superposition eyes, which means they see a single erect image. Butterflies have apposition eyes, which means that the lenses each form a small inverted image which the brain puts together to get a whole image. And the last difference is their color, butterflies are generally more colorful."

When they arrived at the site, Chloe entered the central main entrance to the park and guided them on to where there was a snack and souvenir shop. She had avoided the lower entrance where the museum was and the upper entrance where the Monastery of *Panaghia Kalopetra* was. These were places that children don't particularly care about. They got their tickets and entered the park, following narrow pathway of rock along the river.

Chloe continued with more information about the moths. "The eggs that were laid late in the year begin to change in spring. In April the eggs produce the larva which forms their cocoon. In May, they become flying insects. When it gets hot they come into the valley attracted to the resin of the trees, the coolness of the valley, and the humidity of the water. At the end of summer they mate and the females lay their eggs in moss, shrubs and tree bark everywhere. Each female lays about 150 eggs and then departs. The males remain, resting during the day, clinging to the trees for protection. During this time, they don't eat, storing up their energy for their remigration back to foreign lands to the north. And that is why, whenever we see a group of moths here, we are to remain very quiet."

"Why? Are they sleeping?" asked Melodia.

"Yes, and they must not be disturbed. So, just enjoy looking at them."

Water ran from different places to join the river, sometimes as narrow trickles, or as foot-wide falls, and then fanning out to form small lakes. Some of the lakes were ringed with trees and flowering shrubs, others were filled with waterlilies. They crossed several bridges, and all along the way, they took turns to see who could find the many colorful and distinctive moths, by pointing. When the moth spread its black and white striped top wings, they could see the reddish-orange wings below and the orange body beneath that. With their wings closed, they looked like a striped and pointed Indian arrowhead.

Finally they came to a large group of trees where there were many benches. Signs for people to be quiet were at each bench and a guard put his finger to his lips when he saw them coming, to make sure they remained silent, for this was the heart of the forest where most of the moths came to rest. The tree trunks were covered with the moths, creating a black and white coat.

Melodia's mouth opened in wonderment and then she turned to her parents with a big smile on her face. Chante and Lucien lived for these moments when life could amaze their little girl. After some time enjoying the scenery, they silently walked away, enjoying more moths flying around, all the way back to the entrance.

Chapter Nine

That evening, Lucien had more meetings with members of the dig team at the B&B. The first one was scheduled for 6:30, the second at 7:00 and the third at 7:30, just as before.

Lucien greeted Layland Elias at the door and ushered him through to the back patio. Layland was in his late forties. He was of medium build, but slender, with dark hair and brown eyes, and he wore dark-rimmed glasses.

"Mister Elias, thank you for coming. I know you've already spoken with the police, but I've been hired by UNESCO's cultural division to investigate the theft, and need to pursue the same lines of inquiry."

"That's fine, detective. Glad to help where I can."

"So you are the team's conservator. I understand you are responsible for the finds that are excavated, making sure they are handled carefully and stored properly. Can you walk me through the process you took with the specific finds that were taken?"

Layland took off his glasses and began cleaning them with an eyeglass cloth which he pulled from his pocket. "Those finds were handled in exactly the same way that I handle all finds. After the photos are taken in situ and the item is removed from its position, the archaeologist who did the work records the item's material, along with the date, where on the site it was found, and its general condition. I arrive with a container to place the item in, usually a small box with cotton padding. I walk the item, along with the information, to the storage building. I unlock the door, and decide where to place the item. I like to keep the same type of items together. That is, I keep marble remnants in one place, clay items in another. There are also bone items, ceramics, tiles, and metal. Whatever it is, I try to group it with finds of the same kind. There are specific ways to preserve each of the different kinds of materials, so I am conscientious about that.

"But my job does not end there. Conservation is not just conserving, as there are often interventions that must take place in order to preserve the site in some way. For example, maybe the item or the entire site needs to be covered from the elements, or perhaps a trench needs to be dug to keep rainwater from flooding the area. There is also cleaning and possibly repairing an item. Any coatings or adhesives on an item can complicate the matter. Then there is the investigation of items and the preventive care and maintenance of them. I need to make sure they stay preserved. If the item comes from the sea, it usually must be retained in water. Since everything here is being retrieved from dry land, the challenge is mostly fragility, and exposure to moisture, heat or cold. I make sure each item is secure and properly padded, recorded and stored. I research the item to determine what it is, how it was made and when it was used. If the item is going to a museum, I am the one who makes sure the item arrives safely."

"That's quite a lot. Thank you. I trust that you keep the storage building locked at all times. Of everyone on the team, who has a key to the building?"

"Only myself, Professor Ekonomos, and our most experienced archaeologist, Alec Laskaras, who is in charge whenever the professor is not on the island."

"Laskaras? I'll be speaking with him tomorrow night. I assume you trust the professor and Laskaras, but do you have any reason to think that another member of the team might have had something to do with the theft?"

Layland shook his head. "I have my small disagreements with some of them now and then, but no, I trust them all not to steal. We're in the business of discovery, not thievery."

"I understand that, but someone, not necessarily on the team, had other ideas. In the days leading up to the theft, do you recall anyone who was there and acting suspicious? Did anyone look too overly interested in watching the team, or was there anyone who loitered or asked questions?"

"We almost never speak with the tourists. We're too busy. So, I have to say no. I don't remember anyone like that."

"Well," Lucien said while pulling out his card, "if you recall anything that might be of interest, please call me."

Lucien walked him to the front and waited for the next person. Ten minutes later, the next dig team member arrived.

"Thalia Doukas? Thank you for coming." After saying why he was in Rhodes, he walked her to the back patio and they were seated.

Thalia was younger than the others. He knew from her CV that she was only twenty-nine. She looked younger, with her straight blond hair pulled back into a ponytail, and with no makeup her light blue eyes looked as innocent as a child's.

"I think you are the youngest professional on site. How did you come to be on the professor's team?"

Thalia sat up a bit straighter before answering. "I graduated top of my class seven years ago, detective, and had my choice of where I wanted to work. I wanted to lead my own team to work this site, but the ministry of culture sent me a letter saying they had already accepted Professor Ekonomos' application. But they offered to recommend me for his team. I was a bit put out, I admit. But I soon realized that having on my CV that I had worked for the professor would only make my CV look better. And once I began working with him and the rest of the team, things worked out."

"So you have been on the team since April?"

"Yes."

"Have you any idea how the items were stolen from the storage facility?"

"No."

"I can only assume that you've grown to trust everyone you work with. But have you seen or heard anything that might lead you to believe someone on the team was not being so honest?"

Thalia looked directly at him and paused. "If I tell you something, will you keep it from the other team members?"

Lucien leaned in. Could she be offering a new lead? "I promise."

"I don't hang out with any of them. I don't know them well enough to trust any of them. I will tell you that I have absolutely nothing to base that feeling on. I guess I am still carrying a bit of disappointment at not having my own team. But I greet the team members every morning and I do my job well. I laugh at their jokes, and then say goodnight at the end of the day, and that's about it. When this season is done, I'll apply again to run my own team."

Disappointed, Lucien sat back and considered her words. Her suppressed anger was about something else entirely. If she had stolen the items, she would not have confessed her feelings. It would have put too much suspicion on her. Still, she might be someone to watch.

"I've got another question for you. There are a lot of archaeologists on this dig. Why so many?"

She tilted her head, surprised at the change of subject. "It's a large site. There's the dig at the top of the mound at the acropolis, and there's the trench dig between the acropolis and the lower temple. There is the work at the old stoa and the Nymphaeums. At each of those sites there is a lead archaeologist and an assistant. The others are specialists, but two of them act as assistants. For the size of this job, twelve is the minimum number working here. Because of the pandemic I'm surprised that Professor Ekonomos got as many people to work as he did. When the students were here, they helped, and I can well appreciate their enthusiasm, but they were often more trouble than it was worth."

"What do you mean?"

"They asked a lot of questions and needed extra handling."

"I see. Well, if you can think of anything that might help the investigation, I hope you will call me."

He handed her his card and then walked her to the front. She left him with plenty to think about. A few minutes later, the last team member for the evening arrived.

"Jace Othonos?" With a nod of the head, Lucien led him through, explaining why he was in Rhodes, and then offered him a seat on the patio.

Jace was in his early fifties, had soft brown curls, and wore a blue kerchief around his neck, which matched his dark blue eyes. He was of average height and weight, and had a tattoo on his arm of a whale and star.

"Mister Othonos, I appreciate you taking the time. I've met most of your team members, and they seem to be a good bunch. How did you come on to the team?"

Jace adjusted the knot at his neck before answering. "I've worked with the professor before, in Athens. He called me in February, told me about this dig, and asked if I wanted to join him again. I said yes."

"And did you know any of the other team members before this dig?"

"Only Flavian Hasparas, the pottery specialist, who both the professor and I worked with before in Athens."

"And during the time you've been working on this dig, have you come to trust your team members?"

"I'm not sure I would trust any of the men with a girl I might be dating, but with their own work, sure. They are all good at what they do."

"No one seems to have noticed any stranger hanging around before the theft. Did you happen to see anyone questionable?"

Jace sat back in his chair and thought about it. Then he slowly shook his head. "No, not a stranger, per se, but we did have an unusual visitor."

"You did? And who was that?"

"I don't know his name. I think I've seen him once before. A man came about a week before the theft to speak with the professor. I don't know what about. They stood atop the acropolis hill and talked for about ten minutes. I was working down at the lower end of the trench, so I couldn't hear anything, but they kept looking my team's way."

Lucien got a little excited. "Please describe him."

"He was well-dressed in nice slacks, and had on a dark blue sport coat. He had short black hair and a small dark moustache, but that's all I could see."

Lucien made a mental note of the description. "Thank you." Lucien pulled out another card. "You've been very helpful. If you think of anything else that you can tell me, please call."

They shook hands and Lucien led him out the front door.

Chante came down from their room and met Lucien in the living room.

"Well? Anything helpful?"

"Maybe. I'm not ready to form an opinion quite yet. Not until I've spoken to all of them. Tomorrow after we get back I'll be speaking with the last guard, and tomorrow night the last three members of the dig team.

"Well, Melodia is waiting for her father to tuck her in." She put her arm around one of his. "Come say good night to her, and then Gala has fixed us dinner. I think she's curious about what you are doing."

"Is she? Well at this point there's not much to know and certainly nothing to share."

Chapter Ten

Friday morning, Chloe arrived just as the family was finishing their breakfast.

"Where are we off to today?" asked Gervais.

"Today, I have a plan for both Melodia and the adults. First, we will drive down the western coast to the ruins of the ancient city of Kamiros. Bring your sunhats, sunglasses and good walking shoes, as it is a large outdoor area. Then we'll stop at a nearby restaurant for lunch where you can try their excellent moussaka. Afterward, we'll head inland to the Toy Museum."

Melodia's ears perked up. "Toys? Can I play with them?"

"Many of the toys are old and can't be played with, which is why they are in a museum, but there are some toys you *can* play with."

They packed up their gear and left shortly after nine. Half an hour later and less than twenty miles away they came to the ancient city. Chloe parked in the large dirt parking area and they walked to the edge of the lot where they could see down on to the entire site.

Chloe gave them an introduction. "This ancient city is at least 2600 years old and was built by the ancient Dorians, a large ethnic group among the Greeks. They also had their own dialect and traditions. The city housed about four hundred families and a large assembly of priests operated the temples. You can see by looking at this valley that there are three levels. We are going to walk down that wide central stone walkway on our visit. At the very bottom is a terrace where a Doric temple to Apollo was built. There is a building called the Fountain House, as it had a large fountain in front of it, and across from it was the agora marketplace. There is also a sacred area where many altars were found.

"The second and central level is where most of the people lived, and you can see that they had a regular grid of streets and blocks. At the top of the hill to our right, you can see what is left of the acropolis, a temple complex to Athena, and what was once a large *stoa* or covered walkway. Some of the pillars are still there, but broken. This town was unique in that it was built right over a reservoir that could provide enough water for the entire city."

"What happened to all the people?" asked Melodia.

"They left long ago," replied Chloe. "They probably went to Rhodes city. There was a large earthquake in 226 BCE which destroyed most of the town. The damage must have been so bad that they had to leave." She continued. "A special type of priest lived here, called the *hieropoios,* who was in charge of making sure the sacrifices were performed correctly. Fragments of writing from the third century BCE describe what was sacrificed: goats to Dionysus, pigs to Apollo, and lambs to the god Pharma. Excavations were done in 1852 lasting for almost twelve years, and again in 1928. What was unearthed can be seen in the London British Museum."

They proceeded down the steps and were awed at the symmetry of the streets, the perfect lines of stacked stone blocks, and the distant views of the ocean. The day was already warming up, but the breeze off the coast kept it comfortable. After an hour of wandering they walked back up the steps to the top of the hill and left.

Chloe drove them to the coast road and headed back north, but only for a short while until she found the restaurant she wanted to take them to. They walked around the building and down a side entrance, where they came upon a back patio that faced the beach. Umbrella tables were there, so they chose one and sat. Soon the menus appeared and they ordered. Melodia had a fish sandwich, Chante had a seafood salad, and Chloe, Gervais and Lucien had the moussaka and confirmed that it was delicious.

Back in the car, they headed south on the Eleousas Road, and just past the town they turned north. Melodia saw the building first, with a large clown poster outside in front. The building was built of large stones with green double doors, and it was surrounded by an olive grove. Inside they let Melodia wander. There were vintage toys from the 1950s through the '80s. They consisted of matchbox vehicles, toy cars, trucks, buses, helicopters, trains, even space ships and a space station, most with their original boxes. There were old children's books, stuffed animals, tin and wooden toys, toy robots, dolls from around the world along with their doll carriages and doll houses, board games, play kitchens, toy circuses, and comic books. Gervais laughed when he was reminded of his own Mr. Potato Head, and Chante remembered the small trolls with colorful wild hair. They came out before she was born, but her mother had kept one and given it to her as a child. Melodia liked the small plastic unicorns with pink hair, and the room with lots of toys that she could play with. Her favorite was the toy monkey. With the turn of a handle the monkey did chin-ups and sometimes flipped over. That made her laugh and laugh. Downstairs in the basement were old pinball machines, Pachinko machines, and early computer games, including Pac Man. All of them worked and Lucien enjoyed playing with these. They thought the toy museum would be a place just for Melodia to enjoy, but they all enjoyed the museum and ended up spending almost two hours there.

By three thirty they left and headed back to the city. Melodia fell asleep in the car and was hungry when they returned. Chloe was glad they had enjoyed the day, and was pleased at how much she was enjoying the Reynard family.

Lucien got to the dig site right at six o'clock, in time to meet with Daikonos Lykaios, who was just coming on duty. As Lucien crossed the street, he saw Lykaios standing at the gate. His chest and muscular arms filled his uniform. His dark beard looked freshly trimmed, and his dark hair was tucked under his cap.

"*Ya sas,* Mister Lykaios. Hello. Thank you for seeing me."

The man stood at the gate and nodded. "Detective."

"I know you have been questioned by the police, but I need to ask you some of the same questions, since you were the guard on duty at the time of the theft."

"Yes, sir, I understand. What do you want to know?"

"Please describe for me your movements that night."

Daikonos took a deep breath, trying to stay calm, having to retell it once again. "That evening at six o'clock, I arrived and met Dimitri at the guard shack. There's a book there where we sign in. We chatted for a short time, and then he left. I fixed myself a cup of coffee and took it with me on my rounds."

"I'm sorry to interrupt, but had the dig team left by then? I guess the site is closed by that time."

"Yes, the site closes at five and the dig team members leave anytime between four-thirty and six, depending upon when they arrived."

"All right, thank you. Please continue."

"The first thing I did was start at the top of the hill at the Apollo Acropolis. I walked around it and inspected the lock on the storage door to make sure it was secure. We always tug on it to make sure. Then I walked around the stadium next to the gymnasium, went past the Odeon and down toward the Athena Temple. I walked to the far end of the stoa, and around the Nymphaeums. Then back to the guard shack for a break. I sat for about an hour, and that's how it went all night long, as it usually does on my shift. First, I do rounds and then take a break. At about four in the morning, I needed to relieve myself, so I walked down to where the bathrooms are near the stoa. When I was done, I reversed my round. I walked around the lower part of the site and then I came up to walk the upper part of the site.

"When I reached the storage facility I found that the lock had been cut. I reached for my gun and called out, thinking someone might be in the building, but no one answered. I opened the door, but did not see anything amiss. Still, it was my duty to call the professor and I did. He came quickly, arriving about five fifteen. The front gate lock had also been cut. He was mad at me when he saw it. I had to admit, I had not checked the gate lock. The professor did an inventory while I stood guard and called the police. It took him only about half an hour to finish the inventory. By then, Calix had arrived at six, and then he stood guard, while the professor made me do another round."

"So then the police arrived and you were questioned."

"Yes, sir."

"I know the schedule for the three of you revolves, but I want to ask. In the days leading up to the theft, did you see any tourist staying around longer than usual, or asking questions?"

"No, not that I recall."

"Do you have much interaction with the dig team?"

"Not really. I'm a night person and that's my usual shift, so I'm not often here during the day to see them, let alone interact with them."

"But you were that day. I'm told you were still here when the team arrived at eight o'clock."

"I was, but I didn't speak with them."

Lucien was getting frustrated. There was nothing that Daikonos had said to lead him to think there was anything other than what he had been told.

"Well, thank you again for answering my questions. I won't keep you any longer." He gave him his card.

Lykaios took it, tipped his cap and said goodbye. Lucien needed to hurry back to the B&B for the last three interviews.

Chapter Eleven

Lucien was a couple minutes late arriving back at the B&B, but Goran Hallas was just arriving himself and stood at the side door to the B&B. After brief introductions, Lucien let him in and then took him to the back patio. Goran was in his late fifties, partially bald with a receding hairline and short brown hair around his ears. He had brown eyes, a gentle handshake and voice, and a belly that was rounding out.

"So you are the team's photographer. Have you worked with anyone on this team before?"

"Yes, I worked for the professor twice before on other digs, but the others are new to me."

"So you've had only four months to get to know them. What do you think of your team members?"

"They seem to be a good lot and appear to know what they are doing."

"And during those four months, have you seen any rifts on the team?"

He cocked his head to think. "No, I don't think so. I mean, if a few of us go out and drink we might argue a point or two about the world, but nothing on-site."

"In the days leading up to the theft, did you notice anyone hanging around or asking questions?"

"Not that I can recall. The students asked a lot of questions, but that's normal, they're learning the profession."

"You must be kept pretty busy with several digs going on at the site."

"Yes, I travel up and down the hill all day long. But the exercise is good for me. As you can tell, I need it. I love the calorie-laden moussaka."

"Did you share your photographs of the stolen finds with the police?"

"Yes, the pictures were key, as there was no other way to identify what had been taken."

"I need to have a copy of those photos. Would you please send them to me?" Lucien handed him his card with his email.

"Yes, of course. I also have video that I take to document the dig. Do you want a copy of those clips, too?"

"Yes, absolutely, but not for the entire length of the dig. How about for a few days before the theft and each of the stolen items? And if you remember anything else, please let me know."

"I will, detective."

They said their goodbyes at the front door and ten minutes later, the second person arrived.

"Mister Flavian Hasparas, please come in."

They settled in the back patio.

Flavian was a trim man in his early-fifties with straight light brown hair that was worn short. He had beard stubble and wore glasses. He was wearing a shirt with a pattern of small clay pots all over it.

"Mister Hasparas, you are an archaeologist who specializes in pottery, as your shirt indicates, correct?"

That made the man laugh. "Yes, detective." He ran his hand down the front of his shirt. "I specialize in Archaic and Classical Greek pottery from the Iron Age. That is why I was hired."

"And you know Jace Othonos. You've worked with him before."

"Yes, we worked together with the professor in Athens two years ago."

"Did you know anyone else on the team before you began here?"

"I had read some of their published articles, but I hadn't met them before."

"Does everyone seem to get along, in your estimation?"

"I think so. I haven't had a problem with anyone. The professor sometimes gets on us, but that's his job. Overall, he is well-liked."

"Do you recall if you noticed anyone hanging around or asking questions about the dig? I know the team members are usually too busy to notice, but there must be times when you are standing and waiting to be called. Surely you observe the tourists now and then?"

"Sure. There are often children running around making noise that sometimes distracts my attention from the site. Once in a while I notice a pretty woman walking by. But no stranger that stands out."

"What is your impression of the theft? How do you think it happened?"

"It was probably some kid who broke in for the fun of it. Maybe had a thing for old buried treasure."

Lucien was waiting for the usual line about kids stealing for drugs, but Flavian did not go there.

"Yes, except only certain things were taken. Anything else you can tell me?"

"I'm sorry, detective. I just don't know anything else."

"Well, thank you for your time. If you recall anything, please call the number on this card."

Lucien walked him out and waited. The last person was late. Fifteen minutes later, he finally arrived and Lucien met him at the front door.

"I'm sorry, Detective Reynard. I got a bit lost."

"Mister Alec Laskaras, I presume." They reached out and shook hands. "No problem, come in. We're going out back to the patio. It's more pleasant out there."

Alec was in his late thirties, trim, with a military haircut. He had light brown hair, was clean shaven with brown eyes, and walked with a slight limp.

"Mister Laskaras, you are one of the archaeologists on the team. Do you have a specialty?"

"No, not particularly, but I am partial to Middle Eastern archaeology. I got started in archaeology in Turkey, near the Syrian border. But I was wounded in a border skirmish and returned to Greece. When I got better, I stayed in Greece to work."

"Yes, I noticed your limp. Are you in pain? Does it hamper your work?"

"No, my leg is healed, no pain, and aside from a bit of a limp I am fine in the field. I don't spend a long time on my knees, but I get the work done."

"Did you know any of the other members of the team before coming to Rhodes?"

"No, but I had heard about Professor Ekonomos, so I applied for work and got on to the team."

"You are the only other person with a key to the storage facility. The professor did not previously know you, but trusted you with a key. Can you explain that?"

"It was probably due to my long career in the field, having led several teams, and a high recommendation from my last project supervisor, who knows the professor."

"Has your key remained in your possession this entire time?"

Alec reached into his pocket and pulled out his keys. He fanned through them until he found the key to the storage. "Yep, it's still here. And no, before you ask, no one has borrowed my keys."

"In your opinion, who would you say is responsible for the theft and why?"

"Who? Who knows. Why? Maybe someone thought they could sell the items, or someone was angry with the professor and was seeking revenge. Perhaps someone hired another to break in, so they wouldn't be directly connected, or perhaps another archaeologist, not of this team, just wanted to get one up on the professor."

"That's a lot of possibilities. Have you experienced any anger or ill-feelings from anyone on the team?"

"No, sir. We all seem to get along pretty well. In our profession, we get used to working with people from all over the world with their own ideas, processes, and feelings. The one thing we all believe in is the process of teamwork. None of us can do the work well on our own. It takes a team, especially for as much ground as we are covering."

"That's understandable. Is there anything you can tell me that you were not able to tell the police at the station?"

"Actually, I was not formally interviewed by the police at the station. They briefly questioned me that morning on site, but only asked if I had seen anything. I had not."

"I was told by Inspector Nomikos that she had conducted interviews with all team members. Do you have an idea why they didn't interview you at the station?"

"No, none at all, but then I didn't have anything to tell them anyway, and they spoke to me on site."

"But you're the third person with a key."

"I know, but it's been in my possession the entire time, and besides, the lock on the storage building was cut."

"Well, thank you for coming. If you think of anything, or in the ensuing days you hear talk of anything, will you please let me know?"

Lucien handed him his card.

"Yes, Detective Reynard. I will."

Lucien walked him to the door and watched him walk away down the road. Then he shut the door and sat down in the living room to think. He was joined shortly by Chante and Gervais.

"Well, son, did you get any decent information from those last three?"

"Hi, Papa, I'm not sure. I have to think about it."

Chante sat beside him. "Surely there was something that might have stirred a possibility in you."

"Maybe. The photographer is sending us photos of each of the items that were stolen, along with some video of the team working, but I doubt that will show anything."

Chante squeezed his hand and patted his knee. "Then I will tell you what you always tell us. 'Maybe yes, maybe no.' Now, go see your daughter to bed and come back down for some dinner." She leaned over and kissed his cheek.

Lucien looked at Chante and could not help but fall in love with her all over again. She had a way of making everything seem brighter.

They avoided discussing the case in front of Gala or Nils, who had graciously invited them to their dinner table for a nominal fee. Afterward however, they met in Gervais' room so Lucien could discuss what he had found out and decide where to go from there. They laid out the CVs for the members of the dig team, including the professor. They also had brief notes on the three guards. Those were the obvious suspects, but nothing Lucien had learned had steered him to truly suspect any one of them.

Chante, ever ready to get to the heart of things, began. "Let's look at the three guards first. Hypothesis: One is either working on his own, or perhaps two of them are working together. One goes to the far end of the site and takes his time, allowing his associate to get in and take the items."

"But they all had keys to the front gate," responded Gervais. "They wouldn't have needed to cut *that* lock."

"Or maybe the person cut it just so it would appear to be cut by a stranger," added Chante.

Lucien pulled out his notes. "Okay, here's what I have in my notes for the guards. Dimitri Kouris is the first guard I spoke to. He's young, and said he is hoping to one day join the police. So I don't think he had anything to do with it."

"He might have said that to throw your suspicions off of him."

"I didn't get that feeling. The next guard, Calix Kalogeras. is an older man. He did say something surprising, that he thought it was an inside job."

"Would someone say that if they were guilty?" said Chante "No, they wouldn't. They would say it was some stranger who broke in."

Lucien continued. "The third guard, Daikonos Lykaios, was the guard on duty when the theft occurred. He seems the most likely person to blame, but if he's the thief, where would he have hidden the items which were taken, in the guard shack? Unlikely, as Dimitri was soon arriving and would go there to check in. He looks tough, but I don't think he's guilty of anything more than taking extra time to take a piss."

Chapter Twelve

Chante, Lucien and Gervais continued to discuss the case in Gervais' room, with Lucien reviewing what of interest he had heard.

"So now let's look closer at the twelve members of the dig team. The first one I spoke to was Lydia Karas. She said that the guard Daikonos was sweating even though it was a cool morning, but she reasoned he was just nervous about losing his job. I think it is more probable that he was nervous because he was on duty when the theft occurred and was the most likely to be blamed. Dru Cirillo was the second person, but he didn't seem to know anything and gave no new information. Gregory Andino commented that there were some nice coins unearthed and mentioned a small bronze statue, but had no new information. I spoke to Amara Sideris and Julien Ganas at the site. Amara has known the professor for twenty years, whereas Julien had only met him. He got on the team after being recommended by Professor Philemon at the university. Neither saw nor did they seem to know anything. The next three came to the house. Layland Elias thoroughly described what he does as a conservator, but gave me no other information of interest about the theft. Thalia Doukas said she didn't really know or mistrust anyone on the team, but she does have some residual anger. Seems she had applied to lead a team for the site, but did not get the job. She was recommended for the team and that's how she got on. She further added that afterward she thought it was to her benefit to work under him, so she could get future work. She also explained the need for the number of archaeologists on the site, and explained that each of the four digs has a lead and an assistant, which was good to learn.

"Jace Othonos was next. He had worked with the professor before in Athens, and the professor asked him to be on the team. He also knew Flavian Hasparas, with whom he had also worked in Athens. Of all of them, Jace had the most interesting information. He said that a man came about a week before the theft to speak with the professor, and that they stood atop the acropolis hill and talked, often looking down at the trench team. Jace didn't know what they said, as he was too far away. Then he got busy and didn't continue watching. He was able to give me a description of the man: well-dressed, dress slacks, dark blue sport coat, short black hair and a small dark moustache. We can follow up on him. Goran Hallas was the first person I saw tonight. He had worked with the professor twice before, but had not worked with the rest of the team members before. He has photographs of each of the items that were taken and some video of the teams working on the site, so we will do a review as soon as we get those. The last person on the team was Alec Laskaras, who had not worked with either the professor or the team before, but came with a high recommendation of trust, so he was given the third key to the storage building. The professor and the conservator, Elias, are the other two key holders. Laskaras thought that maybe someone stole the items to sell, or that someone might be angry with the professor and was seeking revenge. Or perhaps an archaeologist from another team just wanted to get one up on the professor. The last thing that surprised me was that he said Inspector Nomikos had not interviewed him. He had been asked a few questions in the morning by the police, but that was all."

Gervais looked at Chante and then back at Lucien. "That's not a lot to go on, son. Let's hope the photographs and video help. The only other thing of interest is the description of the man who came to speak with the professor."

"Yes, I'm going to call the professor and ask him about that person. But for tonight, let's mull over what we've learned and start fresh tomorrow."

Early Saturday morning Lucien called the professor.

"*Kaliméra*, Professor Ekonomos. This is Detective Reynard. I'm calling for a couple of reasons."

"*Kaliméra*, detective."

"First, I want to thank you very much for scheduling your team to meet with me. I very much appreciate your cooperation."

"You are very welcome. Anything that can help you and the police catch the thief is worth it."

"Yes, I have spoken to each of your team members and the three guards."

"Were any of them able to give you anything to go on?"

"Very little, I'm afraid, but one person did mention that they saw you speaking with someone on the site the week before the theft, and I would just like to know who that might have been. He was described as being well-dressed, nice slacks, dark blue sport coat, short black hair and a small dark moustache. Can you tell me who that person was?"

"That sounds like Argus Dougenis. He's from the Department of Antiquities and Cultural Heritage, I believe from Athens. He contacts me now and then to check on the work."

"Does he usually come to the site to do so?"

"No, usually he calls, but he did come once before during the first season."

"Would you be so kind as to tell me what you spoke about?"

"Oh my, that was several weeks ago, but let me think. He said he had come to the island to see a friend and thought he would stop by. I recall the usual questions: how was the work coming along, what things had turned up, and was there anything special."

"When you answered his questions, did you tell him about the items that were later stolen?"

"Yes, because some of the coins were particularly old. In fact, I opened the storage facility and showed him those pieces, and others."

"You did? Did you tell the police about that?"

"No. The Department of Antiquities and Cultural Heritage is the oversight administration for all archaeological excavations in Greece. Of all people, I would think that he should be eliminated from suspicion. They would want those pieces back as much as I do."

"I'm sure he is as innocent as you say. I'm just trying to put as much information together as I can. Please don't think me rude, but did he show any particular interest in any of the pieces? You see, he might have mentioned to someone what he had seen, without realizing what was going to happen."

"Oh, I see. No, no interest in anything in particular. For what it's worth, even though I only met him this spring, I do believe he acts in the best interest of the country."

"Good. Well, thank you for letting me know this information. If I have any more questions, I'll call."

"All right, Detective Reynard. Good luck."

They hung up.

Chante, who had been listening, waited. "So we can eliminate the man who visited the professor?"

Lucien pursed his lips and slowly nodded. "I think so. Ekonomos said he was from the Department of Antiquities and Cultural Heritage."

"Oh. A bigwig. How disappointing."

"Maybe. At any rate, now we know at least one person from that organization, so it wasn't a complete loss. The man's name is Argus Dougenis."

Then they went down for breakfast on the back patio. It would be another warm day.

"Lucien, Melodia wants to go to the beach. Why don't you and Gervais follow whatever leads you want. Chloe asked if we wanted to do anything today and when I asked about beaches, she said she would take us to two nice ones."

Lucien agreed. "That's a good idea."

Gervais was curious. "*Do* we have any leads to follow?"

"I did quite a lot of thinking last night before I could sleep, and came up with something that we could do. I will discuss it with you upstairs later," and leaned in with a low voice, "when our hostess isn't lingering to catch what we say."

Gervais nodded.

An hour later, Chloe had arrived and the women took off, leaving Lucien and Gervais to discuss their options. They sat in Gervais' room at his office desk where they had set up their laptops.

"So what trail do you want to follow?" asked Gervais.

"We need to do a deep search into everyone on the team, and the three guards. On the surface, there is nothing, but there is always something underneath everyone's story."

"All right, then I will start on the team members, and Chante can take the three guards when she returns." Then Lucien's computer dinged with an email.

"Perfect timing. Goran Hallas has just sent over the photographs he took of all the items that were stolen."

"That's great, but it would be nice if the archivist could send over what he has already researched and written up on each item."

"Right, that would be Gregory Andino, whose job is to identify the artifacts as they get unearthed. I'll give him a call right now."

Lucien looked up the man's number and called him.

"*Kaliméra*, Mister Andino. This is Detective Reynard."

"*Kaliméra*, detective. What's up?"

"Sorry to bother you this morning, but I've got a request. Would you please send over everything that you have written up on each of the stolen items?"

"I can, although I have made only the most basic of notations on those items until I can do some deeper research."

"Anything you have would be useful. It helps us to know what we might be looking at. And would you please do so as soon as possible?"

"Right now? Okay, give me a few minutes to put that together for you."

"Please send it to the email address on my card. Thank you."

They hung up and Lucien and Gervais waited. About ten minutes went by, and then Andino's report with the attachments came in. The items were numbered, corresponding to the number on a small placard next to each item in the photos. There were now fifteen pictures and fifteen descriptions. Lucien emailed the pictures and their descriptions to Gervais and Chante.

Gervais and Lucien spent some time looking at each picture and then reading the description of each one. Not surprisingly, they were mostly coins, parts of weaponry, and jewelry pieces.

1. Item #423: Obverse - a man's head in profile wearing a spiked crown / Reverse – an oak leaf, Silver, 15mm, within 1st c. BCE

2. Item #424: Obverse - profile of a man's head / Reverse - a rose Silver Didrachm, 15 mm, within 1st c. BCE

3. Item #425: Obverse - head of Helios with sun rays around head / Reverse - head of an eagle, Silver Tetradrachm, 27mm, late 2nd c. BCE

4. Item #426: Obverse - head of Helios in profile, wearing spiked crown / Reverse - a stamped rosebud in an incuse square with a coiled snake, and a man with the word "Aptemon" above, Silver Drachm, 16.45mm, 1st c. BCE

5. Item #427: Obverse - Alexander the Great head in profile / Reverse - Zeus seated on thrown, holding an eagle, Silver Tetradrachm, 28.37mm, late 2nd/early 1st c. BCE

6. Item #428: Obverse - two drinking vessels in the shape of rams heads; above them, two dolphins swimming toward each other / Reverse - a quadripartite incuse square in the form of a coffered ceiling; each with a dolphin and a spray of laurel leaves. Delphi Silver Tridrachm, 28.42mm, Mid-3rd c. BCE

7. Item #429: Obverse - frontal head of Helios / Reverse - five petalled rose with wreath of oak leaves. Bronze Tetratrachm, 27.15m, 1st c. BCE

8. Item #430: small statue of Colossus of Rhodes holding light above head. 11x6cm, 300 gr., Bronze, 1214 CE

9. Item #431: small elongated and pointed oval spearhead with opening in shaft, 8cm, bronze, 2nd c. BCE

10. Item #432: Macedonian stabbing spearhead, 16.51cm long, bronze, at least 200 BCE

11. Item #433: Sword handle, with a flared hilt covered with a double raised ring pattern, Green patina with earthen encrustation, Bronze, 3rd c. BCE

12. Item #434: Ring, Silver Alexander the Great drachm coin in a vermeil ring setting of 22kt gold plate finish over pure silver. Size 9, late 300 c. BCE

13. Item #435: One earring, gold loop with front in shape of a ram's head, gold, 4cm, 3rd to 2nd c. BCE

14. Item #436: necklace end piece, fine snake link chain with half of a snake closure, 15cm, Gold, unknown (3rd c. BCE)

15. Item #437: bracelet, bird decoration, made from sheet bronze with rounded terminals, 65 mm olive green patina, 4th c. BCE

Lucien and Gervais were impressed by each item, and figured any one of them might be what a collector was after.

"We might need to further consult with Andino to find out the value of these items," suggested Gervais.

"Or perhaps a specialty appraiser might be better," responded Lucien. "Regardless, I think these might be the key to our mystery. I'm beginning to think it's not a person who will lead us to the items, but one of these items that will lead us to the thief."

Chapter Thirteen

Lucien searched online for an appraiser who specialized in ancient Greek artifacts and found one in Athens. The man was Doctor Theron Nicholaides, and on his website was a picture of him in a shirt and dress jacket. He appeared to be in his seventies with short white hair, a wrinkled forehead and light hazel eyes. The website linked to many of the museums that had utilized his expertise along with some letters from museum curators who had thanked him for his work. A news feature on his site said that he was finally retiring at the end of the year, to make it an even fifty years in his career. A phone number was posted on his contact page.

The phone rang five times before it was finally picked up.

"*Emprós.*"

"Hello, Doctor Nicholaides. Do you speak English or French?"

"Yes, I speak English. Who is this, please?"

"My name is Detective Lucien Reynard from the culture department of UNESCO's Paris office. I'm here in Rhodes and I am in need of your expertise."

There was a pause at the other end. "I'm sorry detective, but I am not taking on any more work at this time."

"Doctor Nicholaides, we don't want anyone else. We want the best." Lucien figured that it wouldn't hurt to lay on the praise if it would get the man to change his mind.

"But detective, I'm in the process of retiring and bringing to a close all the jobs I have been working on. I can give you a recommendation of someone else to contact."

"Doctor, let me explain. I am investigating the theft of fifteen specific items from an archaeological site in Rhodes. If I send you photographs of each of the items along with their descriptions prepared by an archaeologist, your valuable opinion might lead us to the thief. Your evaluation could possibly reveal which of the items was the reason for the crime. That knowledge could hopefully lead us to the perpetrator. Surely you would like to end your career with an international headline about how you helped the Greek police. UNESCO is happy to pay you for your time."

At least Lucien hoped that UNESCO would pay for the work. He should have asked them beforehand if they would agree, but couldn't fathom that they wouldn't want to know the value of the items.

There was a longer pause on the phone. "Doctor, are you still there?"

"I'm here. I don't do appraisals on things that I can't examine for myself and hold in my hands. No self-respecting appraiser would."

"I understand that, but this is an important case, and we have precious little to go on. Please, doctor. Even just a preliminary estimation of value would help. You would be of tremendous help to us and the Greek government."

Lucien could hear him take a deep breath. "There are several approaches to determining value: the cost determination of what it would take to reproduce a piece, the sales comparison with anything similar that has sold in the past, and the present value, usually for insurance purposes. I take it you are solely interested in finding out what the thief might expect to get for those items."

"Yes, anything that you could find out for us would be of immeasurable value. It could indicate what specific interests the thief had and what kind of collector or buyer might be interested."

Another deep breath could be heard. "This is highly irregular and not particularly ethical." He paused, again, obviously thinking. "What I tell you could not be printed in the news, or used in court. It can only be used for general valuation and seen internally by the police."

"Of course. We would only use your expertise to get a general idea. We wouldn't use it in court or publish anything you tell us."

"All right, forward what you have to the email address on my website and I'll see what I can do. I can't promise you a complete report, but I'll do my best with what you give me."

"Thank you, Doctor Nicholaides! Can you please tell me how long it might take for you to complete the work?"

"I can't answer that until I see the photographs of the items, but I will get back to you as soon as I can. Perhaps a week, maybe sooner."

"Whatever time you can spare is most appreciated. We are at a standstill here, so if you can get back to us as quickly as possible, that would be great. And one more thing, we need for you to keep this quiet. We don't want the thief or anyone else in the antiquities world to know about our investigation."

"I have my reputation to consider, detective. I won't be telling anyone."

Lucien thanked him again, ended their call, and then immediately emailed him the pictures and descriptions. He also sent a text to Monsieur Teniet at UNESCO's Paris office, so it would not be a surprise when the bill came in.

"That was some smooth talking," commented Gervais. "Let's hope he is as good as he claims."

"I hope so too. What he tells us may or may not lead us to the thief, but regardless, at least it will give us more information on each item." They stared at the photographs on their screens, wondering if knowing the value of the items would make any difference. "In the meantime, there are other things we can do."

"For instance?" Gervais asked. He knew that Lucien never lacked for ideas.

"For instance, I think it might be a good idea to go to that hotel near the acropolis, the Vista, and make some inquiries. And I think it's time to pay Inspector Nomikos another visit."

Soon, Gervais and Lucien found themselves walking into the Vista Hotel. They went to the front desk and asked for the manager. Mister Kellis came out from the back office.

"Yes, sir, how can I help you?"

"Yes, Mister Kellis, thank you for seeing us. I'm Detective Lucien Reynard and this is my assistant, Gervais Reynard. We would like to ask for your assistance. Perhaps you heard about the archaeological theft at the acropolis?"

"Yes, I read about it in the paper, but what does that have to do with me?"

"Mister Kellis, we think it is possible that someone may have stayed here to watch and plan the theft. We need to know if someone arrived within the week before the theft and most likely checked out of your hotel on the night before or the day after the event. If you can please check your records to see if there was such a person, we would be most appreciative."

Kellis did not like the police and was somewhat brusque. "I will not reveal the name of any of our guests without a warrant."

"That is fine, Mister Kellis, and we understand you wanting to protect your guests' privacy, but if you would first check to see if anyone was here during that time, then we would be happy to obtain a warrant to get that person's name. Please Mister Kellis, it is very important. It all depends on whether you want to be cooperative with the police and have your cooperation noted and therefore gain attention for your lovely establishment, or whether you might be mentioned in the local paper as being uncooperative and arrested for obstruction of justice."

Lucien's statement surprised Gervais, but it also put a slight panic on the face of the proprietor. The man went to the reception desk computer, and after asking Lucien for the dates in question, did a search. The search proved advantageous. There were two possibilities. A mister and missus had checked in on the Friday before and had checked out on Monday after the Sunday theft, and a single man had checked in four days before the theft and left the night before. This brought a smile to Gervais and a knowing nod from Lucien.

"Thank you very much for your cooperation, Mister Kellis. We will now obtain that warrant to discover those names. In the meantime, would you be so kind as to show us the room that the single person was given?"

The man silently nodded, glanced again at the booking to get the room number, and then led them to the elevator and up to the fifth floor. Fortunately, the room was unoccupied. Lucien walked straight to the large window that faced west. The whole of the acropolis was visible, but one would need binoculars to see that far away. Their visit was very quick, but enough to confirm Lucien's guess.

"Thank you, Mister Kellis. That will be all for now, but we'll be back soon. Please have the hotel video footage of the man in question arriving and departing ready for when we return."

On the way out, Lucien took the hotel proprietor's business card from a holder on the counter, and he and Gervais left.

When they were outside, Gervais turned to Lucien. "Now what?"

"Now we ask the inspector for a warrant for Mister Kellis at the Vista Hotel, and find out if we have an actual lead or not."

Lucien called the station downtown and left a message for Inspector Nomikos describing what he needed, and requested a short meeting. When Lucien and Gervais arrived at the police station fifteen minutes later, an officer escorted them to Inspector Nomikos' office.

She stood to greet them. "Detective Reynard, nice to see you again."

"*Kaliméra*, Inspector Nomikos. I would like to introduce you to my father, Gervais Reynard, whom I have the good fortune to have with me as one of my researchers. He's a retired professor of history from the University of Perpignan. His specialty is the Byzantine Era and he has written several books on European history."

The two reached out and shook hands.

"It's very nice to meet you, professor. Welcome to Rhodes."

"Thank you. It's warm here, but I am enjoying your pretty island."

Then she paused. "Would you happen to be the same Professor Gervais Reynard who solved one of our country's mysteries several years back, identifying the tomb of a princess in Mystras?"

"I am, but I am now retired. These days, I enjoy assisting my son with his mysteries in crime."

"Well, it is a pleasure." Then she glanced to Lucien. "Detective Reynard, I got your message about the warrant, and if we just sit tight, that paperwork is being rushed through. So you believe you might have a lead on our thief?"

"I can't make any promises, but it is a step in the right direction, as this individual conveniently was registered at the Vista Hotel across from the acropolis. We saw it was indeed possible to watch the site from his fifth floor room in order to plan the theft. We have the hotel proprietor looking for the video of him checking in and checking out."

"That is good news. Now you have successfully brought me to shame, as I had not thought of that possibility."

"Nonsense," he winked, "We are working together, are we not?"

She smiled. "Of course. And how did your interviews with the guards and dig team go?"

"Not as well as I had hoped, but I did glean a few things from them that I would like to share with you."

"Please, have a seat. What did you discover?"

"Several things. One, Jace Othonos remembered a man who had visited the site and spoke with Professor Ekonomos about a week before the theft. The professor said it was a man named Argus Dougenis, a member of the Department of Antiquities and Cultural Heritage. Apparently, the professor took Dougenis into the storage facility to show him some of the items that had been collected. Although the professor speaks highly of the man, it still remains possible that Dougenis might have said something to someone who had a specific interest. Professor Ekonomos said he hadn't told you about the man's visit, but now we know. Then there was Gregory Andino, who commented that there were some nice coins that he had seen, and perhaps they might have stirred someone's interest. Because the valuations are not yet known, I thought it prudent to get an appraisal of the items, so I contacted a top appraiser in Athens who will review the photographs and descriptions."

"So if we know the value of the items, we might be able to see which was the most desirable to obtain. Very good. Anything else?"

"I was surprised to find out that you had not called in Alec Laskaras for an interview, since he is only one of three individuals on the team who possesses a key to the storage building."

She frowned at his insinuation. "I spoke to him directly on site that morning and deemed it was not necessary to bring him into the station."

"That's fine. He didn't offer anything useful, anyway."

At that moment an officer walked in with a piece of paper and handed it to Inspector Nomikos. She scanned down the page, was satisfied, signed it and looked back up.

"We have our warrant. Let's go pay Mister Kellis a visit."

They left in a patrol car, followed by another vehicle with a second officer to assist.

Kellis was shown the warrant and had the tape ready for viewing. The second officer stood at the hotel entrance as the three of them watched the tape. The individual in question approached the desk to check in. The man was unknown to them, but had registered his name as Nicholas Pappas. Then Kellis changed tapes to show the man checking out four days later and paying in cash, which made him look even more suspicious. The tapes were taken by the second officer to the station for further analysis and to have copies made. Inspector Nomikos thanked Kellis for his cooperation and they returned to the police station, where the inspector promised to have Pappas investigated, and whatever turned up she would let Lucien know.

The Lion sat on the second step inside his pool, cooling off from the midday sun, wearing large dark shades and drinking a tall iced wine cooler. The wine was from the grapes grown in the small vineyard below his house. He had hired an Italian viniculturist to manage the rare red Mandilaria grape variety that he had chosen to plant and grow ten years before. He had no wish to sell the limited amount that his vineyard produced, but instead retained what was made for his own consumption. It also made for nice gifts when a job was well done and was often accompanied by an envelope with a payment.

His phone vibrated and he saw that it was his attorney, who had several minions and henchmen stationed around the city keeping an eye on things. "Yes, what is it?"

"Sir, the police have obtained video of my man going in and coming out of the hotel where he stayed near the site."

This caused the Lion to set down his drink a little harder than he intended. The glass nearly broke on the pool tile. He took a deep breath. "Thank you for letting me know. I'll get back to you." He had his ways.

As long as things went smoothly, the Lion maintained a temperate state of mind. But when things went wrong, his tempestuous streak turned him into a fuming animal. To cool his anger, he might stomp around his house drinking his wine. Or he might dive into his pool and swim several lengths to help him think, which is what he did today. By the time he finished his third lap, he had made up his mind. He got out of the pool, dried off and picked up his phone again. He called his attorney back and told him to call a certain person who he knew he could trust to get the job done, and gave instructions.

The attorney answered. "Yes, sir?" That's what he called him, just "sir," never saying his real name. He didn't even know him as "the Lion."

The Lion told him what he needed done, who to contact, and how to pay the man as soon as the job was completed. It was how he usually handled the darker side of his business.

The Lion was a recluse, as many millionaires become. A normal employer would have a paper trail of employee names with their job titles, often knew their families, and supported them as best as possible. But a man of the Lion's stature and mindset had independent people who were not on any legal payroll, had no official title on paper, had no family, were paid in cash, and no one knew his real name other than his attorney. No list, no ties, no connection to him, and no explanations. He had few people with whom he came into contact. One was his full-time chef of twenty-four years, who lived on the property, served him every meal, and sometimes acted as his private chauffeur. He had a housekeeper, the same woman who had come to his home once a week for thirty-two years, though he seldom saw her. He saw his viticulturist only once a year when approving wine from a new harvest. And his attorney, who had his private number and with whom he met now and then on legal matters. There was the occasional middleman the attorney used, with no ties to the Lion. The middleman relayed instructions, then reported when the tasks had been completed. The chef, housekeeper, and viticulturist were simply paid with cash in an envelope. The attorney took his fee from the account which he managed. Others would receive a small package with no return address.

The Lion was simply known as a retired wealthy man who appreciated his privacy. And that's the way he liked it.

There were other men in his line of work who once knew him, whom he used to meet for a drink, swap a good story, and even consult, but they were part of his past and they no longer knew what had become of him.

Chapter Fourteen

While Lucien and Gervais waited at the B&B for Chante and Melodia to return from the beach, they began researching online for information about the stolen items. They doubted that the two spearheads and broken sword would garner much. The statue was not in the best of shape, but to a specialized buyer it might be valuable. The ring and bracelet were in good shape and they might hold more worth, but what possible value could a broken chain have? So they concentrated on the seven coins as the best bet to holding any real market value.

They had been working for about an hour when Chante and Melodia returned. Chloe had taken them to two different beaches and then a small taverna for a simple lunch. Chante was hosting a slightly pink face, but with sunscreen Melodia had not taken on any color, although the sun had made her sleepy. After Chante had gotten Melodia to take a nap, she joined Gervais and Lucien in Gervais' room.

As soon as Chante walked in, Lucien's cell rang. It was Inspector Nomikos.

"I want to let you know that the name our suspect signed at the Vista, Nicholas Pappas, was fictitious. Both names are very common, but no one on the island is listed with that name, nor did any flight or ferry passenger lists have that name."

"Can you run his picture through facial recognition?"

"Way ahead of you there, detective. Our small police station cannot afford such software, but I did forward the picture of him to National Headquarters in Athens, and they are running it through the system. It might take a while."

"Thanks, inspector. Just let me know."

When Lucien got off the phone, Chante finished telling them where they had gone that day, and Lucien let her know about visiting the hotel, getting the warrant, and the searches they were working on.

Gervais was still concerned with what little they knew. "Son, I am very glad that the information we got from the hotel is panning out. If they find him, I assume the police will do a thorough interrogation. But what else can we do until then?"

"We still have the acropolis dig videos to look through. Mister Hallas said he needed to separate out those recordings within the time frame that I requested. Then it may take quite a while to look at everything that he taped." Lucien checked his email. "He hasn't sent the video yet, but I'll keep checking."

"Then," prompted Chante with a coaxing smile, "does that mean we can actually be tourists tomorrow?"

He couldn't resist her plea. "I don't see why not. What did you have in mind?"

"Chloe recommended that we take a tour of the west coast of the island. If we get an early start, we can see two castles and a folklore house, and Melodia can enjoy the Farma of Rhodes petting zoo. Apparently, they are well-known for their ostriches. If we get hungry they have a restaurant. The folklore house sounds good for seeing some of the island's culture. Then down the coast is the medieval castle of Kritinia, built by the Knights of Saint John. Further down is the castle of Monolithos, which was also built in the 15th century. Both castles have great views from the hilltops, and we don't have to walk too far to get to either one, which is good for Melodia."

"That sounds like a full day of fun," nodded Lucien. "Why don't you call Chloe and set that up?"

Chante called, and Chloe said it would be a long day so she would pick them up at 8:30 and they could be at the zoo when it opened at 9:00.

That afternoon Chante and Gervais looked into the professional history of each member of the dig team, while Lucien concentrated on finding the value of the coins. Nothing turned up on the dig team's professional history of interests outside of what their CVs already had listed. When Chloe had time, she would do a search into their social media profiles. For Lucien, the suggested value of some of the coins yielded some interest. He wondered how his values would compare to those of the appraiser.

Sunday morning, Chloe picked them up and they headed half an hour south to the Farma Petting Zoo just off Kalamonas-Psinthou Road. They were the first guests to arrive, and upon entering each purchased a cup of mixed, raw sliced vegetables to feed the animals. There were three large enclosures of ostriches. Melodia was little afraid because they were such large birds, but as soon as she saw the adults feeding them, she wanted to have some fun too. A zoo keeper was there to tell them about the ostriches with some surprising facts. He explained that ostriches have the largest eggs of all birds, with one egg weighing up to the equivalent of two dozen chicken eggs, but they still have the smallest eggs of all birds when compared to their body size. The adults knew that an ostrich could run fast, but they were still surprised to find out the top speed was up to over sixty-nine kilometers per hour. Chloe figured out that that was about forty-three miles per hour. There were three things they found most surprising: ostriches have the largest eye of any land animal, they have three stomachs, and they don't have any teeth, so they have to swallow pebbles to grind up their food.

They circled around the llama enclosure and came to the sheep, kangaroos and camels. Across the way there was a large pen for wild boars. There were three of them in their pen. Two were asleep on their leafy nest. Melodia laughed at the one who was awake making snorts with its long rubbery snout. Then there were donkeys and ponies. Next, there was a pond with ducks, and a place where children could pet baby animals. There were a few small piglets, a baby goat, a baby lamb, and the newest addition was a baby camel—all of which Melodia got to pet. It was hard to get her to move on, but then they came to the fallow deer, and adult sheep and goats. Finally, there were three round cages: one with a porcupine, another with a raccoon, and the third had a lemur with large golden eyes. They also got to see a glass enclosure where there were many ostrich eggs waiting to hatch under heat lamps. The four adults had just as much fun watching Melodia enjoy the animals as Melodia had speaking to the animals.

They spent a little bit of time in the souvenir shop, where there were painted ostrich eggs and ostrich feather dusters, along with cosmetics made from the contents of the ostrich eggs. Chante was surprised to find out the bird has the strongest immune system of any animal in the world, which is found in the yolk of their eggs, thought to be great for anti-aging skin treatments. Gervais was amazed to find out that an ostrich can lay up to 100 eggs in one year. There was also honey, herbs, and locally pressed olive oil for sale. It was too early for lunch, but as much as the adults were amused to see that the restaurant offered ostrich fillets, omelets and burgers, as well as wild boar burgers, Melodia got upset that anyone would eat the animals that they had just seen.

When they got to the car, Lucien received a call. He stood outside the car to answer, as it was from Inspector Nomikos.

"Good morning, Detective Reynard. I thought I should let you know that I heard back from Athens Headquarters with the facial recognition on Nicholas Pappas. His real identity is Cyril Bouras. We've just obtained his local address and I've sent officers to his house to bring him in for questioning."

"I should probably come in and be there, but I'm not presently in town. I'm with my family on the south coast."

"Please, detective. Be with your family and I'll see you at the station when you get back. The interview will be recorded so you can always watch it then."

Lucien hesitated. If he cut the day short, Chante would understand, but Melodia would not. "All right. I'll see you later this afternoon," and he hung up.

Chloe headed back to the coast and then on to the small town of Soroni, where she took them to the Folklore House. It was located in a residential neighborhood, and was painted white on its stone exterior. They rang the bell and a woman let them in. The owners were away on holiday but she was taking care of the house and could admit them. She explained that the owners had created the collection in 1992, and the house had been open to the public ever since. The interior was furnished in the traditional fashion of many of the older village homes. White-washed walls with a large arch separated two rooms. In one room were kitchen items and decorative local plateware on wooden shelves, while another shelf held an assortment of clay jugs with rounded handles. A woven brown and beige striped carpet lay in the center of the wooden floor, and large hand-woven baskets leaned up against the wall. On the rug was a small wooden table and wooden bench seats. A line was strung above, holding many locally-woven cloths and other textiles.

In a second room was a small bed with a colorful quilt, and another quilt was hung on the wall. There was a dark chest, and manikins stood to either side, dressed in native costumes full of traditional Rhodian embroidery patterns. Most interesting were the corn dollies that hung on the wall. They were actually bound wheat stalks, representing old pagan gods that were the spirit of the crop. Chloe explained that they were fashioned from the last of the season's crop to carry the enlivening spirit over the winter and into the spring where they were thrown into the furrow for the next crop. The entire folk collection was colorful and lent an excellent view into an older Rhodian home.

Only twenty minutes down the coast road, they turned off toward the village of Kritinia. They climbed a hilltop covered by a pine forest which offered panoramic views from the road. They drove past a white-washed village and then took a dirt road that led almost all the way up to a castle. A parking lot was on a level area next to a small café and tourist shop. Chloe recommended a small lunch there after they saw the castle. A wide set of inlaid stone stairs rose toward the ruined building. Upon ascending the steps, Chloe filled them in about some of the castle's history.

"The village owes its continued existence to these castle ruins, which bring in the tourists. It was built by the Knights of the Order of Saint John in the Venetian style of the mid-1400s. This location was strategic, as it allowed an excellent view of the sea to spy on any approaching enemy or pirate ships. When it was first built, it housed two Grand Masters: Giovanni Battista Orsini, who was the Order's Grand Master from 1467 to 1476, and Pierre d'Aubusson, who occupied the castle in 1476. Four years later in 1480, however, was the Siege of Rhodes by the Ottoman Turks. That year 100,000 soldiers came to destroy the castle. Although the knights were greatly outnumbered and suffered through many battles, the Turks ended up retreating, leaving the castle in uninhabitable ruins.

"The Grand Master did not waste time, but had the castle rebuilt to its original state, and in 1503 the next Grand Master, Emery d'Amboise, took up residence until 1512. To mark the castle's history and to honor its past masters, two coats of arms were placed above the entrance. During the mid-1500s a chapel devoted to Saint John was built, and frescoes were painted on its walls, remnants of which can still be seen. Today there is not a lot left of the castle, but the Greek Archaeological Service is taking steps to conserve what is left and renovate some sections to make them safer for tourists to explore."

They climbed many steps up to the imposing stone walls, topped with crenellations. Once inside, the shell of the building was all that was visible. On that level there were a few remaining tall thin window frames, and a partially destroyed six-sided tower rose to the rear of the castle. Paths linked the far end of the ruins so that its length could be explored. Crumbling rocky steps rose to one side where a platform could be reached that had a low stone wall. From that height the view was breathtaking, allowing the eye to stretch across the sky-blue Aegean Sea to Chalki Island and other small islets. The breezy cool air refreshed their moistened brows from the growing heat, and the vista rewarded every step they took.

They returned to the lot and went to the café, where they put two tables together to sit in the shade and enjoy the view of the castle to one side and Mount Attavyros on the other. They ordered fresh squeezed orange juice, grilled slices of eggplant with melted cheese on top, Greek salads, and yogurt with honey for dessert. Afterward, they perused the small shop which had local products for sale.

During dessert, Lucien got a call back from Inspector Nomikos, so he excused himself and stepped outside.

"Hello, detective. Unfortunately, there won't be an interview with Cyril Bouras. When officers arrived at the scene, they found him in his apartment with a gunshot to the chest."

"Suicide or murder?"

"We are in the process of determining that with an autopsy. We're checking for gunpowder residue and anything else the coroner can tell us. Sorry, but it seems we've hit a dead end, again."

"On the contrary, Inspector Nomikos. It tells us that we are getting closer, but to what and why, we don't know yet. If it is murder, then we know that someone certainly did not want us to question him."

"All to be determined, detective. Talk to you later."

There was only one more stop for the day's explorations and that was further south to Monolithos Castle. A half hour later they reached the village of Monolithos, which was nestled like an amphitheater on a broad angle to the sea. Then they drove through a pine forest for about two miles, passing small tourist stands on the roadside selling jars of honey, the distillate alcohol Souma, and olive oil. Shortly thereafter, they came to a parking lot at the base of the castle's hill.

"So that is how the castle got its name, mono-lithos," said Gervais, "it truly is perched on one huge outcrop of white rock."

"Indeed, professor, all 300 feet of it. And from that rocky castle are some of the best views on the whole of Rhodes."

The path up to the castle was only 500 feet, but it was steep. Chloe suggested that Lucien either hold Melodia's hand the entire way or carry her, as some of the walkway was slippery with loose pebbles and worn smooth by centuries of people's steps, and she could not guarantee the safety of the hand rails. As they slowly progressed, with the sun at its zenith, they were graced now and then by the shade of some pines and tall shrubs. Along the way they saw hundreds of small piles of rocks left by tourists as tokens of thanks. Chloe also filled them in on the history of this castle.

"Historians say that the first buildings on this rock were a Byzantine fortress and the Church of Saint Pantaleimon, both erected in 1476. Around the fortress, the Knights of Saint John's Grand Master d'Aubusson built a Venetian castle. One can only imagine how difficult it must have been to bring in building materials, transport workers to this remote spot, and construct it on this rocky plateau. Like Kritinia Castle, it was an excellent outpost for watching the Aegean Sea. Unlike Kritinia, Monolithos had a more difficult access route, but strategically it could be better defended, and did its job when the Ottomans came in 1480 and tried to take it. Its walls were never breached."

When they reached the castle walls, access was by a staircase cut into the rock. After they entered, even though many outside walls still remained, most of the inside walls were in ruins due to time and the elements. Chloe pointed out where cisterns used to hold water for the outpost. In the center of the fallen stone were two chapels. A smaller one dedicated to Saint George was in complete ruins. A second white-washed chapel, still in operation, was dedicated to Saint Panteleimon. They stepped inside to get out of the sun, but there were only a few faded paintings, an icon and some plates hanging on the walls.

"Who was Saint Panteleimon?" asked Chante. "I've not heard of him."

Chloe smiled apologetically. "That may be because he is actually a Russian saint who was co-opted and brought to Greece. In Western Europe in the mid-1300s he was known as the patron saint of physicians and midwives. But when Christianity considered his healing antithetical to the church's belief that God was the only true healer, he was murdered. Afterward, he came to be regarded as one of the Fourteen Holy Helpers and a guardian martyr. His name means "mercy and compassion for all.""

They stood at a broken stone arch and looked out over the sea for a magnificent view of a few small islands and Fourni Beach. The view alone was worth every step. Regardless, it seemed one too many castles for Melodia, who wanted to leave. They revived her with an ice cream from the small taverna when they reached the parking lot. After which, she promptly fell asleep on the hour and fifteen minute drive back to Rhodes city and their B&B.

Chapter Fifteen

Lucien wanted to tell Chante and his father what he had heard from the inspector, but didn't want Chloe or Melodia to hear it. When they returned that afternoon and Melodia was out of earshot, Lucien told Chante and Gervais about what had happened to the man at the hotel, and that he was waiting to hear back from the inspector whether it was ruled suicide or murder.

"Are you kidding me?" Chante responded with a bit of a shock. "It's murder, for sure. Someone didn't want him talking."

"Or," Gervais added, "he may have killed himself because he failed to go undetected. It could be that whoever he worked for would have done the same to him anyway, so he preferred to do it by his own hand."

"Either way, we won't learn anything from him now," noted Chante.

Then Lucien had an idea. "I'm not so sure about that. Tomorrow morning I'm requesting access to his apartment. I think we can learn something about his life. I also want Inspector Nomikos to check his phone and bank records. Perhaps they can trace whom he might have spoken to and who was paying him."

"There might be surveillance videos around the apartment," considered Gervais. "Ask the inspector to check on that, too."

After dinner Gervais checked his email to see that Goran Hallas had sent video clips that he had taped at the dig site. There were several from three days before, plus recordings of each of the fifteen stolen artifacts being unearthed. It took the three of them, dividing up all the footage, to survey it all. They carefully watched each clip, hoping to catch a stranger paying too close attention in the background, and conversations between the dig team. With great interest they focused on the moments when the team discovered each one of the pieces that had been stolen. But nothing revealed itself.

Finally, Chante was too tired to continue and Lucien agreed to follow her to bed. It was nearing midnight, but Gervais was still awake and decided to keep going. He skipped watching again the footage of the coin discoveries. Instead, he focused on the other items, looking frame by frame. He was about to give up when something caught his eye. He replayed one segment over and over, frame by frame. Yes, he was sure of it. After the small piece of gold chain had been removed from the trench, he could swear he saw something shiny still in the ground. While it may have just been the glint of the sun on a shiny pebble, it struck him as odd when the excavation leader called for the ending of that day's work. But he couldn't see who that leader was. All he could see were legs in the trench. In itself, ending the day's work would not be so unusual. The timestamp said 4:17, so it's conceivable that it was close enough to the end of a work day. Still, something about it bothered him. He would bring it to Lucien's attention in the morning.

Before breakfast Monday morning, Gervais called them into his room to share them what he had spotted the night before.

"Now watch carefully. I'll go frame by frame so you don't miss it."

He forwarded the frames slowly. "There! You see that?"

"What is that?" asked Chante.

"It could be anything," responded Lucien.

Gervais had to grin at them both and remind his son of something Lucien was always fond of saying. "Maybe yes, maybe no. But it does have a golden sheen to it and is certainly worth following up."

Lucien nodded his head in agreement.

After breakfast, Lucien called the police inspector and made his requests.

"*Kaliméra*, Detective Reynard. Sorry, no cell phone was found on Cyril Bouras or in his apartment and he didn't have a landline. A person without a cell phone these days is unlikely, but he could have lost it, or someone could have taken it. I will have phone and bank records searched with his fake and real names. I asked the apartment manager about any security cameras on the premises, so we could see Bouras' comings and goings, but was told that there is no surveillance system."

"Well, thanks for checking."

"I did get the coroner's report and she determined that there was very little gunpowder residue on the man's hand, even though he had a gun in his right hand. He wasn't licensed to have a gun and no registration for the gun could be found, which means it came from outside the country. There were no prints on the gun except the victim's, so if it was murder, the person wore gloves. The coroner could not say conclusively, but chances are it was murder, as the angle of the shot was downward, as if someone stood over him at close range. A suicide would have the angle of the shot from the right side toward the heart, or slightly upward."

"I understand. That makes sense. Someone could have placed the gun in his hand after it was fired. Can I get into the man's apartment?"

"We didn't find anything of interest inside, but you're welcome to look. I'll send an officer to meet you at the apartment in one hour. I'll text you the address."

"Is there anything else you can tell me about this man?"

"Sure. He wore workmen's clothes, ate a lot of take out, and had no living relatives that we could find. The coroner said his hands were rough so he might have been a day laborer, and he brushed his teeth with mastic and herb toothpaste."

Lucien knew the inspector was making fun of the man with that last comment, but Lucien had learned to take every scrap of information and file it away in his head. He thanked the inspector and signed off.

Gervais wanted to come with him to the apartment. Chante was just as curious, as she was good at spotting inconsistencies, but instead she decided to keep Melodia occupied and take the day to do some tourist shopping.

Lucien and Gervais borrowed Gala and Nils' car and followed the directions to Cyril Bouras' apartment, which was eight miles south of Rhodes City in Faliraki Village. The apartment listing online gave it a two-star rating. They arrived to find a police vehicle out front. The building badly needed painting, and the landscaping was minimal. They identified themselves to the officer, who took them to the apartment and unlocked the door. The officer showed them where the man had been shot, sitting in a living room chair. The blood was still awash against the back of the chair. Then he waited outside in the hall while they looked around.

"Okay, Papa, we need to look closely and think about who this man was."

They carefully looked at everything. The furniture looked used, worn dark curtains were at the front and bedroom windows, and the trash was overflowing. But the apartment was not without its comforts. There was high-end alcohol on the kitchen counter, a nice painting of a seascape hanging on the living room wall, deluxe Egyptian towels in the bathroom and nice sheets on the bed.

When they met back in the living room, Gervais offered up his opinion. "It looks like he was living on the edge, with money only coming in sporadically. When he did make some money, he tried to reward himself with good booze, art and some nice linens. This makes me think he worked only part time."

"But at what?" asked Lucien. "Inspector Nomikos said he didn't have any living relatives, so that would explain why there are no family photos. But three things did catch my eye: one—the newer bath towels were dark blue with small white anchors, two—the photograph leaning up against his bedside lamp was of him standing dockside next to a large ship, and three—the painting in the living room was of a ship at sea. I think he might have worked at the docks. The inspector also said he had rough hands."

"Son, there are probably a dozen or more working docks around this island, though we could start at the ones nearest to his apartment. But he could have worked at any of them. We could ask workers at each one to identify his picture, but that would take a long time."

"I don't think we need to go to *any* port. There is only one large shipping port for goods and tourist lines, the central port just outside of Saint Catherine's Gate in the old city." Lucien went to the picture in the bedroom and took a close up picture of the photograph with his phone. He came back and showed it to Gervais. "See at the edge of this photo the side of the dark blue ship with just the edge of a name showing? All we can see is "An," but we may be able to look up all the ships that come to Rhodes and find one that has a name that starts with those two letters."

"That's a great idea! Then we can find out what company unloaded that ship."

They took a few pictures of the man's belongings. They looked in his closet for the maker of any suits, but the man didn't own a suit. Then they left, thanking the officer for his time.

While Gervais was driving back, Lucien called the Port Authority and put it on speaker so Gervais could listen.

"Hello, my name is Detective Lucien Reynard and I am working with the Rhodes police on a case. We need to speak to someone who can give us the name of a ship that came into your main harbor in the last month that begins with 'An'."

"Just a moment, let me call up the list of vessels that came into this port." The man was silent for a few seconds and then he came back. "There are eight cargo vessels beginning with those two letters that came into our harbor. The Anastasia from Athens, the Andonia and the Andria from Rome, the Andromeda from Croatia, the Angelina from Barcelona, the Anisia from Tripoli, the Anna Marie from Monaco, and the Anthea from Tunis."

"Wow, okay. Can you tell me if any of them have a dark blue hull with white lettering for their name?"

"Give me a minute. I'll need to check each one." A minute later he came back. "There's only one, the Anastasia out of Athens."

"Excellent. And how often does that ship, I mean vessel, dock in Rhodes?"

"She's a cargo vessel that comes in once a month."

"How many people would you say work the docks loading and unloading the cargo vessels? And how many shipping companies operate out of the central port?"

"There are hundreds of dockworkers who are employed both part and full time for about a dozen different companies at the loading docks."

"Oh, well thank you very much for your time and assistance."

"Not at all. Happy to help the authorities."

After Lucien ended the call, Gervais whistled. "That's a lot of men and a lot of companies. I guess we could call each one of those companies, speak with their human resources department, and find out if they have an employee named Cyril Bouras."

"Yes, and that's exactly what I would like you to do when we get back. If nothing else, you can inform them that one of their employees will not be coming back to work."

Gervais nodded. He had a feeling that was coming.

Lucien had Gervais text Chante to let her know they were returning and Gala and Nils would have their car back soon. She responded that she would tell them, and that she would see them back at the B&B, as she was out picking up lunch.

After they returned and had finished eating, and while Melodia took her nap, Gervais got busy making a list of Rhodes shipping companies, and Lucien went back to his notes to find out which dig site manager had been working the trench.

The only note he had on who worked where indicated that Jace Othonos worked in the trench. He was going to text him, but realized that the dig teams probably don't answer their phones when their hands are dirty. Lucien knew that several of the dig specialists went back and forth between each of the dig sites, like the illustrator, archivist, geologist, conservator, and photographer. Now, however, Lucien felt it was time to pair each dig leader with their assistant.

In the meantime, he left another message for Inspector Nomikos, letting her know that they were chasing down a lead on where Bouras might have worked. Chante called Professor Ekonomos to find out who worked on the different teams, but he didn't pick up and there was no immediate response. It wasn't until after five o'clock when he replied by email. Then they gathered in Gervais' room to go over the new information.

Chapter Sixteen

Professor Ekonomos listed the teams in his email. He was the leader at the acropolis dig and Thalia Doukas was his assistant. Amara Sideris was the leader on the stoa dig team and Julien Ganas was her assistant. Alec Laskaras was the leader on the Nymphaeum dig team and Falavian Hasparas was his assistant. And on the trench team, Jace Othonos was the leader and Lydia Karas was his assistant.

Lucien quickly remarked. "It *was* Jace who called the trench site to a close that day."

Gervais followed. "So the photographer, Goran Hallas, would have been immediately called to take a picture of the find once a part of it was revealed but still in the ground."

"And then he apparently switched to his video camera to record the item being taken out, and that is when a second piece might have been spotted," added Chante.

Gervais added, "Do you think Jace got so excited when he lifted the piece of gold chain out of the trench that he didn't notice the additional sparkle still in the ground? Do you think it's possible that while all eyes were on the first piece, Lydia might have seen it and retrieved a second piece when no one was looking?"

"Good question," responded Lucien. "Jace would have removed the first piece of chain and probably stood, holding it up to get a good look at it. I suppose it's possible Lydia might have had a moment to remove a second piece before the conservator arrived to take the item to the storage building."

"Son, didn't you say it was Lydia who told you that on the day the theft was reported, she thought the guard Daikonos Lykaios looked suspicious? Sounds like she might have been trying to divert attention away from herself and on to him."

"But after the piece of gold chain was taken from the ground," added Chante, "wouldn't *any* intrigued archaeologist have insisted on digging just a little deeper to see if there were any more pieces like it still in the ground?"

"You would think so," agreed Lucien. "If Jace did see a second piece, it might have been the reason he purposely called an end to work that day, so that once Lydia left he could take a second piece out without anyone seeing."

"But wouldn't Lydia have seen it in the ground?" asked Chante.

"Not necessarily," responded Gervais. "It depends on the angle of the sunlight shining into the trench. Lydia might not have seen anything reflective from the angle where she was, and the same could be said for Jace not seeing it."

They cast glances at one another wondering who had seen the golden gleam.

"I still don't get it," remarked Chante. "What possible value could a broken piece of gold chain have? I mean, sure, it may have been old, but with the small amount of gold that any necklace might have, it still wouldn't have amounted to *that* much, would it?"

Gervais did a quick online search for the price of gold on the market. "As of today, a gram of gold is worth €52 or $57, and an ounce is worth €1,650 or $1,786. A simple short chain of gold could cost several hundred dollars, a heavy gold chain could cost several thousand, and if you were one of those rock or rap stars who wears a really large-linked, heavy gold chain, it might cost at least fifty grand."

"But we can tell from the photo that the chain was more delicate," Lucien reminded them. "The description was," he looked it up on his computer, 'a fine snake link chain of almost six inches with snake head closure.' It was only a small piece."

Chante angled her head with a slight shake. "That may be so, but we have no idea what the rest of the necklace might have looked like, or how long it may have been when it was in one piece."

"That's true," answered Gervais. "For all we know it may have been quite elaborate and dripping with precious jewels."

"But would either Jace or Lydia have taken the chance of being caught taking a find?" queried Chante. "I mean, it would ruin their reputation, they'd be kicked off the team, and even be subjected to jail for stealing an artifact."

Lucien agreed. "It would be taking a large risk. In your background searches on both Jace and Lydia, was there anything to suggest that either might do such a thing? One would need to be fairly desperate. Was either of them hurting financially? Or did one of them know something that no one else did?"

Gervais knew he and Chante had found nothing in their general searches. "We looked into each team member's professional past and didn't turn up anything like that. But we don't have the means to check into their financials. Inspector Nomikos would have to do that."

"I don't think any of them were paid poorly," said Lucien. "Depending upon their experience and years in the field, I believe an archaeologist makes anywhere from €14 or $15 to almost €28 or $30 per hour. Still, if one had large expenses, a gambling habit, or some other need for additional funds, they might be tempted. Seems we will need to make further inquiries with both Jace and Lydia."

"But let's not overlook the fact that we could be wrong about what we thought we saw," Gervais reminded them.

"Nonetheless, it would be interesting to see their faces if I showed them the video and asked each one what they thought that gleam might be."

Chante added, "I don't think that the photographer, Goran Hallas, has viewed this video, or wouldn't he have noticed that gleam and said something?"

"Maybe not," replied Gervais. "I only saw it going frame by frame."

"What matters is if Lydia or Jace saw it." Chante and Gervais agreed. "So, I will ask them tomorrow."

The next day was Tuesday, and when Lucien checked his email before breakfast, he saw that there were several emails sent to him from the appraiser, Theron Nicholaides. They had come in at 3:03 in the morning. Chante called upstairs to let him know that breakfast was served. So when they got seated, Lucien let them know that they had appraisals to go over after breakfast.

Chante's eyes lit up. "Great! Let's look at the gold chain first thing."

They hurried with breakfast, and while Melodia was playing with a new doll she had received the day before on their shopping trip, the adults gathered in Gervais' room to review the appraisals.

The first attachment was ten pages long. It consisted of a short introduction, the intended use of the report, the identity of who was asking, the ownership, the type of value ascribed, relevant dates, the scope of the work, his approach to the value of the items, the conditions encountered, two pages of disclaimers and terms, along with a statement of confidentiality. The man was taking no chances and being very clear. Those pages were followed by the appraiser's professional profile, his academic and professional background, the various associations he belonged to, and a selected list of high-profile clients that he had done work for. The last page was his invoice for the work completed.

Finally, there were three separate emails, each with five attachments, one for each of the items.

"I know that we all want to see what he said about the gold chain," instructed Lucien, "but we owe it to the board members of the Hellenic Ministry of Culture, to UNESCO's Department of Culture, to the Rhodes Police Department, to the country of Greece, and to Professor Ekonomos, to know what every piece might be worth. So please have patience. I feel sure that we *will* find some surprising information."

Chante and Gervais nodded in agreement.

Lucien opened the first file. "All right, here we go."

The window opened to show a small picture reproduced from the photographer's original. What followed were two sets of descriptions: one was what the team conservator had written up, and the other was Nicholaides' more elaborate description. Afterward was listed the method of analysis used to determine the value, and a signed certification which included a statement that he was not biased or interested in the item himself. He also included information on the technology of ancient coin production and wear and tear, a write up on the general history of rulership during that time, and a list of the types of coins that were minted in the Hellenistic Period (336–31 BCE). The subheadings for each item were: age, authorship, condition, functionality, historical importance, the maker or artist, material, provenance, the quality and grade, rarity, size, and style. His completeness proved his long-standing professionalism.

All of that was of interest but could wait. They hurried through the attachments, past all the descriptive text, and directed their focus to the bottom line with the estimated values. The nine coins varied in a present day value from €23 or $25 to €600 or $650.

After they had looked at all the coins, Chante added up their value. She asked if they could speak in terms of dollars as she was having to convert from euros every time, and they were fine with that. "The total of the nine coins comes to less than eight thousand dollars. That hardly seems worth stealing."

"Let's keep going," soothed Lucien. "There's more to see."

The small bronze statue of the Colossus of Rhodes was in poor shape and was only valued at $425. The Macedonian spearhead was valued at $450, the other spearhead at $650. The bronze sword pommel and grip came to just under $1,000, even though its condition was poor, its bronze decoration was elaborate. The thick ring was valued at just over $1,000. The one gold earring was $250. The bracelet was considerably more, valued at $15,000. But when they got to the snake chain necklace, the value was undeterminable, as it was incomplete and the weight was unknown.

"Oh, this is so frustrating," said Chante. "I so wanted to know more about that piece."

"Look what it says under style and quality," said Lucien. "It says, 'This fragment of snake chain is of exceedingly fine quality. Even though it was found in the Hellenic Period layer of soil, it would be considered near impossible to be fashioned at that time. Have never seen anything like it. At one end of the chain the snake head clasp is most likely missing gemstone eyes. What little remains was exquisitely made. I believe this piece was once owned by royalty.' So what do you make of that?"

Chante was speechless, but Gervais was the one to comment. "It's a lot of fancy words that tells us very little."

"And it's possible that it is not the piece we should be focusing on, anyway," added Lucien.

"So what now?" asked Chante. "You are going to ask Lydia and Jace about the gleam, but what can we do?"

"Chante, I want you to see what you can find on both Lydia and Jace. I want to know how creative they are. Do they have any hobbies, collections, specific likes or dislikes? Try to determine their state of health, note any travel comments or pictures, and see who their friends are on Facebook."

"And me?" asked Gervais.

"I want you to keep calling the port shipping companies and find out what company Cyril Bouras worked for. I'm taking my laptop to the dig site to show the video clip to both Lydia and Jace. If either of you find out anything, text me."

Lucien took a minute to forward all the emails from the appraiser to Chante and Gervais for their records, and to Monsieur Teniet at UNESCO's Paris office. With that, he closed his computer, put it in his backpack and left the B&B. He would also get the information to Inspector Nomikos when next he saw her.

The day was pleasant so he decided to walk to the site. Besides, he wanted to think over everything he had learned so far. Now that there had been a murder, this case had taken a major step beyond theft. That meant someone of importance had learned about his inquiries at the hotel. Had it been the hotel manager, Mister Kellis, who reported the police's interest to the man's higher up? He didn't think so, as the manager didn't seem to know Cyril Bouras, alias Nicholas Pappas. Someone else must have hired Bouras to be at the hotel to scout and then steal the artifacts. That contact had to be the person who took possession of the finds, as they were not at Bouras' apartment. And that same person must have continued to watch the hotel or hired someone to watch, or how else would they have known that the police had been there and went to cut their connection to Bouras so quickly. It had to be a middleman, as Lucien felt it was unlikely that the boss behind the operation would have personally committed the crime.

On the way to the site, Lucien decided it might be prudent to inquire with Professor Ekonomos about the video first. He quickly texted him to let him know he was on his way and could he please be admitted at the gate in ten minutes. By the time he arrived at the site, it was a quarter after eleven. Dimitri Kouris was the guard on duty, and he greeted him and unlocked the gate.

Lucien walked up the hill to the acropolis dig. Seeing him approach, the professor waved.

"Hello, detective. What's new?"

"I assume Inspector Nomikos told you about the man who had been watching the acropolis hillside, and his subsequent murder?"

"Yes, I was very surprised to learn someone had been watching us like that, and of course that it also ended with his death."

"In the meantime, we received a copy of Mister Hallas' photographs and video, and found something curious on the tape from the day the piece of gold chain was found. Would you mind taking a look and letting me know what you think?"

"Of course."

Lucien played the segment frame by frame when it came to the frame where it showed a golden glimmer. "In your best guess, what could that be, professor?"

The professor slowly shook his head and asked Lucien to play it again.

"I have no idea. It could be another find, or just the soil. The entire hillside is made up of limestone rock that dates to the Late Cretaceous period. Any number of other components could be embedded in the limestone."

"Like what, professor?"

"The most likely is aragonite, a crystal formation that can be yellow and orange, which could look like that when light hits it."

"Do you mind if I show Jace and Lydia this tape segment and also get their opinions, since it was in their dig site?"

"Go right ahead."

Lucien thanked him and walked down the hill to the trench site.

"Hello, Mister Othonos, could I tear you away for a minute to look at something and give me your opinion?" Jace nodded and followed Lucien about six meters away so their conversation would not be overheard. Lucien was also careful to have both of their backs to Lydia, so that she could not see Jace's facial expressions, and their backs hid the screen.

When Lucien played the video, he carefully watched Jace's face.

"Wait, what was that?" Jace said when it came to the golden gleam.

"I don't know. I was hoping you might have an idea." Jace had definitely shown concern and curiosity while viewing the segment.

"I honestly don't know. But I know I did not find anything below the small chain that was retrieved. I remember my back was killing me that day and so after the find, I called it a good find on which to end our day."

"Well, thank you. I appreciate your interpretation. Do you mind if I ask your assistant, Miss Karas, since she was next to you that day?"

"That's fine with me."

Jace walked back to the trench and told Lydia to go see what Lucien wanted to show her. When Lucien played the segment, he also carefully watched her face. Her pupils quickly expanded and she took in an almost imperceptible breath, so something had surprised her.

"Can you tell what that gleam is?" he asked.

She took a small step back and paused before responding. "I have no idea. It could just be the reflection off some shiny silica. The only thing I remember finding that day is the small piece of gold chain."

"Well, thank you very much for your opinion. I was just curious what it might be. I'll let you get back to work. Good day."

Lucien walked back up hill, Dimitri unlocked the gate to let him out, and Lucien walked away still not convinced either way.

Chapter Seventeen

Chante picked up lunch again, so when Lucien returned they all sat down to eat. Gervais and Lucien dived for the skewers of pork, while Chante forked into her courgetti patties, cutting pieces up for Melodia.

"Well?" asked Chante. "What did Lydia and Jace have to say?"

"I decided to show the video to Professor Ekonomos first. He thought the gleam might be aragonite, a yellow and orange crystal formation sometimes found in limestone, which underlies most of the hillside. Jace looked genuinely surprised and didn't know what it was. But at least now I know why he ended the day a few minutes early. He said that day his back was hurting him. And Lydia thought the gleam was a reflection off some shiny silica, also sometimes found in sandstone. But it was her reaction that got my attention."

Gervais leaned in, "Why? What did she do?"

"She seemed surprised to see it. Her pupils dilated and she took a step back."

"So?" followed Gervais.

"They are reactions of surprise and avoidance."

"So you think she *did* know what it was?" asked Chante.

"I'm not sure. What did you two find out?"

Chante saw that Gervais' mouth was full, so she responded first. "I found a couple of things on their social media profiles. Jace attended a conference last year in Athens on ancient weaponry."

"That doesn't seem out of the ordinary for an archaeologist," replied Lucien.

"Yeah, but one of the speakers gave a presentation titled A Comparison of Roman and Greek Spearheads of the Hellenistic Period."

"Oh, that is interesting. What else?"

"It seems that Lydia has an aging mother. A month ago she posted on Instagram that she was searching for a good rest home for her mother in Thessaloniki, where she keeps an apartment. She was asking her followers if any of them knew of a place with a good reputation. Rest homes can be expensive."

"That's one possibility for each of them. Papa, did you find the shipping company that employed Cyril Bouras?"

"That took quite a few calls, as there are a lot of Greek shipping companies. But I concentrated on the top twenty that operate in the Mediterranean, and on my fourteenth call, I found him. The company is called Med-Isle Shipping. Bouras was listed as a part-time dock hand in Rhodes. He had worked for them just over a year. I didn't say much, only that he had passed on. They were sorry to hear of his death, and thanked me for letting them know."

"Good," acknowledged Lucien. "Now get me all you can find out about this company."

"Already done. I sent you an email with a link to the company's website. I checked out the dates when they are scheduled to load and discharge the Anastasia, and assumed the similar dates ahead were similar to dates in the past, as the Harbor Master mentioned that the cargo vessel came in only once a month."

"Papa, that's amazing. Thank you. You get a raise."

"Really? Are you paying me?"

"Uh, no, that was a joke."

"Oh, so now what?"

"I think it is time for me to check in with Inspector Nomikos. You two already did a day's worth of work. Any thoughts on what you would like to do with Melodia today?"

"Nothing specifically for the day," responded Chante. "A trip to Lindos might be nice, but it's already too warm for an outdoor visit. How about if we hang out in town today, and I'll call Chloe for a trip to Lindos tomorrow."

"What's to see in Lindos?" asked Lucien.

"There is a large acropolis with a Temple of Athena, an ancient sanctuary, a Roman temple, old churches, a castle, a Byzantine museum, a lovely wide bay, several scenic beaches to choose from, and some really nice restaurants. We could definitely make a day of it, and it's less than an hour from here down the eastern side of the island. We might even see some Rhodian deer, as they hang out near the acropolis."

"Deer, Mama?" put in Melodia, who was listening.

"Would you like that?" asked Lucien.

"Yes, Papa."

"If Melodia approves, then that's great. Sounds nice."

"I'd like to go with you to the station, son."

"That's fine with me. Chante, are you two good without us for a few hours?"

Chante turned to Melodia. "What do you think, Melodia? Want to do some more shopping today?' Melodia nodded enthusiastically.

After lunch, Lucien texted the inspector, saying he wanted to come to the station to fill her in on what they had discovered. She replied that she would be back at the station at two o'clock and she looked forward to seeing them.

At the appointed time, Lucien and Gervais arrived at the station and the inspector met them at the front desk.

When they were seated in her office, Lucien began.

"My father and I went to Cyril Bouras' apartment and discovered a few things there. A painting of a ship on the sea and a picture of him standing in front of a ship proved fruitful. We were able to determine the name of the ship from only two letters showing in the photograph. After speaking with the Central Harbor Master, we found out that it was a shipping vessel named Anastasia, out of Athens. Since it only comes into Rhodes' main port once a month, Gervais was able to call Greek shipping companies that work the island. He spoke with their human resources departments and found out which company unloaded that vessel. That is how we found the company Mister Bouras worked for as a dockhand, the Medi-Island Shipping Company. Gervais let them know Bouras was dead, but did not elaborate."

"Wow, that's some nice detecting. Congratulations."

"That's not all. Goran Hallas, the photographer and videographer on the dig team, was able to get us photographs and video of each of the items that were stolen, and the conservator, Layland Elias, sent his preliminary descriptions for each item. As I mentioned before, we found a top-notch appraiser in Athens, sent him copies of the pictures and the descriptions, and he provided a preliminary appraisal of each item." Lucien reached into his pocket and pulled out a thumb drive with all of the information, minus the invoice. "You may want to get that information to your officer who watches the coin and antique shops, in case any of the fifteen items show up."

"There were some surprises as to the valuations on some items. The statue had a relatively low value, the spearheads more, the coins ranged in value from €23 to €600, but not totaling more than €7391. The value of the chain could not be determined, as it could not be weighed or closely examined, and the most expensive piece was the bracelet, valued at €13,858.

"Again, gentlemen, good work." She took the thumb drive and placed it on her desk. "I'll make sure my officer gets what he needs."

"There's more. It took a while, but the three of us viewed all the video that had been taken at the four dig areas at the acropolis site. We focused on the week leading up to the theft, looking for anyone in the background to see if there were any obvious outside observers paying too much attention to what was found, but we did not see Bouras. Then we closely watched the minutes when those fifteen items were pulled from the ground. Gervais found something of interest. Here, let me show you what got our attention."

Lucien pulled out his laptop, opened it up to the video of the chain being extracted, and then paused on the frame that showed the golden gleam.

"There, see that gleam?"

"Yes, what is it?"

"That's what we were wondering. So I showed it to Professor Ekonomos, and the two people who were working that trench pit, Jace Othonos, the leader, and Lydia Karas, his assistant. We thought that perhaps there was a second piece of gold chain under the first, and it was taken out when no one was looking. None of them claimed that it was anything more than a mineral or stone in the soil that happened to catch a reflection of the sun. However, when watching Miss Karas' response to viewing this, she seemed surprised in a particular way that seemed questionable to me. I may have misinterpreted her reaction, and one of the others may have been lying, but I wanted to let you know."

"That was very observant of you. Do you want one of my officers to look deeper into their personal histories?"

"That has already been done, inspector. Chante discovered that Mister Othonos attended a presentation on Hellenic spearheads at a conference in Athens last year, and Miss Karas may have needed some extra money as she has been looking for a good rest home for her aging mother."

"Well, well. Those indicators are very promising. It sounds like I should get a warrant to look into their financials. There's not enough proof to get a warrant to search the place where either is staying, but perhaps we could keep an eye on both and see if they attempt to sell anything."

"The financials might be a good idea," Lucien agreed. "I doubt either would try to sell anything on Rhodes. There's too much focus on the theft. But they might try to go on the dark web to sell things at a later time."

"All right. I'll start searching their financials. Thank you, detective, and thank you Professor Reynard, for *your* work on this case. Please extend my thanks to your wife as well, detective."

Lucien closed his laptop. "That's it for now."

"Well, *I* still have some questions, Detective Reynard. I'm curious why someone hired a man like Bouras and then felt the need to murder him? Why not just pay him to watch the site and let him go? Or maybe Bouras committed the theft, but took one of the pieces for himself and that was enough to get him killed? It's obvious there is a third party involved."

"I'm with you there," returned Lucien, "I am curious who Bouras was working for when he was not working at the port. It seems like he might have been only a part-time gopher. He obviously had connections to someone, probably a middleman. I doubt a man with influence, connections and wealth would deal directly with such a man. That is my next line of pursuit."

"If you are as successful as you have been so far, judging by what you told me today, I've no doubt you will eventually learn that as well."

"I hope so, Inspector Nomikos. I hope so." Nomikos reached forward to shake Lucien's hand and ever so slightly lingered in her glance. Then Gervais shook hands with the police inspector and he and Lucien left.

That evening after they had dinner and Melodia had gone to bed, Chante, Lucien and Gervais sat downstairs in the B&B living room and chatted.

"I liked Inspector Nomikos," Gervais told Chante. "Smart and attractive, with a no-nonsense way about her. She was appreciative and complementary to us."

"She was?" asked Chante.

"Yes. She congratulated us for doing good work." Then he looked to Lucien. "And judging by the way she looked at you, I think she likes you."

"No, Papa. I think she was just thankful that we made some headway on the case."

Chante looked from Gervais to Lucien, not sure about the comment.

"What's next?" queried Gervais, in an attempt to change the subject.

Lucien pulled his stretched-out legs toward him and sat up. "We have some time yet before Inspector Nomikos can get any financial information on Jace and Lydia. So for tomorrow we will take a short break and go to Lindos."

Chapter Eighteen

On Wednesday Chloe arrived at 8:30, had some coffee with the Reynards, and then they all departed heading south. Forty-five minutes and thirty miles later, they arrived in Lindos. Chloe explained that they could walk from the parking lot all the way to the Lindos acropolis, but it would be too far for Melodia and the path was steep. Instead, she thought it best to park south of town in the large public parking lot and take a taxi to the north end of town nearer the old acropolis. It would be tight in the taxi and Melodia would need to sit on someone's lap, but it would be a short ride. Then they could walk up the shorter and less steep path to the top of the hill where the site was. After they were finished exploring the acropolis, they could walk down the steeper path into the heart of town to find a restaurant for lunch. When they were ready to head back, they could get another taxi back to the car.

They parked, Chloe called for a taxi, and they were deposited where the paved road up to the ruins ended and became gravel. It was the furthest the taxi would take them. It was not far up the hill and the first thing they came to was a huge stone relief of a large ship. Chloe explained that the stone carving was of a Rhodian trireme, which was a type of ancient galley. It had been manned by 170 rowers who worked three rows of oars. It carried forty armed archers, soldiers and seamen. Unfortunately, the stone carving had partially deteriorated over time. Nonetheless, it was large and impressive.

Up a rampway they came to an old Byzantine church. Chloe began with her description of the site. "The oldest part of the acropolis was burned down in 391 BCE. The Byzantines came and built a small castle over the already ancient acropolis site in the thirteenth century, but when the Knights of Saint John came, they enlarged the entire area into a fortress with terraces, staircases and pillared halls. The small church became a chapel dedicated to Saint John. The chapel is now in ruins, but if you look there, you can see where the small altar had been."

Next to it rose the Propylaia stairway. Up some wide steps they came to the larger acropolis plateau where they purchased tickets to see this area. There was plenty to see. Part of a building which had been the headquarters for the medieval knights was open. There was a large stone house with arched gates that had some reliefs on them, built in 280 BCE. Passing through, they could see up into a spiral tower, but it was blocked off because it was not safe for visitors to enter.

A long portico opened up to the area of an ancient stoa. Chloe related some of its history. "During the second century of the site's Roman Period, it was built with an Ionic colonnade. Four complete pillars still stand, along with a partial fifth one." She pointed out the sign in English describing the builder named Seleukos, who had dedicated it to an oracular demon named Psithyros. He was not to be honored with any donation less than one drachma.

Higher on the plateau was the large Church of Saint John, where Chloe continued her history of the site. "When the Turks came to the island, they turned the church into a mosque. Archaeologists have been at work, and now the entire inside of the church has been excavated down fifteen feet to the original church floor."

Chante held Melodia's hand tightly as she could have easily fallen in. Next to it was a large open area where the Temple of Athena Lindia once stood.

"Here, thousands of votive offerings were found. Only a few pillars remain, but the plateau was carefully leveled and a low stone wall was partially rebuilt on the eastern side, so that amazing views of the sea, of the town of Lindos, and the surrounding countryside can be seen."

They all leaned against the wall and enjoyed the overlook.

By then it was nearly eleven o'clock and the heat was becoming strong, so Chloe led them down the steeper path into Lindos town. The Reynards wanted to explore the shaded alleyways of the whitewashed village and then find a place for lunch. Along the way, Chloe pointed out some of the older mansions in the town which dated to the seventeenth century, having grand arched wooden front doors. They went into several shops as well. One was well-stocked with leather goods, another with traditional embroidered cloths, and a lot of locally made jewelry filled the windows. As they headed down the street toward the coast, they passed lots of tourists at that north end of town taking donkey rides and heading up to the acropolis. Melodia kept pointing with glee and claiming "there's a donkey!" Chante could not resist when they came across a tourist shop that had small stuffed animals and purchased one that was a donkey. Melodia wanted to hold on to it and ended up cradling it the rest of the day. Also of interest were colored pebbles embedded in many of the walkways forming mosaic designs, mostly of the Rhodian rose.

Chloe ended up taking them to a rooftop terrace café with a bayside view. All that walking had increased their appetites and the menu offered many options. Gervais went for marinated octopus as an appetizer and then had a steak. Lucien had some mussels for an appetizer and then seafood pasta. Chloe just had a seafood salad, and Chante and Melodia shared some salad and grilled salmon. Then they all shared a combination dessert platter. After their large meal and feeling the heat of the day, they got a taxi back to the public lot. But Chloe had the taxi end their ride just before the parking lot. She told them they were close enough to the car and she wanted to show them something.

Once the taxi driver was paid and left, Chloe pointed up the southwest slope of the acropolis to show them an ancient amphitheater. It had nineteen rows of seats carved from solid stone. Chloe said it had been built in the fourth century BCE and once held almost two thousand spectators. One could still see the circular area where the orchestra had sat. She added that besides theatrical performances, the theater had also been used for athletic competitions and many festivals, one of which was to honor Dionysus.

After they got back into the car, their original plan was to go to Saint Paul's Bay beach so Melodia could play in the water, but as soon as the car got moving, she fell asleep, clutching her new stuffed toy. It was too hot to have her out in the sun, anyway. They drove northward, meandering along the coast to see the seaside views, and returned to the B&B by mid-afternoon.

While Melodia continued to nap with her toy donkey, Gervais, Chante and Lucien sat in Gervais' room to decide their next step on the case.

Lucien began. "Last night I looked through the Medi-Island Shipping website but didn't see anything that we could pursue. Again, I keep getting the feeling that it's not the people we should be following up on, but the stolen finds."

Gervais agreed. "I know what you mean. It seems following the lead on the gold chain was a bust, but I continue to feel that there is still something we're missing concerning those items."

"I keep asking myself," said Chante, "what was it about those particular finds at that particular time? The dig team had been working the site since April, and since then they had uncovered hundreds of items. What was so important about those particular fifteen items? What made them different?"

"Well, for one thing," reminded Gervais, "the cheap statue was the only piece that came from the Common Era. All the rest were much older, between the first and fourth centuries before the Common Era."

"That's true," confirmed Lucien. "Were those fifteen items taken at random, or carefully selected? The only really valuable item was the bracelet."

"I know what you mean," said Chante. "It seems odd. A cheap statue, two spearheads, a really broken up sword handle, a chain worth very little, a single earring, a ring, a bracelet and a bunch of coins. It almost seems like the coins were taken as a decoy."

They opened up their laptops and all three stared at the fifteen items on their screens.

Lucien tapped his brain with two fingers. "Let me ask you both. If you really wanted to steal something, but you didn't want anyone to know what it was that you were really interested in, how would you go about it?"

Chante and Gervais looked at each other, thinking about his question, but it was Gervais who responded first.

"I would definitely throw off suspicion by taking a lot of something else, like those coins. So, I think we can safely say it wasn't the coins that the thief was after."

"Clever. I agree. So let's take them off the list. There were seven coins. So that leaves eight more items. Chante?"

"Well, I would make sure I took at least one really expensive item to make it look like that was the item I wanted. Even though the $15,000 bracelet would have been a good start on a deposit for Lydia's mother at a rest home, it still wouldn't have been enough, so I don't think the bracelet is it."

"Okay, now let's say the bracelet is out. That leaves seven more items," concluded Lucien. "And really, unless the small statue had something hidden inside of it, which is unlikely, for how would anyone know that, I don't see that item being anything of real interest. It just seems like it was made for tourists, even if it is old, and it was the youngest item in the lot and not worth much, anyway. Let's take that off the list. That leaves six items."

"So now," said Gervais, "that leaves the two spearheads, one broken sword handle, one earring, a ring, and a broken chain."

"Based on what I found out about Jace Othonos attending that lecture on spearheads," reminded Chante, "it's possible he may have wanted them. There is that tie to those two items."

Lucien had to agree. "Those spearheads were only of moderate value; one at $450 and one at $650, but maybe he was a collector? Let's keep them on for now. The sword pommel and grip were in poor condition and received a value of just under $1,000, and only for their decoration. I just can't see anyone wanting a broken sword and two damaged pieces of spearheads, especially when there are so many sword pieces for sale online in much better shape."

"I agree," said Gervais, "but I think they should stay on the list."

"So besides them," Lucien added, completing the list, "we have the gold earring at $250, the ring at just over $1,000, and a small part of a gold chain with no assigned value."

Chante was slowly shaking her head and frowning. "To continue to disguise the specific items taken, I would make the item that I really wanted the very least likely. I know it seems strange, but I'm going to say that it was one of the jewelry pieces."

"Hmm," nodded Lucien in return. You may have something there. We've been going on the premise that the items were taken for resale, and that their monetary value was of the most significance. But what if it wasn't what they could get for the item or items? Maybe there was another reason?"

"Like what?" said Chante.

"I don't know. But what if it matched a piece in a set, like a match to a second earring that had been found in a previous dig? And all this time, someone was just waiting for more of a set to show up? We need to get a list of items that were unearthed from the 1946 dig and compare them. Maybe we'll get lucky."

The one thing they could do was once more pay a visit to the Archaeological Museum and speak to the museum's historian. If anyone knew what had been found during those early years, the museum's historian was sure to know.

Thursday morning, while Chante took Melodia to the Rhodes Aquarium, Gervais and Lucien went to the museum. They were instructed to head to the museum's small theater where the historian was about to complete a short lecture to a class of fourth graders. All of a sudden, the doors burst open and a crowd of children flowed out the door. When the group and its teacher cleared the room, they saw the man collecting his notes at the podium.

The man was spritely, in his seventies, with longish white hair that he had pulled back into a ponytail. Lucien and Gervais walked down the short incline.

"Doctor Manikas?" Lucien called out.

"Yes?" He looked up to see who was approaching him.

"I'm Detective Lucien Reynard and this is my father, Professor Gervais Reynard. We are conducting an investigation into the theft at the Rhodes Acropolis and have some history questions for you."

He quickly studied them with bright blue eyes, and then shook their hands.

"Oh, yes. I heard about that." He cocked his head a bit. "You don't sound Greek. French?"

"Yes, we have been asked by the cultural department of UNESCO in Paris to work with local authorities."

"How can I help? I'm only too glad to help anyone who has questions about Greek history."

"We're doing some background research and are curious about the finds from the early archaeological digs. We understand the museum has some of those finds and we are wondering what they are."

"Yes. We have quite a few, but many pieces went to museums out of the country. Walk with me to my office and I'll look in my files for the lists of earlier finds."

"Thank you. That would be great."

While they walked, the doctor gave them a rundown of what he knew.

"Archaeological work on Rhodes and many of the Dodecanese Islands has been carried out for over a hundred years. The one thing we don't know is whether the Turks, during their 390 years of rule, had unearthed anything from the acropolis site. We don't have any records from that period. I believe the Turks were far more concerned with possessing all things valuable above the ground, and retaining governmental control. The Italians then took control of the island in 1912 and held it for thirty-three years. We know they began excavations then and we have some photos from the 1912 dig. Although the photographs are few, there is nothing to suggest that the ground had been previously disturbed in any way archaeologically. Later, of course, the ground was pockmarked from explosives during the Second World War when the Germans came briefly in 1943. Then the British came at the end of the war and were here until 1948. In 1949, Rhodes came under Greek authority, and we have excellent records since that time."

By then they had reached his office. He unlocked the door and bid them enter and have a seat. He opened his file cabinet and searched through his files. Then he searched again. He looked up with a deep frown. "I don't understand. The files from the 1912 dig are here, but the ones from the 1946 dig are missing."

Lucien and Gervais were not surprised. Someone was doing all they could to keep any link to the past a secret. Now they knew more than ever that whoever was behind the theft was doing their best to keep that link to the 1946 dig severed.

"Do you want a copy of the items found in 1912?"

"No. It seems the list we want was from the 1946 dig." Then Lucien got an idea. "Don't you keep copies of those records?"

"With new research and finds coming in all the time, it is all we can do to get that newer information into our files. For older digs, we just haven't had the time or people to do it. Our curator will have the list of items that are on display in the museum from that dig, and there are boxes in the basement with some of the finds that did not go on display. I can contact the museums in other countries that received finds and get lists from them, but it will take some time."

"Doctor Manikas, it would greatly help us in our investigation if we had those records. Would you please do what you can to collect the information from the 1946 dig and get back to us?" Lucien gave him his card. The doctor said he would do his best. They shook hands and Lucien and Gervais left.

Chapter Nineteen

Chante and Melodia took a taxi to the northernmost tip of the island to the Hydrobiological Station of the Rhodes Aquarium. She was surprised to find the building in its original art deco style with curved lines in bright yellow with red borders, circular windows and a prominent cylindrical tower. They entered the building, bought tickets and immediately began to experience its unique interior with large wall murals of underwater scenes. In the lobby an introductory sign greeted them with a short explanation about the aquarium, stating that the institute had opened the exhibit in 1937 to study the flora and fauna of the Aegean and Eastern Mediterranean Seas.

A paved floor made of black and white pebbles illustrated various marine animals and led down a corridor inlaid with stone and shells. It immediately gave them the feeling that they were entering an underwater passageway, as fish tanks appeared recessed along the cave-like walls. The biodiversity and ecosystems of the Dodecanese Islands were showcased with examples of the different sea sponges, marine grasses, jellyfish, sea turtles, seahorses, sea slugs, and eels. As they went along, the tanks got larger and so did the marine animals.

Melodia ran from one tank to the next, excited to see all the different marine life.

"Look Mama, we are below the water. Mama, look at that funny fish. The shells are so pretty. Mama, look, that one has a long head. Wow, Mama, see that yellow one?" It was an endless running dialogue about everything she saw.

At one point she ran so far ahead that when Chante turned the corner, Melodia wasn't there. A panic immediately came over her and she ran ahead calling Melodia's name. But soon she saw her staring up into a large shark tank.

"Melodia, please stay with me."

"Mama, a man put this in my pocket," and she handed it up to Chante.

It was a folded piece of paper that read: "Leave Rhodes, or you will be sorry."

Chante immediately turned pale and quickly looked around. Only another couple with their young son was coming into the room. She had to ask.

"Excuse me. Did you see a man go past you?"

The man and woman looked at each other and back at her. "No" he said.

All Chante could do was keep a tight hold of Melodia's hand and coax her through the exhibit and back out the front door. While waiting for a taxi, she called Lucien. Gervais and Lucien were just leaving the archaeological museum.

"Hi love, are you and Melodia enjoying the aquarium?"

Chante did all she could to keep from crying. "Someone put a threatening note into Melodia's dress pocket."

"What? What did it say?"

"I can't say right now. I'll show it to you when we get back to the B&B."

Now worry was in Lucien's voice. "We are on our way back right now. We'll meet you there."

When they were all back at the B&B and Melodia was in their bedroom playing, they went to Gervais' room and Chante showed them the note.

"This is not good. Was Melodia able to describe the man?"

"Not really, but she said he must have been washing dishes because he wore white plastic gloves."

"Now I know we are getting closer to the thief and/or the murderer."

Gervais was equally in shock. "Yes, but close to finding out what? We haven't the faintest idea who the thief is, or the murderer, or who they work for.?"

"Should Melodia and I leave the island?" asked Chante, very concerned.

"That won't do any good, as whoever is behind this wants me to stop my investigation. I'm calling Inspector Nomikos and telling her what happened."

He picked up his phone and dialed her number.

"Inspector, this is Reynard. My wife and daughter were at the aquarium today and a man put a threatening note into my daughter's pocket, warning us to leave."

"Oh, then someone *is* getting scared that you are getting too close. Should we analyze the note for fingerprints?"

"My daughter said the man was wearing gloves, so I doubt there are any prints on the note."

"You will need to review every place you've been and every inquiry you've made in order to get an idea where the threat came from."

"We will. And one more thing, inspector. My father and I just came back from the archaeological museum, trying to get a list of artifacts that came from the 1946 acropolis dig. We thought perhaps if something similar had been found back then we would know it was related to one of the items recently taken. We met with the museum's historian, Doctor Eugene Manikas, to get the list of items, but it was missing."

"Then I guess that answers your question. It must have been related. But to which piece?"

"We think we have narrowed it down, but until we have that list of 1946 artifacts, we can't prove it."

"Detective Reynard, where are you staying?"

"At Gala and Nils Lindgren's B&B. Why?"

"Because there has been a threat to your family, and no matter how much you might disagree, I'm having a man posted to watch the residence."

Lucien could only take a deep breath and agree. He couldn't be with his family all the time to protect them, so it might just be the best insurance.

"All right, Inspector Nomikos. I agree. I just hope we can solve this case soon, as my family won't like being watched for long."

"Good. I'll have an officer nearby starting tomorrow morning."

"Thank you."

"Oh, and even though Cyril Bouras is dead, there is no cell listing on the island for him. He must have used a burner phone, if he had one. If he was paid to watch the dig site, he was paid in cash. And we looked into the financial records of Lydia Karas and Jace Othonos, but nothing turned up of note."

"At least now we know. Thank you for checking."

They ended the call. Lucien let Chante and Gervais know the results of the financial checks, and about getting assigned an officer to watch the B&B. Lucien would inform Gala and Nils.

Gervais was anxious. "But what can we do in the meantime?"

"We stick together tonight and have dinner here. Then, first thing tomorrow, I think it's time we spoke with someone at the Greek Archaeological Service in the Ministry of Culture, and find out what organization, private or public, has been financially supporting the acropolis digs. Someone is getting reports on the finds and I think finding that person is the key."

Friday morning at eight-thirty, Lucien got online and found the Ministry's website. He already knew that it was responsible for all Greek excavations, preserving the country's archaeological heritage, and museums. He clicked on the link to the archives and was surprised to find out that the archives were founded in 1832 when the modern Greek state was established. Sure enough, there was a link to a modern article titled "The Protection of Antiquities During World War II." But when he clicked on it, the file was not available. However, the website also linked to the Central Archaeological Council, which was the body that oversees all archaeological sites for excavations, restorations, conservation programs and a host of other departments. He found a page that said its business was conducted by a Board of Directors and listed seventeen officer positions: a Director General, a Secretary General, a legal counselor, five archaeologists, seven professors and one architect, but their names were not listed. On the contact page a phone number with an Athens prefix was given, so he called it.

"Parakaló. I Ellinikí Etaireía Nomikís kai Archaiologías"

"Hello. I'm sorry. I don't speak Greek. Do you speak English?"

"Yes, sir. How can I help you?"

"I need to speak to someone about the looting of an archaeological dig on Rhodes."

"I will transfer you to our legal counselor, Kostas Samaras."

Lucien was put on hold for a few seconds, and then the line picked up.

"Hello. This is Kostas Samaras."

"Hello. This is Detective Lucien Reynard with the culture department of UNESCO. I've been assigned to work with the local authorities to investigate some stolen artifacts on Rhodes."

"Oh? You sound French. Are you from the Paris office?"

"Yes, sir. I am."

"Oh, then do you know Monsieur Teniet?"

"Yes, of course. He is the one who assigned me to come to Rhodes."

"Excellent. Yes, well, how can I assist you, detective?"

"There may be a couple ways. One, would your council happen to have a list of the archaeological artifacts that were unearthed from the Rhodes acropolis dig in 1946?"

"Hmm. That information would need to come from the historical archives. But there should be a record of that at the Archaeological Museum."

"Yes, there should have been, but it seems that file has disappeared. I suspect it was taken on purpose so as to hamper any investigation."

"Oh dear. I see. Well, let me put in a request and have the information forwarded to you. What else?"

"I understand that the council is the entity that approves all archaeological digs within Greece, and I am hoping to find out who funded the past and present digs at the city acropolis."

"I will need to get permission to access that information."

"That information seems to be a well-kept secret. No one in Rhodes is saying, nor could our local authorities find out. I understand that it could be an archaeological research corporation, a special monuments organization, a particular museum that wants to acquire whatever is found, or perhaps a wealthy collector with a specific interest in the area."

"Yes, any of those could be true."

"But you don't know? The problem is, Mister Samaras, it is looking like someone wealthy, well-connected and well-informed has been receiving information about what is being pulled out of the ground at the acropolis since 1946. And that person may be responsible for the fifteen items that were recently stolen. I would very much like your assistance helping me find out who that person might be. Is there any way that we can form a cooperative endeavor to do so?"

Kostas Samaras paused on the line. "I can see how this must be difficult for you. Let me see what I can do. Can I reach you at this number?"

"Yes, at any time. I would very much appreciate your help and am happy to relay your greetings to Monsieur Teniet. I'm sure he would especially appreciate your cooperation in the matter."

They shared emails and ended their call.

Gervais was smiling. "That went well. Let's hope he is as forthcoming as he sounds."

At that point, Chante, who had joined them during the call and stood at the doorway, offered a suggestion. "I have an idea. How about if we use this time to lie low and wait for information to come in? We can search online for famous lances, swords, earrings, rings and necklaces, our prime items of interest?"

Lucien and Gervais both looked at her with admiration.

"That is an excellent idea," answered Lucien. "Let's get started right after breakfast."

Chapter Twenty

Gala and Nils were shocked to hear that Melodia had been approached in such a way and were concerned for her, but they were taken aback when they heard that the authorities were going to be watching their home and business. Lucien assured them that it was only a precaution. While they ate breakfast, a uniformed officer arrived and was escorted to the back patio by Nils.

"*Kaliméra*, my name is Officer Tavoularis. I've been assigned by Inspector Nomikos to keep an eye on your family."

Lucien stood and introduced him to everyone around the table.

The officer gave each of the adults his card. "Keep that card handy, and if you have the slightest concern about someone suspicious or need assistance, call me immediately. I will be parked in the nearby lot and familiarizing myself with the neighborhood. If you need me to accompany you anywhere, just let me know. I will be relieved by another officer every night at six, until I return in the morning. A third officer will take over to relieve us. If you need help during the night, call the second number on that card, which goes directly to our main office and they will alert the officer on duty here to quickly attend to your needs."

Lucien thanked Officer Tavoularis and then the officer departed.

"That makes me feel better," said Chante. "But I already feel pretty safe here at the B&B. Gala or Nils are almost always here. What about you, Lucien? Who's going to protect you when you are out on your own?"

"I'll make sure that I'm not alone. I'll either have Papa with me or I can ask for an additional officer. Now, let's finish up and get to work."

On the last shopping trip, Chante had bought a fairy flower garden for Melodia to assemble and play with. It was now the second week of August and many of the businesses were already closed for a respite after the busy summer season. Gala said that the only other couple staying at the B&B was departing that day and Nils would be checking them out. She was happy to sit and watch Melodia play with the toy garden in the back patio for at least an hour so the Reynards could work. Chante was hesitant, but Gala welcomed the change from her daily routine and she had grown to adore Melodia. Besides, it would be difficult to get by the officer out front, get past the locked front door and through the house where Nils was in the front office doing paperwork, and extremely difficult for anyone to scale the high wall in the backyard.

Relieved of some worry, Chante, Gervais, and Lucien took their second cups of coffee upstairs and assembled in Gervais' room with their laptops once again.

"All right. So, Chante, if you would focus on searching for famous swords, and Papa, if you would search for collectable spearheads, I'm going to make a list of all the people we have spoken to and where we've been so I can get a feel for where we might have been compromised. I don't like that someone has threatened us, so I need to concentrate on that."

Despite the relatively short time they had been on the island, the list that Lucien came up with was fairly long. An hour later, Chante went to check on Melodia and found that all was well. Gala had been reading a book and was happy to continue. She said to check back in a half hour, when she would begin to prepare lunch. Due to the added threat, Lucien offered to pay extra for Gala to provide their meals at the B&B, and Gala agreed.

With fifteen minutes left until Chante would again go downstairs to relieve Gala, they had a reporting session, which they had for many years adopted for their research work.

Chante began. "I need to preface that there are hundreds of famous swords throughout history, so I decided to focus just on swords with a European history or Turkish connection to the island. I eliminated swords that had any mythological or fictional story, like the sword in the stone of Arthurian legend, and just concentrated on real historical swords. I eliminated swords that have been preserved intact and are still on display in collections and museums. I also eliminated any sword that came from a country whose travelers had not come to Greece, which were quite a few. And last, I had to eliminate swords that were missing but recovered after 1946. When that was finally done, I was only left with two possibilities.

"One is the Sword of Islam, known as the Protector of Islam. It was a ceremonial melee weapon which came from the Berber collaborators in Italian Libya, and was given to Benito Mussolini in 1937. Since he came to the island, I included it. It disappeared in July of 1943 from his summer residence after the Italian Resistance destroyed his home. The second sword is the original Investiture Sword of the Prince of Wales, used since Tudor times, and replaced by a newer sword in 1911. I could not find out why it was replaced. It could have been stolen or it might be in some royal or private Welsh collection. No one from Wales that I could find came to Rhodes, but as it is part of the United Kingdom and fit the time frame, I left it in.

"But I'm afraid that's it. Unless someone was chasing after a sword that was fictional, it wasn't a sword that the thief was after. And on that, I believe that anyone with the money and means would only be going after what they were sure had once existed."

"Well, that answers that," said Gervais. "Now let's look at spears. Like you, Chante, I had to eliminate the mythological and legendary fictional spears. Though we may want to go back to this group, as there are many famous mythological spears. We can't completely discount the idea that even if they were of legend, someone may have made a replica claiming authenticity, and that may still have some value. The Greek god Hephaestus, for instance, produced a long list of magical weapons. And although the existence of the spear of Longinus, said to have pierced Christ on the cross, is pure conjecture, someone may have had one made to pan off as real.

"But first to the real and factual. This search has been more difficult because spears have been around since 200,000 BCE, then made of bone, flint or obsidian. I eliminated spears like them, as the historical layer where the two spearheads were found, was much later. The two spearheads that were taken from the dig site were made of bronze. That means the thief may have been looking for spears made within the Bronze Age, which was between 2,400 and 500 BCE. Or the thief could have been waiting for an Iron Age spear, which overlaps the end of the Bronze Age by several hundred years. Iron spears were first used in battle in the 7th century BCE. Iron is stronger than bronze and holds a sharp edge longer, and that period fits within the time frame of the level at which the stolen items were found.

"Three different spearhead shapes were developed during that time frame: the triangle shape which was much like an arrowhead, the lozenge shape which was still pointed and very elongated, and the leaf shape which had a long point and was rounded at the base. There were thrusting spears used in close combat, and throwing spears used for longer distance. The thrusting spears were used more during the Mycenaean period, from 1600 to 1100 BCE, and the throwing spear during the Archaic period, from the eighth century to 480 BCE. At least twenty distinct spearheads were developed with different shape variations. In short, it's nearly impossible to know exactly what the thief may have been looking for, so I had to limit the search. I first concentrated on types of spears used in Greece, and found the Dory used by Spartan Hoplites in ancient Greece, which puts the date from the eighth to the seventh century BCE. And the Hasta spear was used by Roman legionaries from the first century BCE through the third century CE. Both spears were made of iron.

"Still, the list of those kinds of spears is much too long, and many of both types of spears have gone up on auction sites. Some can be had for as little as $100 and I found one for as high as $1,000, but as auctions go, that price might be inflated. I narrowed the list again, to spears that have gone missing from museums. Aside from American Indian, Australian, African, and Hawaiian spears taken, I found nothing about a stolen European spear. So I'm sorry, it doesn't look like the most desired item of those taken were the spearheads."

Lucien understood his father's frustrations. "Okay, let's take a break and we'll tackle searches for rings, earrings, bracelets and necklaces after lunch. I'm sure Gala could do with a break in order to get lunch ready for us."

Gala fixed a Greek salad, a vegetable stew, and some seasoned lamb patties. She also made a golden apple pie in phyllo dough. As usual, everything was delicious.

Just after lunch, Lucien got a text message from Kostas Samaras, the counselor he had spoken to that morning.

The text from the councilor read: "The Director General has instructed one of our archaeologists in charge of historical records to forward to you the list of finds from the 1946 acropolis dig. Not sure how long that will take, but it should be within the next twenty-four hours."

Lucien texted back: "That's great. Please relay my thanks. Any word on getting me the name of the organization that financially supported the 1946 dig and is presently financing the 2021 dig?"

A minute later, Counselor Samaras responded. "The council meets once a week, every Tuesday morning at 10:00. Will ask for their consensus on permission to get that information and relay it. Will let you know."

At least he, Chante and Gervais would soon have the list of finds from the 1946 dig.

While Melodia laid down for a nap, Chante, Lucien and Gervais continued their searches in the next room.

"Before we move on to our research, I want to go over with both of you the list of people who might have had connections to someone threatening us. First, I think we can rule out Gala and Nils. They seem far too busy running their B&B to get involved with anything."

"True," said Gervais, "but they are also the two people who know what we are doing and where we are going every day. Let's not rule them out completely."

"All right. So from now on, let's not disclose what we are doing from day to day, unless we have to."

"But there *is* Chloe," added Chante, "who takes us around, and she could be telling them where we are going."

"True, again. I suppose we could test all three of them. We could schedule another driving trip on the island and have Officer Tavoularis follow us at a discreet distance. That way, if anything looked suspicious, he would be nearby. But let's continue with the list. There is Professor

Ekonomos and his entire archaeological team: Thalia Doukas, Jace Othonos, Lydia Karas, Amara Sideris, Julien Ganas, Alec Laskaras, Favian Hasparas, Dru Cirillo, Gregory Andino, Layland Elias, and Goran Hallas. Detective Nomikos did background checks on all of them, and you two have done further checks, and I think we've learned what we can from them."

Gervais again had his concerns. "Yes, but all of them know why we are here, and what we are trying to discover. We don't know if any of them made calls to a third party with our information. All of them are on the suspect list for good reason."

"Okay, agreed. Then there are the three guards, Daikonos Lykaios, Dimitri Kouris, and Calix Kalogeras," added Lucien. "Each knows the same thing about us. Then there is Theron Nicholaides, the Greek appraiser, whom I think we can rule out."

This time it was Chante with some hesitation. "Although we haven't met him in person, he knows exactly what we are doing and the value of those things. It's possible that the thief may have contacted him for a general valuation of some of the goods that the thief didn't want to keep, but wanted to sell. And just because he seems above board, he is retiring soon, and may have been paid to keep quiet about any further inquiry into those items."

"Okay, again. Then there is Professor Philemon from the University of Thessaloniki. Even though we have not met with him, he may have manipulated the school into getting a team here in Rhodes so he could keep an eye on the finds being unearthed. And there is Mister Kellis, the proprietor of the Vista Hotel. He didn't seem to know anything about Cyril Bouras, alias Nicholas Pappas, but maybe that connection was well-hidden, or some unknown person was keeping an eye on Bouras."

"And," added Gervais, "don't forget Argus Dougenis. He visited the site and spoke with Professor Ekonomos, and the man was shown the finds in the storage building. I don't know if he necessarily had anything to do with keeping an eye on us, or having Chante and Melodia followed, but I think he is a good candidate for having something to do with the theft."

Lucien came to the bottom of his list. "Then there is the Archaeological Museum's historian, Doctor Eugene Manikas, but I think we can rule him out, as we were with him when Chante and Melodia were at the aquarium."

"But," Chante reminded him. "Wasn't that perfect timing? You did contact him that morning for an appointment, and he could have removed the folder from his files before you arrived, and told someone to follow us when we left the B&B."

The three exchanged looks.

"There is only one person left," continued Chante. "Inspector Nomikos. She's known everything, every step of the way. She did not bring in that one archaeologist for an interview, and she did not follow up on all the leads that we discovered."

Lucien smiled. "Now, I think that might be going a person too far. First of all, I investigated her past and found her record exemplary, she would not have been so quick to issue that search warrant, she just doesn't make that much money to be involved in paying killers, and she is an officer of the law. So aside from her, we just listed twenty-five people, and any one of them could have been the link to the man behind the scenes."

Gervais agreed. "Then we have twenty-five good reasons to be on our guard."

Chapter Twenty-One

The Reynards continued their discussion.

"Now that we have finished that unsettling list of possible suspects, we need to continue our research on the stolen items. Papa, please do a search for special rings that went missing. Chante, if you would take both earrings and bracelets. Since we already know what one of the earrings looks like, maybe you can find a match for a pair that went missing. And see if you can find any bracelet similar to the one that was taken. Look for the shape, stone cuts and type of setting. Then all that will be left are necklaces, which I will take." Lucien looked at his watch. "It's 2:00 now. Let's take an hour and then we'll share what we've come up with."

They turned toward their screens and began to tap away at their keyboards. Forty-five minutes later, now awake from her nap, Melodia wandered into the room. Chante took a few minutes to get her to play in their bedroom until they had finished, then returned, but left the door open to listen for her. As protected as Chante felt within the B&B, for Melodia's sake she was not taking any chances.

When Lucien called time, they took turns reporting what they had discovered. Chante nodded to Gervais to begin.

"I was not very successful in my search for rings, mostly because there is an overwhelming list of them. I could find some rings listed of recent note that were missing. But to find an ancient ring online that has disappeared or was stolen, not so much. Rings are a very ancient form of jewelry. People of class wore them to show wealth, rank, and status, but later they were also worn as a token of love by commoners. Rings of course were often buried with the dead, but I wasn't aware that rings, like coins, were sometimes dedicated to a god and left as an offering in a temple.

"There are lots of notable rings of questionable history: King Solomon's magical ring that was buried with him, although his tomb is yet to be found. The Howard Carter Ring of Protection, known as the Ring of Ra, which he said he found in Aswan in the tomb of a priest. The ring was bought in 1860 by the Egyptologist Marquis d'Agrain, but where it is now is unknown. There's Charlemagne's Love Ring with a little story attached to it. It was left on his German lover when she lay dead and he was mourning her. The Archbishop Turpin came to comfort him and when he saw the ring he took it when no one was looking. Love went with the ring, for it is said Charlemagne then directed his love toward Turpin, who felt something was very wrong so he threw the ring in a nearby lake. Charlemagne was then entranced by the lake, built a palace next to it, and was later buried there. The ring might have been retrieved from the lake, but there is no indication that it was.

"There is the 4th century gold Silvianus Ring, once owned by a British Roman named Silvianus. In 1785, it was found in a field in Hampshire by a farmer and sold to the Chute family. The ring was also referred to as the Vyne Ring, as that was the name of the family home. In 1929, the archaeologist Sir Mortimer Wheeler was doing excavation work at a Roman temple in Lydney Park in Gloucestershire, England. There he unearthed a plaque concerning the Silvianus Ring. Apparently, Silvianus found out that a man named Senicianus stole his ring, so Silvianus put a curse on it. It's said that Wheeler consulted Tolkien about the name in the curse, and that is how Tolkien was inspired to write *The Hobbit* about a ring to rule all others.

"And of course there are many mythological rings: Aladdin's magical ring of Arabic lore and Angelica's ring of French myth, both of which made one invisible. The Ring of Euned in the Fortunate of Welsh legend, and the Nibelungen ring of German mythology. There are lots of ancient rings for sale on auction sites, many from early Egypt and Greece, but surprisingly not with particularly high asking prices. There was an ancient Roman ring with a coin design of Emperor Julius Caesar, dating between 100 and 44 BCE, but it's in a museum. There are lots of reproductions of famous rings. But I have my doubts that it was a ring the thief was after. So, unless they were going for a mythological ring, I didn't find one that was rediscovered in Greece before or after 1946."

Chante nodded and took it from there. "Okay, earrings. I'm in the same going-nowhere boat. Earrings and pierced ears are ancient customs among men, women and children. The first mention of earrings is in the Bible. In the story of Aaron, he commanded the Israelites to have their wives, sons and daughters remove their gold earrings, which he melted down and forged the golden calf. This dates the story between 538 and 332 BCE.

"Egypt, of course, had men and women wearing earrings from 1550 to 1070 BCE. There were two things that surprised me about earrings. One is that they were most notably worn by men to display wealth, from 550 to 330 BCE. And two, they were often worn by sailors in case they were shipwrecked. Once their bodies were recovered, the gold would pay for their burial.

"As Gervais discovered, many earrings were made from ancient pieces of jewelry and even from Roman glass, which seems to have been popular. And also there are famous earrings with a mystical story. There are the Karna Kundala earrings, the Makarakundala earrings, and the Shiva Kundala earrings, but all are of Hindu mythology. One cannot explore the topic of famous earrings without mentioning Johannes Vermeer's painting, *Girl with a Pearl Earring*, painted in 1665. This of course came from the artist's imagination. Pearls were the one jewel that designated purity.

"There is one notable pair of earrings from England's Georgian era, dating from 1714 to 1830. They were rough cut diamonds placed in sterling silver, but nothing written describes one earring having been stolen. So, I have hit a blank trying to match anything close to the one unearthed earring.

"Now we move on to bracelets. There *are* some famous bracelets from history. There was Queen Victoria's bracelet given to her by Albert on their wedding day in 1840. It featured a cameo, and it is said she never took it off. She died in 1901, but it is now most likely in the Crown Jewel collection. There is the famous Duchess of Windsor's panther bracelet, but that design is entirely different and produced much later in 1952. And in famous paintings, a simple gold bracelet is shown in John Singer Sargent's 1892 painting, *Lady Agnew of Locknaw*. There is no history on it. There is a website that shows pictures of many reproduced authentic and medieval bracelets, but none of them match the art of the one unearthed. That's it."

Lucien took a deep breath. "All right. Thank you, Papa and Chante, for your work. The search for famous necklaces is without doubt exhausting, as millions have been produced throughout time, and many have been described, portrayed and written about. There are plenty of famous diamond necklaces which have not been lost, like The Black Orlov with its so-called curse. Then there is the Indian Sancy diamond, which has been lost and found several times. The last time it turned up, it was during an autopsy of a robber when he tried to escape. He had swallowed it and died, and it was found in his stomach. It's now in the Louvre. There's another Indian piece, the huge pear-shaped Patiala diamond necklace. It was constructed in 1928 but disappeared in 1948. It was apparently disassembled, as a part of it showed up in a thrift store in London, but the remaining parts have not been found. Of course there is the Tiffany Diamond, fashioned in 1878. In 2012 it was reset into a necklace, but it is now at Tiffany's in New York.

"The Florentine Diamond, another large Indian diamond, has been missing since the early 1900s. There are lots of stories surrounding this one. It's documented to have belonged to Ferdinando II de Medici in 1657, then went to the Habsburgs in 1736. When the Austrian Empire fell in 1918, it went to Switzerland, but was stolen later that year. It's said it went to South America or the U.S., but no one knows for sure. Also, there was the 'affair of the diamond necklace' of Marie Antoinette. The story goes that King Louis XV had a gold chain with hanging diamonds made for his mistress, Madame du Barry. But he died during its construction and the jewelers went bankrupt because it hadn't been paid for. They tried to sell it to King Louis XVI, who was married to Queen Marie Antoinette. Publicly she refused, but behind the scenes a wild story took shape about a female con artist who closely looked like Marie. She forged letters as if from the queen, the story involved a Cardinal, and the case went to trial. The necklace ended up going to England, where it was disassembled and sold in pieces. There was also Queen Victoria's large diamond necklace that was worn at her coronation, but as far as we know it is housed in the Crown Jewel collection.

"We can't discount the idea that many historical male figures wore necklaces, too. For instance, a 1514 portrait of Henry IV shows him wearing several heavy gold chains around his neck, and there are countless others.

"Then there are famous necklaces seen in paintings that were supposedly real. There's the German George Pencz's *Portrait of Lady*, painted sometime in the first half of the sixteenth century, in which a lady is shown with her neck adorned by several gold chains. It sounds like I found the same website for medieval and ancient jewelry that you found for bracelets, Chante. They show only reproductions. Even though they are not originals, they might give us some idea of what the original looked like. But they don't show any ancient Greek pendants on snake chains of gold. If they had, I might have been able to look up their history, but even in the medieval representations, the pictures mainly show the pendant with little of the chain showing.

"I didn't bother to research mythological necklaces. I ran out of time. If one of you wants to take the time and explore that avenue, you're welcome to do so, but I don't think it will help us, as we are looking for something genuine."

Gervais reasoned. "This has been an interesting search session, but I'm not sure how much it has gotten us any closer to the real reason why those fifteen items were taken."

"Oh, I don't know," responded Lucien. "We learned a couple things. One, it could have been a ring that was brought to the temple as an offering, if not also the other pieces of jewelry. And two, I think we can safely say that it was an item that was more ancient than modern. That is, most of the things taken were from as early as the Bronze Age, and could have been from the Iron Age to Classical antiquity, up to the late Roman Republic."

"But what about the statue?" asked Chante. "That was much more modern, having been produced in the High Middle Ages in 1214. That is a complete anomaly."

Gervais nodded in agreement. "That's true, but I have a theory about that. I think that sometime during the Middle Ages, someone came to the temple and decided to dig a deep hole and bury it. Maybe they decided they didn't like the statue they recently bought, or maybe they wanted to leave an offering?"

"I suppose that's possible," thought Lucien. "I can't think of any other reason why one piece would be so out of place for the time period with those other items."

They were interrupted by Melodia running into the room with her dolly and declaring it was play time.

Chapter Twenty-Two

That evening before dinner, Lucien discussed with Chante and Gervais a possible plan to test Gala, Nils and Chloe. Because it was of the highest priority to secure the safety of their family, and since the family was in the hands of those three people the most, Lucien felt that they needed to make sure they could be trusted above all others. They came up with a plan and decided to put it in play that evening.

At dinner, Gala made her mother's recipe for moussaka and everyone declared it the best they had ever had. She then offered her grandmother's recipe for Revani cake, made with semolina flour soaked in lemon honey and sprinkled with coconut. Since Gala and Nils were sitting with them, they refrained from talking about their progress in the case.

"What should we do tomorrow?" asked Chante, setting the scene.

Lucien set the bait. "The weather looks like it is going to be nice. We haven't seen a lot of the east coast. Why don't we plan on taking a trip down the eastern side to the end of the island?"

Gervais added to the ploy. "Lucien, do you really think we need Officer Tavoularis to follow us? We'll be out of the city and in Chloe's good hands. Do you think we can dispense with him for one day?"

"I suppose we could," responded Lucien. He turned to Nils and Gala. "She can be trusted, can't she?"

Nils quickly responded. "Yes, of course. The drive sounds lovely. I'll give Chloe a call and see if she is available." He pulled out his phone and called her immediately. When she answered, he made the inquiry. "They want to take a drive down the eastern coast. Yes, that's right. Okay, see you in the morning at 9:00. Bye." After everyone understood that she had agreed, it was set.

It had been a lovely evening and everyone was so full after dinner that they opted to sit on the back patio, enjoying the cooling breeze and the glittering stars, with lovely stretches of silence. As Lucien described the experience later to Chante, "It felt like we were hanging from the sky, waiting in limbo, not knowing where this investigation was going, but at the same time, it was as if we were just waiting for the right time for the sky to open and show us the answers."

Saturday morning, there was still no response from Doctor Manikas from the Archaeological Museum, nor from anyone from the Central Archaeological Council. Lucien gave Officer Tavoularis a call from his room and told him the plan. He was to follow them in an unmarked car. Tavoularis understood. He would be ready, and told Lucien to text him if there was a problem.

An hour later, Gervais and Lucien waited in the living room with Nils for Chloe to arrive, while Chante was upstairs getting Melodia ready for the day.

Melodia and Chante came downstairs carrying a basket of beach towels, then said goodbye to Gala and Nils and departed, with Officer Tavoularis following at a distance behind them.

The sky was clear blue and the sun was already out. Lucien sat in front with Chloe, and Gervais and Chante sat in back with Melodia in the middle. Chloe drove south on Highway 95 and they finally came close to the water at Faliraki Bay. Chante, Lucien and Gervais were on their phones searching for things to do—not in Lindos, but in Archangelos.

About ten minutes from Archangelos, Lucien found just what he was looking for. "Melodia, how would you like to see some ponies?"

This immediately excited Melodia. "Yes, Papa, please. I want to see ponies."

"Where are the ponies?" asked Chante.

"Just down the road in Archangelos is a place called the Faethon Miniature Horse Farm. Do you know it, Chloe?"

"Yes, the breed is endangered."

By then Chante had found something that interested her. "Oh, and apparently Archangelos is well-known for its ceramics. I'm looking at some beautiful hand-painted bowls. There's a workshop that offers tours. Oh, Lucien, I would love to see them."

Gervais had something to add. "There's also a lovely place just inland from there called Seven Springs. I've seen this advertised in a brochure. It looks cool and inviting. Why don't we make it a day in Archangelos instead of going all the way down the coast? We can save that drive for another day."

Chante and Gervais said yes at the same time, and Melodia repeated, "ponies, ponies, ponies."

Lucien watched Chloe's face. She was frowning. "Well, we have already passed the turnoff to Seven Springs."

"That's all right," said Lucien. "We'll go to see the ponies first, then into town for the ceramics shop and lunch, and then go to the springs on the way back."

"Sounds good," said Chante.

A few minutes later, Lucien saw a roadside grocer. "Stop here. The website says the farm depends upon people bringing offerings of food for the horses. Chante, would you mind running in and getting some apples and carrots?"

"Sure. Be right back," she said as the car came to a stop.

Lucien expected Chloe to reach for her phone. Lucien had discussed the possibility with Chante and Gervais that if Chloe was working in tandem with another, she might try to call them to let them know that their destination had changed. But she did not pick up her phone. Chante was quick and returned with a bag. They were off again, and shortly up the road Chloe turned on to the Rodou Lindou Road. They finally saw the sign for the Faethon Miniature Horse Farm, and went through the gate.

Lucien quickly texted Officer Tavoularis that it would be better for him to wait outside the gate. The officer responded that he would park under a nearby tree.

Chloe pulled the car into a dirt lot near the horse corals where several ponies could be seen.

When Melodia saw the ponies she was so excited she could hardly contain herself. At first, Chloe said she would wait in the car, explaining that she wasn't fond of horses. But Lucien coaxed her to come with them. He said he had read that a Greek-speaking person might be needed to translate for them, as the owners spoke only Greek. She came with them, leaving her phone in the car, and she *was* needed to translate. A ranch worker was raking one of the pens, but stopped when they pulled up. He began to tell them about the ranch and Chloe let them know what he was saying.

"He welcomes us to the ranch of the Rhodian Pony. He says the ponies are very special, as there are very few left in the world, and this sub-species is found only on Rhodes."

There were round wooden corrals with enclosed horse stalls against a back wall. The ground in each corral was lined with bricks to make it easier to hose down, but the ponies were also allowed to graze in a nearby alfalfa field. The striking and sweet looking equines were indeed small but had large heads and soft brown eyes, and were well-shaped with rich brownish red coats, wild bushy manes and long thick tails.

As Melodia continually stroked each animal and fed them the food they had brought, the farm worker continued to explain things while Chloe translated.

"He says that only two hundred years ago there were a lot more of these kinds of horses. Every family had one for their farm, but then they started to diminish, so the Phaethon Association was established to protect them."

When the group walked down the line of corrals, Melodia whinnied hello to each of the horses as she greeted them, and then she did it all over again saying goodbye when they walked back up the line.

Against an office building there was a table with information about the Faethon Miniature Horse Farm and a box where visitors could leave a donation. Lucien was generous, as he measured the reflection of joy on Melodia's face.

When they got back in the car, Chloe started to go for her phone, but Chante stopped her.

"No need to search for a shop to go to, I know the one I want. It's just up the road."

As they drove out of the fenced property, Lucien saw Officer Tavoularis and glanced his way to follow.

A minute later, Chante saw the shop. "There it is."

Chloe pulled up and before she could beg off coming in, Lucien prompted her to join them. "Chloe, I'm hoping you can show us the best buys, and perhaps help us pick some things out."

She surprised him. "Of course, I love this shop. I bring tourists here all the time."

After letting the family and Chloe enter, he turned his head to see Officer Tavoularis pull over and park.

The shop had tables and shelves full of ceramics, some with a modern design and some which were copies of ancient originals. The modern ones had designs of animals; deer were prevalent, but there were also birds, fish, and an octopus. Others had leaf and flower decorations or a Tree of Life. A few had anchor designs or full ships, some were geometric, and others had a mixture of designs. The colors ranged from white to beige, turquoise blue to dark blue, tan to dark brown, yellow to orange, and lavender to red. There were broad heavy cups, coffee mugs, napkin holders, vases, jugs, large and small plates, and bowls. The really expensive pieces were copies of traditional ancient art amphoras, with figures delicately painted on bands of mottled tan over dark brown backgrounds. The ancient style with high looped handles was very different from the modern vases with a simple loop.

Lucien got a text from the officer saying all was good, and no other vehicle had been spotted following them.

They took a great deal of pleasure and time looking at all the colorful pieces in the shop. Lucien kept an eye on Chloe to see if she went for her phone. She had removed it from the car as they were in a tourist area and theft was always a possible hazard. But she left it in her purse and walked around with Chante. She and Chante continually chatted together about the styles and what they liked. At long last, Melodia picked a small blue plate with a deer in the center, after realizing there were no plates with a pony on them. Chante chose a larger turquoise plate that had lavender vines holding two white doves. She said it represented her and Lucien's love for one another. Gervais wanted a brown and blue mug that had an olive branch on it. Lucien decided not to purchase anything for himself, but heard from Chante that Chloe liked a small bowl with colorful fruits and flowers, so he decided to buy it for her without her seeing, as a gift of thanks.

Lucien made their purchases while Chante and Chloe stood outside and talked about where to go for lunch. Chloe recommended a place nearby, so that's where they went. The restaurant was a lovely taverna with murals of Greek beaches on the walls and fresh flowers on the wooden tables. Lucien secured their packages below his feet and then texted Officer Tavoularis to tell him to get something to eat, as he thought they would be at least an hour in the restaurant. He would text again when they were leaving.

Because of the day's heat, Melodia and Chante had lemonade and the rest had beer. Then it was baked goat feta, some spinach pies, and olives with delicious bread. After that they shared a large pot of baked pasta with *soutzoukakia* sausages made from spiced pork. Chante ate around the meat, as usual, but the pasta was delicious with a creamy herb sauce. For dessert, Chloe suggested the restaurant's specialty, locally gathered apricots, cherries, plums, and quince that had been preserved in sugar and placed in vanilla syrup, served with almond cookies. After he got the bill, Lucien texted Officer Tavoularis that they were getting ready to leave.

After lunch, they were all full, happy, and ready for their next adventure. Chloe took a drive north on the 95 highway and then turned west on Kolumpion-Archipolis road. There was a parking lot and quite a few cars were already there. It was a favorite place among tourists and locals alike in the summer. Lucien quickly texted Officer Tavoularis to let him know where they were headed.

"We'll be walking a bit," said Gervais. "Son, do you have your flashlight with you? We'll need it to walk through a tunnel."

"Yes, right here on my belt."

"And I have one, too," said Chloe. "I always keep one in the car."

They filed out and Chante grabbed the basket with towels and water. They followed Chloe through the entrance under pine and plane trees, then across a wooden bridge over a stream. The water ran below in a pleasant flow across both wide flat areas and between rocks, creating a mixture of a soothing rush and babbling brook. The temperature turned at least ten degrees cooler. A peacock paraded on the far side, which Melodia immediately pointed out, as it strutted just out of the crowd's reach. They came to stone steps that led down to an aqueduct. It would take them to the falls and a pretty lake. Chloe said that the aqueduct had been built by the Italians in 1931 when they occupied the island.

On a side bench, everyone sat to remove their shoes and carry them. Chante put hers, Melodia's, and Lucien's in her basket, while Gervais and Chloe held theirs. The water rushed down a smooth decline headed for a tall arched stone entry into darkness. Melodia didn't like the look of the dark tunnel or the rushing water, even though it was just a couple of inches deep. But Lucien agreed to carry her while leading them through with his flashlight, and Chloe followed up the rear with her light. It was dark but nice and cool as they sloshed through the water. Thank goodness it was only one way, as the tunnel was only wide enough for one person, but had a high ceiling. Gervais said it was 164 yards long with a few curves, but it took only five minutes and was kind of fun to go through.

When they emerged on the other side they were met by the picturesque sight of a shady waterway lined with flat stones. Lucien got a text from Officer Tavoularis saying that two men had arrived and were rushing toward the entrance. He was going to follow them. But a minute later, he had seen them take each other's hands, so he texted Lucien back and wrote: "False alarm, it was two gay men on holiday."

Chloe and the Reynard family stepped out and joined the other tourists who walked down a side path to another lovely area where a wide sheet of water fell from about fifteen feet above them down into an aqua pool. A pathway of flat stones curved toward the falls and then went under it. Then about fifteen feet out the water fell from another wide stone wall and dropped about two feet. They followed the side path further and the water fell again into a small lake where ducks ruffled their feathers while bathing and geese swam and periodically ducked down to grab small *gizani* fish. They found a shady spot to sit and relax. Melodia dangled her feet in the cold water and laughed at the geese. It was truly an enchanting and most relaxing time had by all.

Lucien took a minute to check his messages to see if he had received any other texts. He saw that Officer Tavoularis had texted that only families and couples had entered and all looked fine. He would wait at the entrance. After an hour, the family was ready to go and walked the upper path back to the car. Once they were on their way, Melodia's head began to nod, tired from their outing. Less than an hour later they were back at the B&B and Melodia laid down for a nap.

Along the way Lucien thought about the day and was pleased to learn that Chloe had not used her phone once, even though she had had plenty of time to do so at the shop, the restaurant, and at the falls. When they arrived back, they thanked her for a lovely outing and her time. Then Lucien handed her an envelope to pay her for driving them around that week, and Chante surprised her by giving her the bowl Chloe had liked in the pottery shop. She was very appreciative and profusely thanked them.

After she left, Lucien went out to meet with Officer Tavoularis and thanked him for his discretion and his time. They were satisfied with how their guide had been.

That night, Gervais, Chante and Lucien agreed: it seemed as though Chloe, Gala, and Nils could be trusted.

Chapter Twenty-Three

Saturday evening, Gala decided to make her version of burgers and fries. The only difference was that she put the cheese inside the ground beef instead of on top, and the usual sesame seed bun was a yeasted dinner roll instead. She made a special fish burger for Chante, and for dessert she made chocolate cake.

All through the evening, Lucien hoped that he would receive the list of items found in the 1946 dig, but he did not hear a thing. But Sunday morning when he checked his email just before breakfast, he received a large file from the Central Archaeological Council. He opened it to find a message from Mister Samaras, the legal counsel.

Detective Reynard,

Please find attached the list of items recovered from the 1946 archaeological dig. Our archaeological historian was too busy to send it himself and forwarded it to me since I was your contact on the council. The list is not long, as the primary task of the field work was to a) remove artillery pieces left over from the war, b) remove anything close to the surface that had been disturbed by the destruction of explosive shelling, and c) to grade and level the area to make it less dangerous for visitors to walk the site. I hope this report helps your investigations.

Sincerely,
Kostas Samaras

Lucien immediately let Chante and Gervais know before they went down to breakfast, but they could hardly contain themselves and tried not to rush their meal when all they wanted to do was look the list over. Melodia had insisted that she eat her bread on her new small plate and announced that she wanted to eat off her plate for every meal. Gala sweetly assured Melodia that she could do so. Then Chante asked if she would be so kind as to watch Melodia in the garden after breakfast for about an hour, and she was happy to spend time outside with the child and continue reading her book. This time, Chante was feeling much more secure about having Gala watch her.

When they assembled upstairs with their laptops, Lucien forwarded the file to both Chante and Gervais so they would all have a copy. They were surprised at the number of items. Samaras had said it was a short list, but it still had 147 objects listed. They had to chuckle. Of course that was probably short compared to other digs, as this *was* Rhodes and items must have piled up for centuries. They divided up the list into forty-nine pieces for each of them, and went to work comparing the descriptions from the catalog of items unearthed in 1946 to the fifteen items that had been stolen that year. Listed were lots of pottery shards, some from vases, some found to be roof tiles, other clay bits, and two small broken clay statues. There were small amounts of metal items, another ring, metal shards from what were thought to be pieces of weaponry, lots of coins and a bronze cup. A few bones joined the list, all from animals, including a roaming deer, stray dogs, and one cat. There were ceramic chips from broken plates, cups, and some broken mosaic pieces still with touches of paint on them. And a broken ivory comb.

For almost an hour they compared the descriptions, but as they neared the end of the list, they were becoming disheartened. Suddenly, Chante yelled "Got it! One piece of fine snake chain seventeen centimeters long. But here's the odd part. It says dating is inconclusive, possible date between 4,000 to 3,000 BCE."

"Isn't that impossible?" asked Gervais. "I thought the oldest jewelry in the world was found in Babylonia, and that find was from 2500 BCE."

"I still don't understand," added Chante. "How could an object that old get found in a First and Second century BCE layer of soil? It just doesn't make sense."

"We obviously need to do more searching," concluded Lucien. "In the meantime, I'm texting Doctor Manikas to see if he can locate that piece of chain in the museum from the 1946 dig. It might be good to get a closer look at it to see if the two chains actually match." Lucien took a minute or so to do that.

Chante looked at her watch and stood. "I need a mental break. I'm going to go sit in the garden, chat with Gala and watch Melodia. You two think on it and I'll come back in a while."

"Papa, can you please do a search on snake chains? Find out their history and any other style of chain that is similar. Anything you can find. I'm going to keep looking for ancient necklaces, even if I have to search for mythological ones."

After forty-five minutes, Gervais felt he had the information that Lucien requested.

"Okay, here is what I have. Snake chains have been made by hand for centuries. No one is sure for how long, but at least to the Early Modern Era, sometime between 1450 and 1750. But it wasn't until the 1840s that they became very popular and at least four different styles of snake chain were made. In the early 1850s chains were beginning to be made by machines. The first patent for machine-made snake chains was issued in 1856 by an American in Rhode Island." Gervais looked up at Lucien.

"Odd isn't it? Rhode Island, and here we are on the island of Rhodes finding this out. Never mind. That's silly." Then he looked back at his notes. Another name for the snake chain is the braxiliaa, with two 'a's' at the end. I was curious why the style took on the name braxiliaa, and discovered a single reference, braxilia with one 'a,' which is a flowering plant."

This caught Lucien's attention. "That's interesting. You would think the chain would have been named after the genus of some kind of snake, not a plant."

"There's more on the plant aspect. I tried to limit my search to stems or leaves that had a scale-like appearance, the flower being yellow or golden, and anything about the plant, the stem or leaf that might appear snake-like. You may remember that the taxonomy of a plant runs from the plant kingdom of plantae to the phylum, to the class, to the order, to the family, and then the genus of a plant. Braxilia is the genus in the family of Ericacea, in the group of flowering plants called angiosperms."

Lucien lifted his eyebrows with a questioning look and wondered where this was going, so Gervais continued.

"Regardless, at first, I thought the spelling was Latin, as most plants have their root word from that language, but the spelling of that name was not found in Latin, and in fact the spelling is called into question. So I looked for the closest spelling in Latin which brought me to the genus of Brassica, which are plants of the mustard family. But also, Pliny the Elder says it is named for several cabbage-like plants, and so both are true. As you can imagine, the list is long, 338 plants in that genus. I looked up quite a few of them and found the common rapeseed plant, which has bright yellow flowers and the pod which holds the seeds is like a long green bean with nodules and could resemble a baby snake. And when the shell begins to open, the so-called fruit makes the pod look like a small striped snake. I looked at the stem but it's smooth, and the leaf is blue-green and feather-like, and not scale-like. It felt like I was getting close but it just didn't seem close enough. Then it occurred to me that maybe I should focus on Greek plants, and found the Brassica nivalis, that is part of the Braxilla group of plants, and it just so happens to grow on Mount Olympus. But that took me right back to the cabbage and mustard family.

"I widened my search a bit and went to the Ericacea family and found something called the *Calluna vulgaris* that also grows on Mount Olympus. I wasn't specifically focusing on plants of Mount Olympus, but there happens to be a good website that lists the plants of Greece and since most of Mount Olympus is protected national lands, the park rangers must have studied the area and so they had an extensive list of plants. Calluna vulgaris is of the heather species but still in the Ericacea family. Lo and behold it has small scale-like leaves. Now its flower is most often white, but its leaf in the fall becomes a golden yellow. The plant is a good food source for deer and sheep, it has been used to dye wool yellow and to tan leather, its stiff branches have been used in making natural brooms for sweeping, and from its flowers a dark amber honey is made. But it was the next piece of information that let me know I had come about as close as I could get. I found a close-up of its leaves and stems and read they were used as a raw material for making sentimental jewelry.

This made Lucien sit up straighter. "Really?"

"That seemed to me to be a very close step for someone looking at the plant with an artist's eye and deciding to fashion some gold that looks like the plant for the same reason. Only with gold it would be considered a more valuable gift. I didn't stop there. I found a website that still produces Scottish heather jewelry with sterling silver fittings. *And*, they produce a gold necklace. Now granted, their jewelry pieces are mostly of Scottish and Celtic design, but I was struck by one necklace in particular that happens to look similar to the necklace designs of ancient Greece."

"Wow, Papa, you have outdone yourself."

"I did what I could. Sometimes one thing just leads to another. How did you do with your research?"

"I first wanted to continue searching for old gold necklaces that really existed, so I found the world's largest and oldest golden jewelry, which was from the northern shore of the Black Sea in Bulgaria, the Varna gold treasure. The gold in that trove was dated from 4,560 to 4,450 BCE. It was a huge find of over 3,000 pieces and there were several gold beaded necklaces.

"There was also the Hotnitsa gold treasure, found in a prehistoric cave in Central North Bulgaria. It was a necklace of large thin gold rings and it was dated from between 4,300 to 4,100 BCE. Another gold treasure was the Durankulak gold treasure found at a lagoon with the same name, also on the northern shore of the Black Sea in Bulgaria. It was 4,650 to 4,200 BCE. There wasn't an intact necklace, but there were gold beads. There are other gold treasures, but they were in other forms and not beads or complete necklaces. The Sakar gold treasure was found in Southeast Bulgaria with an age of 4,500 to 4,000 BCE. Those pieces were small flat rounded gold appliques, like buttons, once attached to some kind of cloth. Then much later, I found a set of clasps. I noted this because we have a picture of one side of a gold clasp of a snake, but this was a 5th century BCE necklace clasp found of two Greek lion heads of gold, and it sold in 2008 at Christie's Auction house for $20,000.

"So far, these have been very old discoveries of real gold necklaces, but there are stories of necklaces that verge on reality, brought to us by ancient writers. For instance, in

Homer's odyssey, there is the poetic story of Serena and her necklace. Her husband Stilicho was the cousin of the Roman Emperor Flavius Honorius. When the emperor was very young he was tutored by Stilicho, and to strengthen his power he had the emperor wed both of his daughters. When Honorius got older, he realized how treacherous Stilicho was and had him executed, which left Serena with a questionable future. In the end she was put to death, but there are several stories that say why. One version, told by the Byzantine historian Zosimus, is that it was due to her vanity, as she was seen stealing a necklace off a statue of the vestal virgin Rhea Silvia, the mother of Romulus and Remus, Rome's founders. It is unknown where it ended up, but the story is immortalized in John Waterhouse's painting, *Penelope and the Suitors.*

"Chante mentioned one treasure of Charlemagne, a ring worn by his German mistress, but there is another story of him and a necklace, also from the early 800s in the Common Era. Apparently, he was a very religious person and believed that possessing a sapphire would get him to heaven and grant him eternal salvation. He claimed to have gotten a sliver of Christ's cross and he had it placed between two sapphires in a golden pendent. He was buried with it in 814, but Emperor Otto III was determined to include that pendent in his treasury, so he had the 200-year-old tomb opened and took the pendent. Then sometime between 1789 and 1799, during the French Revolution, it was taken by the people and it ended up in the hands of Napoléon Bonaparte II, who gave it to the church. When the bishop received it, he gave it to the new emperor's soon-to-be wife, Joséphine, who in 1804 wore it to Napoléon's coronation. It eventually went to Napoléon III, and when he died it went to the Archbishop of Rheims. After that, there is no history of it.

Another story of a diamond necklace and Napoléon exists, and it has an even more twisted story. In 1811, when Napoléon's second wife Marie-Louise had a son, he gave her a necklace with 234 diamonds. When Napoléon went into exile she returned to her ancestral home in Austria, and when she died the necklace went to her sister-in-law, the Archduchess Sophia. When she died it went to her son Charles Louis, and after his death it went to his third wife Maria Theresa. In 1929 she had it put up for sale in New York, but with the Wall Street crash a diamond dealer bought it for a fraction of its worth. Maria Theresa went to court and got the necklace back. Finally in 1948 she sold it to another dealer and it eventually went to Marjorie Post, the owner of General Foods, who ended up donating it to the Smithsonian Institution, where it still resides. Just an amusing note, she was the original owner of the Palm Beach mansion, Mar-a-Lago."

"Wow," returned Gervais. "History sure has its twists and turns."

At this point, Chante and Melodia entered and announced that lunch was ready.

"All right," responded Lucien, "then we will continue this after lunch." And they all went downstairs for their afternoon meal.

Chapter Twenty-Four

After lunch, they went back up to Gervais' room. Melodia settled next to Chante on the bed and they and Gervais prepared to listen to more of what Lucien had to report.

"When I left off before lunch, I had finished describing ancient finds of necklaces that are real or said to have been real. So I had to start looking at gold necklaces from mythological sources. I thought about it and Papa was right. Even if a necklace was known to have been mythical, someone could have replicated one to pass off as real. Forgeries have been known to be created for thousands of years.

I'm not a fan of mythology and had never heard of any of these necklaces I'm about to tell you about. But I felt I should look them up, if for no other reason than to satisfy my curiosity. There were many and I admit I began to get bogged down in fascination with each one.

"Metaphorically, gold has been associated with the sun and masculinity, and so there are a host of mythological goldsmiths. Most known are the two Germanic mythologies: Thor with his hammer, and Wayland the Smith, maker of weapons and armor. There was one notable female, Brigid, the Irish patroness of blacksmiths. Hephaestus was also a big name from Greek mythology. He made lots of magical weapons and other items.

"As far as famous necklaces, there are many possibilities with long stories but I will relate only the most notable. First is the necklace of the Norse Goddess Freya. The story goes that she wanted something of gold after the trickster Loki had tantalized her with a gold hoard he had obtained from a group of giants. So one day she left and went looking for the giants to obtain her own gold. Instead, she found four dwarves, who had in their possession a beautiful gold necklace with amber and rubies, called the Brisingamen. She was dazzled by it and her vanity made her believe that wearing it would dazzle anyone who saw it on her. The dwarves said she could have it, but only if she slept with each one of them. She wanted the necklace so badly, that each did have their time with her. She put the necklace on and went home, but because she had been gone so long, her husband had left her. She searched but never found him. She wore the necklace everywhere she went, but now it was seen as a weakness, a sign of her greed and as guilt for losing her husband.

"Next is the story of Penelope, the wife of Odysseus. While waiting for Odysseus to return from his travels, Penelope was approached by 108 men, all of whom claimed that Odysseus would never return. Because of that, she must marry another. Each man proceeded to try and win her over and make her his wife. But she kept them all at bay by claiming she would only marry once she had finished weaving Odysseus' burial shroud. So she wove by day, and unraveled what she had done by night, for three years. A man named Eurymachus got tired of waiting. To make her quickly change her mind, he thought he could win her over with jewels. So he presented her with, and I quote from the story, 'a magnificent chain of gold and amber beads that gleamed like sunlight.' We don't know what happened to the necklace, but upon Odysseus' return, he killed Eurymachus with an arrow. To be noted, another suiter also gave her a necklace, a man named Peisander, but nothing else is known about it. And another suitor, Eurydamas, gave Penelope a pair of earrings, so Chante you can add that one to your list.

"Another story is of the Lady of the Lake, part of the Arthurian legends. One of the Knights of the Round Table was Sir Pelleas. The most popular story is about his love for Nimue, the Lady of the Lake in Thomas Mallory's story of *Le Morte d'Arthur*. But there is another tale about how he helped an old woman cross a river. As a reward for helping her, she gave him a jeweled necklace that would enchant any woman who saw it. This was good news for Pelleas, as he wanted to win the love of Nimue, which he did, but nothing else is known of that necklace.

"There are two Japanese stories of bejeweled necklaces. One story is about the Magatama necklace from 1000 BCE, which had curved beads but they were said to be made of jade. And the other was the Mikuratana-no-kami necklace, which was given to Amaterasu, the Japanese goddess of the sun. The reason I am relating this second story is because Amaterasu was also considered a snake goddess. The story goes that she had taken the form of a snake and had slept with the goddess Saiō, as scales were found in Amaterasu's bed the next day. She is linked to a snake cult which existed at the time. Perhaps a necklace with snake heads was fashioned to honor her?

"The last story I'm going to tell is a little long and twisted, but I found it striking, so bear with me. It is the story of the Necklace of Harmonia. It was made by the Greek god Hephaestus. I was not familiar with this god or the necklace, so I had to look up this legend in some detail. It's a surprising story so I think you will find it of interest. First, I became familiar with Hephaestus. Despite the fact that Hephaestus was born with crippled feet to the Gods Zeus and Hera, he was talented; becoming the chief metal worker and artisan of the Olympian Gods, and he was married to Aphrodite. He's famous for making many things for the gods: Achilles' armor, Agamemnon's staff, Aphrodite's girdle, Eros's bow and arrows, Helios' chariot, Hermes' winged sandals and helmet, and many other items.

"One day, he discovered that Aphrodite was having an affair with Ares, the god of war. This enraged Hephaestus, so he devised an unbreakable chain-link net that was so fine it was nearly invisible, and he threw it over them while they were engaged in love-making. Entrapped, the couple was dragged to Mount Olympus, where they were laughed at by the gods. Both were shamed, but Poseidon convinced Hephaestus to release them. Hephaestus' bride price was returned, and Ares had to pay the fine for being an adulterer. But from that union, Aphrodite and Ares produced a daughter named Harmonia. The infidelity was never forgotten, so Hephaestus decided that one day he would find a way to avenge the affair and the subsequent birth of Harmonia.

"When Harmonia became an adult she fell in love and became engaged to Cadmus of Thebes. Hephaestus saw this as his chance to get even, so he fashioned a magical necklace as a wedding gift. The necklace would allow Harmonia to keep her youthful beauty, but along with the gift was attached a curse. All of her descendants who received and wore the necklace would also be granted the same gift, but also experience a great misfortune. When Harmonia died, her daughter Semele inherited the necklace. When her grandmother Hera visited and saw the necklace on Semele's neck, she inferred that Zeus was not really Semele's grandfather. Semele went to Zeus demanding the truth, but for her insinuation, she met her end.

"There is a gap in the story of several generations, but by that time the necklace had become an object of desire for its power to retain youth and beauty, especially by the women from the House of Thebes. The next time the necklace appears is in the story of Queen Jocasta, the daughter of Menoeceus, the king of Thebes. You will know her story when I tell you that after her husband died, she ended up unknowingly marrying her son, Oedipus. All of their descendants came to their own tragedies. One of Oedipus' sons, Polynices, inherited the necklace, while his brother Eteocles took the throne of Thebes and exiled Polynices. So Polynices gave the necklace to a woman named Eriphyle as a bribe to have her husband Amphiaraus march against his brother Eteocles, so Polynices could get the throne. One of Eriphyle's sons, Alcmaeon, joined in the fight, along with a man named Phegeus, but in the end, the two young men and Eriphyle were killed.

"However, by way of another of Alcmaeon's sons, the necklace was passed on to one of Phegeus' daughters, named Arsinoe. Then it passed on to two other sons, who dared not give it to any woman. Besides that, they were tired of the family feuds, the deaths the necklace caused, and the curse it brought, so they dedicated the necklace to the Temple of Athena at Delphi. But the story does not end there. One of the generals of that region, named Phayllus, stole the necklace from the temple and gave it to a woman who lived in Delphi, to win her over and make her his mistress. Again, she retained her youth and beauty. But one day while he went off to fight in the Third Sacred War against Thebes in 356 BCE, the son of the mistress set fire to the house, which killed his mother, and that seems to be the last we hear of the necklace of Harmonia."

There was a pause as they were all taken by the tale.

"That is some story," commented Chante. "Any description of the necklace?"

"Not that a mythical tale can be trusted, but it is said it was wrought of fine gold with the clasps being the heads of two snakes with jeweled eyes."

Gervais was shaking his head. "That's a long and crazy story, but to think that the small piece of chain that was unearthed is the same as in the story couldn't be possible."

"Why not?" asked Chante. "If a skilled metal worker could make a net so fine as to hardly be seen, why couldn't he fashion a snake chain necklace?"

"There does seem to be some symbolism here," added Lucien. "A poisonous snake will bite and leave the victim in peril. If Hephaestus could make magical weapons, what's to say he couldn't imbue a snake chain with destructive qualities?"

"But," reminded Gervais, "the gods of Mount Olympus are myths, not real people."

"Let's talk about that," said Lucien. "All the early Greek stories were told through oral storytellers. It wasn't until the late eighth century BCE that the Phoenicians produced the first written characters that eventually became the Greek alphabet. And it wasn't until Homer wrote The Iliad and The Odyssey that stories of the gods came to be known. Historians believe the stories weren't actually recorded until the sixth century BCE. And the first story, The Iliad, was about the Trojan War, which occurred between the twelfth and thirteen centuries BCE."

Gervais, who had gotten back on his laptop, shared what he had just found. "The Greek Hesiod poet tells of a Golden Age when the god Cronus ruled and humans first roamed the earth. Saint Jerome says this was from 1710 to 1674 BCE. Then there was the Silver Age when Cronus' son Zeus ruled, said to be from 1674 to 1628 BCE. These were followed by the Bronze Age, the Heroic Age, and the Iron Age. Of course, now we know that humans roamed the earth long before 1710 BCE. But the Gods of Olympus were specifically believed to exist solely by the Greeks, and they are exclusively that country's story of origin, so it wouldn't be too hard to believe that the stories were based on real people who took on an embellished story of greatness."

"So," continued Chante, "you're saying that some man with an advanced knowledge of metalwork, alive sometime between the Neolithic Age and the Bronze Age, may have indeed fashioned a gold snake necklace, but mystical aspects were added to make the story more exciting?"

"Yes," confirmed Gervais, "which would put that period of time in the Helladic chronology dating system between 3200 and 1050 BCE."

"And," Lucien continued, "If the Durankulak gold treasure was from around 4000 BCE, why would it be so hard to believe that a more intricate gold necklace wasn't fashioned a thousand years later?"

Now Chante was shaking her head. "But that would mean that whether the necklace is real or mythical, whoever stole the chain believes it *to be true*. Otherwise, why wait...what...from 1946 to 2022, seventy-five years, for another piece?"

"Exactly."

"Okay," she continued, "let's say it *is* real. We may now know *why* someone took it, but that doesn't bring us any closer to *who* took it."

"That's true," said Lucien. "We are either looking for an elderly person, or someone who got the information from an older person and continued the quest."

At that point Lucien's phone dinged with a message, which he quickly read.

"That was Doctor Manikas. He looked in storage for that piece of gold chain in the museum, and it is also missing."

"That's not good," remarked Chante.

"It's not good because we won't be able to compare it to the one found this year, but in a way, it is good news, as it means that it must have been a match. I am truly hoping that once Mister Samaras meets with the Central Archaeological Council, I will be granted the information of who funded the archaeological dig in 1946 and who is funding it now. That person, whoever they are, is hiding behind an organization and obviously doesn't want their name revealed. I think I'm going to have to go to Athens and plead before the council to reveal the name of the organization and the person behind it. And I'll have to work fast because the council is meeting in two days."

Chapter Twenty-Five

On Monday, Lucien thought about contacting Inspector Nomikos. He was actually surprised that she had not checked in with him and wondered why. He thought it might be for several reasons. One, that she had already run through her leads and had nothing new to share. Two, that because Lucien was there with Chante and Gervais she could put her officers to work elsewhere. Three, because Officer Tavoularis was watching over them, so nothing else was needed. Lucien also thought it was possible that Officer Tavoularis could be reporting to the inspector and letting her know where the Reynards were and went at all times. Just the same, he felt he should check in with her, tell her about the list of older finds, and at least thank her for the protection that his family was being given. He called her but it went to voicemail, so he left a message.

"Hello Inspector Nomikos. It's Detective Reynard. Just a courtesy call to give you an update. We received a list of the items from the 1946 dig and have been searching through them to compare them with the list of stolen items. Only one thing showed a connection, the gold chain, but we're not sure if that will lead to anything. I also want to sincerely thank you for sending Officer Tavoularis over during the day and for the men guarding us at night. It is much appreciated and we do feel safer. If anything comes up, just give me a call or text. Thank you."

For some reason, he decided to withhold the information about him flying to Athens to meet with the council, and he decided not to call Kostas Samaras to let him know that he would be there in the morning. He called the airline and booked the earliest morning flight to Athens. He planned to be at Samaras' office early to request a meeting with the council to directly plead his case. Then he decided to call Monsieur Teniet in Paris.

"Detective Reynard. Good morning. How are things going?"

"A true mix, sir." Lucien explained everything that had happened working with Inspector Nomikos, all the interviews, the missing list of archaeological finds and then getting the list from another source, the murder and the threat, little about the comparative searches they had made, and the discovery of the link between an item from the 1946 dig and the present dig. He explained that the only people who would have been receiving reports from both digs would be those who were funding them. The local authorities had tried to get that information, but were met with resistance. Then he explained that he was heading to Athens to try to meet in person with the Central Archaeological Council and find out the name of the funding organization, because whoever was behind the theft had to have known about everything that had been pulled from each dig. Was there anything the Monsieur Teniet could do to convince the council to cooperate and release that information?

"Well, I can't demand they give that information to you, but I know the Director General and could emphasize the need for international cooperation on behalf of UNESCO. When are you meeting with them?"

"I'm flying out very early tomorrow morning before they meet, and hoping I can get permission to speak with them. I haven't actually asked yet, as I was afraid if I asked ahead they would say it wasn't possible. So I was planning to just show up, and hoping that being already present would add weight to pleading my case."

"I think we can do better than that. Tonight I will personally call the Director General, Filipe Linardakis, to let him know that I am sending you to speak with the council on an important matter, and to please have them assist you."

Lucien was glad he called. "Yes, sir. That would be great. Thank you."

"You're welcome. Let me know how it goes. Please say hello to Chante and Gervais for me. And how is the little one?"

"Melodia is six and a half, and she is a loveable handful."

"Sounds about right. Well, take care." Then they signed off.

That evening after dinner, Lucien called a meeting with Chante and Gervais.

"I've got a 7:35 flight out tomorrow morning and should arrive in Athens an hour later. I've already booked a taxi to take me to the airport in the morning and a driver in Athens to take me directly to the downtown building where the meeting is taking place at 10:00. I'm booked to come back on an afternoon flight. I don't want anyone but you two to know where I'm going. So, at breakfast when Gala and Nils ask where I am, just say that I had an early meeting downtown. I want you two and Melodia to stay here while I'm gone. It is the safest place for you."

"But Lucien, what about the officer outside watching the B&B? Won't he see you leave?" asked Chante.

"I'm going to text Officer Tavoularis tonight and let him know that I have an early morning meeting and ask him not to follow me. It's more important for him to stay to watch the B&B and protect you here." Chante nodded. "One more thing. While I'm gone, I need one of you to search for anything on Argus Dougenis, the man who visited Professor Ekonomos at the dig site. By the way, I found out who the Director General of the council is, Filipe Linardakis. I need background on him, too."

They agreed. Gervais was worried about Lucien going alone to Athens, but he knew his son could not let a thread of information dangle without pulling it. Chante and Gervais wished him good luck with the council, and promised that they would stay put and wait for his return.

Early the next morning at daybreak, Lucien met his taxi out front and waved to Officer Tavoularis, who was sitting in his car and watched as the taxi passed. He gave Lucien the okay sign. The flight went smoothly and Lucien was able to quickly spot the driver at arrivals in Athens, who had his name on a card. Lucien arrived at the downtown building early enough to quickly cross the street and have a cup of coffee at a café. Then he returned to the building. A directory of the businesses in the building was located on a wall near the elevator. He pressed the button for the floor of the Central Archaeological Council. No names were listed, but he would ask when he got there.

When he came out of the elevator he saw a reception desk at the end of the hall and approached an attractive young woman behind the counter.

"Kaliméra. Pós boró na se voithíso?"

"I'm sorry. Do you speak English?" he asked.

"Yes, sir. How can I help you?"

"I'm looking for Mister Samaras' office. Is he in yet?"

"Yes, sir. Is he expecting you?"

"He should be, my boss called last night to inform the council of my arrival today."

"What is your name please?"

"Detective Lucien Reynard, from UNESCO's Paris office."

"One moment, please." She picked up the phone, briefly spoke in Greek, and then hung up. He'll be out in a moment."

Lucien thanked her and glanced around, but it did not take long for Samaras to come out of a door down the hall and approach him with a handshake.

"Detective, Director General Linardakis said to expect you. I am afraid you are not allowed to be in the room during our meeting. However, you have been granted a few minutes to address the council right after the meeting."

"That's fine. I am very happy to hear that I will be able to address them. Can you give me some idea how long your meeting will last?"

"It usually lasts no longer than one and a half hours." Samaras looked at his watch. "The meeting is beginning in about ten minutes. Would you care to wait here or downstairs in the lobby?"

Lucien saw two blue chairs by a window with magazines. "I'll wait over there. Thank you."

"Fine. I'll come and get you when we are ready to receive you."

Lucien thanked him again, then Samaras walked away and Lucien made himself comfortable. He sent a text to Chante and Gervais. *"I've been granted time to address the council, but only after their scheduled meeting. Hoping to get in to see them by 11:30. Text me if you find out anything about the two men."*

"Will do," was the response.

The wait seemed long, but that was only because he was anxious to get the information he needed. He kept rehearsing over and over in his mind what he would say. Finally, at 11:45, Samaras appeared. On the way down the hall he reminded Lucien to keep his visit brief. Then Samaras led him into a large room where a long dark wood table was surrounded by the seventeen members who formed the council. Lucien assumed that the man at the head of the table was the Director General, Filipe Linardakis. He also guessed that the man next to him with the laptop was the Secretary General. The rest had to be five archaeologists, two of whom were women, seven professors, two again who were women, and one architect. The legal counsel, Samaras, stood next to Lucien.

"Director General and members of the Council, this is Detective Lucien Reynard, a representative from UNESCO's Cultural Division in Paris who wishes to address you. He has been working with the local authorities in Rhodes to investigate a theft at the Rhodes Acropolis."

Then Samaras sat at his chair next to where Lucien was standing.

Linardakis addressed Lucien. "Detective Reynard, welcome. It was good of Monsieur Teniet to let us know that you were coming. He said you have something to share with us and something to request concerning your work in Rhodes."

"Yes, sir. First, I would like to extend my thanks to the council for allowing me to address you, and Monsieur Teniet on behalf of the Paris UNESCO office also relays his thanks. I will be as succinct as possible about what has happened and what we have discovered, which will lead to my request.

"On July 16th, sometime between 3:30 and 4:00 a.m., a person cut the chain to the secured area around the Rhodes acropolis and then cut the lock on a storage building and took fifteen items. Each of the twelve people on the dig team at the site are professionals with experience and were questioned by Inspector Lex Nomikos of the Rhodes police and by me. The three guards who work the site were also questioned by both of us. There are no indications that any of them are suspects, so each has been eliminated as such.

However, someone was watching the site in order to learn the timing of the guards' rounds, and this was most likely the person who committed the theft. That person had a clear view of the site from a distance, and I found the hotel where he had stayed. With the aid of the police, we got the hotel's video of a man paying cash for the room for several days before the theft. We even discovered who that person was. He had used an alias upon checking in. But before we could get to him and proceed with questioning, he was found murdered in his apartment. Obviously, whoever hired the man did not want to take the chance that he might say anything."

Worried expressions appeared on the faces of most of the members before him. One person even repeated the word, "murdered?"

"A professional photographer took pictures of each of the items unearthed during the dig, so we have pictures of each of the pieces that were stolen. I got the idea that perhaps it might be prudent to compare the items taken this year with the items unearthed in the last known dig in 1946. But when the historian at the Archaeological Museum, Doctor Eugene Manikas, tried to find the list of items, the file was missing. It was becoming evident that someone was doing their best to keep us from discovering what those items were, but they did not anticipate our resourcefulness and your cooperation in supplying the list from your records. So thank you very much for your help.

"When we compared the items that were stolen with the list from 1946, only one item matched, a gold chain. So I had Doctor Manikas search to see if the gold chain from 1946 was still in the museum's holdings, and he found that it was also missing. Those two pieces of gold chain must mean a great deal to someone, because they have been watching and waiting for more of the same since 1946. The digs are seventy-five years apart, so either that person is in their eighties, or most likely the search has been carried on by a second person. Whoever it is, is well-funded, well-connected, and well-informed about all items being pulled from that site. It has to be someone who is receiving reports of the artifacts being unearthed in order to know when to take those items.

"It seems plausible that someone is receiving reports of the discoveries in order to recover more of the gold necklace. For what reason, we don't know, but he has gone to quite a lot of trouble. I am not accusing anyone, but I would like to know who funded both digs, or at least the name of the organization involved."

The General Director spoke again. "Detective Reynard, I hope you are not intimating that the Central Archaeological Council, which approved the organization to fund the digs, has had anything to do with hiding this individual. I can assure you, it has done nothing of the kind."

There were concerned looks on every face around the table, and Lucien was taken aback at the accusation.

"And I can assure you, sir, and everyone here, that the thought never crossed my mind. All I know is that there is someone who is willing to commit murder in order to keep their identity hidden from the authorities, and if all of us don't do something, there is no telling to what lengths this person might go."

The Director General turned to his legal counselor. "Mister Samaras, please escort Detective Reynard out of the room to wait while the council discusses what we can do."

At least they would think about it, thought Lucien. "Thank you, sir, ladies and gentlemen."

Samaras led Lucien out of the room and returned him to the blue chairs near the reception desk. Twenty minutes went by before Samaras returned with an envelope, which he handed over. Lucien was confused and looked to Samaras for clarification.

"The council is and has been under a strict agreement never to divulge the identity of any individual. The fact of the matter is, they don't know the name of the person who runs the organization. They are in contact only with an agent who works for the organization. However, after much discussion, the council finally agreed that they were not obligated to keep the name of the organization a secret. In that envelope is the name of the organization that funded both the 1946 and the 2022 digs. I'm afraid that is all that we can do for you."

Lucien nodded in thanks. "Well, it's a start. Please relay my sincere thanks."

Chapter Twenty-Six

By the time Lucien emerged from the building, it was only 12:30 and he still had three and a half hours before his flight back to Rhodes. He decided to grab an early lunch. When he found a nearby taverna, he asked for a quiet booth in the back where he could have Wi-Fi. He sent a text to Chante and Gervais asking to Skype with both of them as soon as possible. They texted back that they would connect with him in ten minutes. That gave him plenty of time to order before and plug in his head phones. His food arrived just as the Skype began, but he set it aside.

"How did the meeting go?" asked Chante from her laptop, where she and Gervais sat together.

"They did not give me the name of any person, but I got the name of the organization." Lucien read from the paper in the envelope. "Write this down. It is called Ellinikés Politistikés Epicheiríseis," which Lucien spelled. "It translates as 'Greek Cultural Enterprises'."

"Hold on," said Gervais as he grabbed his computer. "I'll look them up." There was a short pause, then he continued. "They have a website and it says they are, quote, 'a privately owned non-profit philanthropic organization with a focus on Greece's cultural heritage through research for the purposes of promoting knowledge and education.' And surprise, surprise, it says it was established in 1945."

"And likely," interrupted Lucien, "it was set up just in time to get an archaeological dig to begin the following year. And what better excuse than to say its primary purpose was to clean up the mess the war had caused on the acropolis."

Gervais continued. "There is a page that lists the museums and universities where it contributes its 'knowledge and discoveries,' with a picture of a rosy-cheeked young man holding a diploma, and a picture of a museum curator standing next to a good-sized statue. There is a contact page for emailing inquiries, but there isn't any physical address for their headquarters, no phone number, and nothing that says who owns the company or who its board of directors are."

"How do we find out who owns and runs the organization?" Chante inquired.

Lucien thought about that. "Well, if it is a legally established corporation, even if it is a non-profit, it has to have filed within the regional city-state, which I would guess is Athens."

"Isn't a corporation required to list its directors?" queried Chante. "In the U.S. they are."

"Apparently not in Greece," answered Lucien. "But there has to be someone who can field inquiries and file tax forms every year, and someone's name must be on the business license."

"I suspect," speculated Gervais, "that the organization has a registered agent who handles all that, and that person is no doubt an attorney who works for a law firm that specializes in corporate law. I would think that each region's secretary must have a database of at least the name of the registered agent of the corporation."

"True, and there must be a commercial registry here in Athens that lists all businesses. I have some time. Maybe I can find them and ask. In the meantime, what did you find on Argus Dougenis and Filipe Linardakis?"

"I can answer for Filipe Linardakis," responded Chante, "I actually found a lot on him. He is highly thought-of and well-respected. His history seems to be impeccable. He graduated from Athens University of Economics and Business with honors in two degrees, one in Business Administration and another in Accounting and Finance. He's married and has a grown son and daughter, and I found an article that mentions him playing golf with one of Athens' heads of state. It seems his position on the Council is fairly secret as I found no reference to him being attached to that organization. I can understand why, because a person in that position could be put under undue pressure to give someone an advantage in some capacity. But that's about it."

"Good. He seemed like an upfront guy, but you never can tell. Gervais, I assume you did the search on Dougenis."

"Yes, I did, and I think you will be interested to know that he *is* from the Department of Antiquities and Cultural Heritage, but *not* from the office based in Athens as Ekonomos thought, or even the one in Rhodes, which would have been the most likely. Argus Dougenis is from the antiquities office located in Delphi."

"Really? Well, that *is* interesting. Why would *he* be here visiting Professor Ekonomos, and not the representative from Rhodes?"

"He is an ephorate, by the way," corrected Gervais. "That is something like a magistrate. I can only assume he is working with someone behind the scenes. I wondered why he would be on Rhodes, so I made a call to the Ephorate of Rhodes. I didn't get to speak to him directly, but I spoke with his secretary, who was very helpful. I told her that I was part of the investigating team working on the Rhodes acropolis theft, and asked if the Ephorate of Rhodes had had a chance to visit the acropolis site of late.

She said no, but he had been on the phone with the Rhodes police and asked to be kept informed of the investigation. Then I asked if there was a reason for the Ephorate of Delphi to visit the site. She was surprised to hear it and couldn't think of a reason why."

"Well, that's the third possible link to Delphi," mused Lucien.

Chante was confused. "The third? There's the necklace supposedly from Delphi and the ephorate from there, but what is the third?"

Lucien did a quick check to recall the details. "Here it is. There was a coin, a Delphi Silver Tridrachm, dated mid-third century BCE."

"Oh, yes," remembered Chante. "The one with dolphins on it. So you think that might help substantiate the idea that the necklace came from Delphi? Although the necklace may have been much older, because a coin from the second century BCE was found, that tells us when the necklace arrived?"

Gervais nodded. "That does seem most likely."

"Okay, I feel we are getting closer. When I'm done speaking with you both, I'm going to find the Commercial Registry Service in Athens and get the name and contact information of the Agent of Service for E.P.E, that is, Greek Cultural Enterprises. I can say that I want to discuss a future business opportunity and that I'm not getting any response from the website's email. What is that email by the way?"

Gervais read it from his notes. "InformationX3 at EPE.com. That looks like some kind of extension with an 'X' in it."

"Really? That sounds like a fake email. Send a blank email and just put 'test' as the subject."

"Really? Are you sure?"

"Yes. I'm betting it bounces right back. Just do it."

Gervais did and a few seconds later he whistled in surprise. "You were right. It did bounce back. How did you know?"

"Because false emails are often given to appear approachable, but the party still wants to remain hidden, so they provide a bogus email address and it bounces. The 'X' in the address was a giveaway."

"Wow, that's sneaky," commented Chante.

"Yes, and amateurish. I'll see what I can get from the registry office. If I'm lucky I may get the name of a law office. Maybe even a phone number. Then I need to know what to say to the Agent of Service representing the organization. I guess I can repeat the desire to discuss a future business opportunity and request that I meet with him, but what would that business opportunity be? It has to be something enticing."

Chante had an idea. "What if one of us sent a short video of the sparkling gold from the dig and a still photograph that shows it better, and say that we have something that the organization might be interested in?"

Lucien chuckled. "That's pretty bold and risky, and the agent might not know what we are referring to. Besides, the video doesn't show a clear picture of a chain, only a shiny gold color. And we would need to leave some kind of contact number so they could call us back. They could easily track the number back to us and find out that I'm an officer of the law."

Gervais went one further. "If we get a phone number, we could do a reverse search to find an address. Do you suppose we could have the agent's phone bugged? If the agent thought it might be a legit inquiry, he or she might contact the person who makes the decisions in the organization, the one who is searching for more of the necklace."

"I doubt the agent would use his office landline to contact that person," responded Lucien, "and if I get a phone number it would be for the law office. No, the agent would probably use their personal cell phone to call the owner."

Gervais was catching on. "Then could the police put some kind of tracking system on the agent's cell? Could Monsieur Teniet get that done?"

"I sincerely doubt that Monsieur Teniet could get an international warrant without proof of a crime. And I don't think the agent would do anything illegal, at least not on the surface. But I believe if we just get the name of the agent, we could forget the landline and have Inspector Nomikos find out what phone numbers are owned by that agent. What we need is a cell number."

"But doesn't that mean someone would still have to get a hold of that cell phone to load some kind of tracer on it?" pursued Gervais. "Even if we could get access to the agent's cell phone, it would most likely have a passcode."

"Yes, but we wouldn't need to physically get into their phone or be anywhere near it."

"What do you mean?" Chante was more than curious.

"I could use a special app I know that would send me the number of all calls that he makes without him knowing."

"But what if the agent texts a message instead or drives to that person's location to speak in person?" asked Gervais.

"The app allows me to also see any texts sent and it also has a GPS tracker. I can listen to a conversation if I want to and even have the person's phone take a picture of them and have that sent to me, as well."

Gervais and Chante stared at Lucien with new eyes, and then Gervais could not help but comment. "It seems you have been learning new things this past year, more than just reading about old cases."

"Papa, I do have access to certain tools in order to find thieves who steal antiquities. There's more than one way to see where a thief goes."

"I believe you, son. You've become more enterprising by the day."

"All right. Got to go. I'm going to try and get that phone number for the agent now. I'll see you later this afternoon. I'll let you know what I find out when I get back."

They said their goodbyes and Lucien did a search for the General Commercial Registry Service in Athens. This ended up being easier than he expected. He found the website. They required the tax identification number, the registry number, a person's name or the company name. Now that he had the company name, he just typed it in. Within two seconds, a copy of the business license appeared on the screen with the agent's name and signature. Lucien took a screenshot and closed his laptop. He could not help but to beam with satisfaction.

Finally, he was able to get to his rather lukewarm lunch, but enjoyed every bite. Then he took a taxi to the airport, caught his flight back to Rhodes, and arrived by taxi back at the B&B by 4:50.

Chapter Twenty-Seven

When Lucien got back he reviewed everything with Chante and Gervais, and they decided that Lucien would visit Inspector Nomikos the next day. He texted the inspector requesting a meeting and she responded that he could come in the next day at eleven o'clock.

On Wednesday morning, Lucien was met by the inspector in the police station lobby, and they walked to her office where they sat down.

She kept it formal. "I take it you have an update for me, Detective Reynard."

"I do indeed. Remember when I asked you to find out the name of the organization that funded the dig, but you were unable to discover what it was?"

"Yes, were you able to?"

"Yes, but in order to get that information, I had to request a meeting with the Central Archaeological Council in Athens, which is the entity that approved the application for the dig at the acropolis, both in 1946 and this year. Monsieur Teniet from the UNESCO office in Paris was helpful, as he knows their General Director and was able to pave the way for me to get an audience with the council. I gave them an overview of everything that had happened, and I think that telling them about the murder opened their eyes and made them more open to sharing with me at least something."

"And did they give you the name of a person?"

"No. They explained that they were only in contact with an agent who worked for the organization, and they were under obligation to never disclose that person's name. The amount of leverage or money used to secure permission to dig the site must have been substantial. However, the council did give me the name of the organization, as they were not obligated to keep that a secret." Lucien handed the inspector the paper that he had received.

"Ellinikés Politistikés Epicheiríseis—Greek Cultural Enterprises."

"Yes. So, now knowing the name of the organization, we were able to find its website. We found out that it is," and he read from his phone, "'a privately owned non-profit philanthropic organization with a focus on Greece's cultural heritage through research for the purpose of promoting knowledge and education,' which was established in 1945, the year before the 1946 dig was begun. But their email is fake. There is no physical address given, no phone number, and their Board of Directors is not listed. But I was able to go online and check with the General Commercial Registry Service in Athens for the name of the organization listed in their system. I was able to pull up a copy of the business license which has a name attached."

"Well, what is the owner's name?"

"That's just it. There is only an Agent of Service listed, but it is a name, nonetheless. Now I need your help, inspector. If you can find a cell phone number for that person, we'll be that much closer to discovering the man behind the agent."

"All right. What is that person's name and I'll see what I can do."

"That is exactly what I was hoping you would say. The name is on the back of this envelope." He handed over the envelope.

"Axios Milas. Okay, but wouldn't he simply be listed online as an Attorney at Law with some firm?"

"Yes, but it would be a landline. I need a cell phone."

"Hmm, I'll see what I can find out. I'll let you know if I can locate the number or numbers. Then what are you going to do?"

"It is better if you don't know, inspector. If my plan works, then you might want to have a search warrant issued to find the stolen items, either in that name or another."

"By the way, Detective Reynard, were you ever able to determine what the gold speck was in the video?"

"No, and most likely it was just what Professor Ekonomos, Jace Othonos and Lydia Karas thought it was— a piece of stone with a metallic luster."

Lucien and Inspector Nomikos stood up and shook hands, and Lucien returned to the B&B for a pleasant lunch in the back garden under the shade of a linden tree. After lunch, Chante watched Melodia play with her games in the yard and Gervais read the paper and sipped his coffee. All Lucien needed to do was wait.

Two hours after Lucien had left the police station, he got a text from Inspector Nomikos. She wrote that there was only one cell number listed for Axios Milas, and she forwarded it to him. Then Lucien went online and put his plan into action. He activated the monitoring system. He wanted to track all texts, calls, emails, and GPS use. He also set up an alert for whenever the agent used the word "council."

When he finished, Chante could not help but comment. "You look like the bird that swallowed a canary." Lucien looked confused, as he didn't know that American idiom.

"It means you look very pleased with yourself. What's up?"

"Let's just say, I am the cat that has set the mouse trap." Now Chante had a confused look, so he explained. "I've just received the cell number for the agent, and whatever communication he sends or receives will be forwarded to me."

This got Gervais' attention. "What happens next?"

"We wait, and I continually scan and read everything he says or writes and any replies he receives. No doubt, most of it will be personal and nothing I want to know about, which I will delete immediately. I'm only interested in the calls he makes to or receives from his boss at E.P.E. I get the feeling, at least I'm hoping, that someone from the council will contact the agent and tell him that I was there. If not that, then the agent is bound to receive the latest report from Professor Ekonomos on the finds from the past month, which I'm betting gets sent on to the man behind the scenes."

"But how long could that take?" asked Chante.

"I don't know, but I wouldn't think more than twenty-four hours."

Gervais was still curious. "What else can you get from his phone?"

"The most important thing is his phone's contact list. I'm downloading that now."

"I have to ask, son, is it legal what you are doing?"

"Yes, Papa. I am a registered user of the police tracking system. I have a special account that allows me to access it, but only for professional reasons. I cannot use it for anything of a personal nature or use anything I record in court. I have to adhere to strict regulations, and after a case closes everything is wiped clean."

A look of relief came over his father's face. Then just as quickly, Gervais went back to reading his French newspaper, which he had specially delivered. Chante and Lucien watched Gervais become absorbed again, then they looked at each other and shared a grin.

But Lucien needed to concentrate on work. "My love, I'm going upstairs to download the contact list onto my laptop and examine the results."

"Okay. We'll be up soon, as it's getting close to Melodia's nap time."

By the time Lucien got upstairs and signed in, the app had finished downloading on his phone, and he transferred the file to his laptop. He needed a larger screen to scrutinize and assess the information.

No call, email or text had been detected using the word 'council.' The next thing was to go through Axios Milas' contacts. Lucien glanced at the bottom of the list and saw that there were a total of three hundred and twenty-two names. That was quite a lot and it would take some time to go through each name. Lucien discovered that the man was good about listing his relationships with his family and those included full names and addresses, so he ignored them. There were many professional listings for people, probably business associates or clients, with their full name, business title, and the address of the company they represented. There were a couple dozen listings that had either only a first name or a last name, with only a phone number and no address.

As he went along, he happened to notice that some listings had a small 'c' in the notes section. At first he thought it might be a 'c' for cousin, but so far, his family members, including one cousin, had already been identified. Once Lucien found three names like this, he thought that the 'c' might stand for 'council' instead. So he jumped ahead to the 'Ls' for Director General Linardakis' last name, and saw he had a small 'c' in the notes field. To confirm it, he saw that Samaras, the legal counsel, also had one. So Lucien started a separate file with a list of each of the last names and numbers with that notation. When he was done, he had a list of seventeen council members' last names and phone numbers. Now he could cross-reference any of their phone numbers with those of recent communications. That was easy to do as all his recent texts were still available to view.

Axios Milas was obviously not on close terms with most of the council members, as he only had a texting history with Samaras. That made sense, as both were lawyers keeping in touch behind the scenes. Samaras had texted Milas the day before. Judging by the time stamp, it had to have been shortly after Lucien left the building. His text read, "*A UNESCO detective was here asking who was funding the Acro dig.*" Milas had only replied, "*No matter, since no one knows but me, he will find a dead end.*" This amused Lucien because it meant that Samaras was fulfilling his duty to report to him, but at the same time he had not mentioned the fact that the council *had* given Lucien the name of the organization. This left him wondering if Samaras was fully on board with the charade or not.

Lucien went back to his searches. He found one contact that had only two initials, which perplexed him. It could have been a secret girlfriend for all he knew. He looked for more, but there was only one. He wondered if it could be the primary officer of Greek Cultural Enterprises. What made it suspicious is that in place of phone numbers there were symbols. Since that made the listing even more mysterious, Lucien decided it was the most important number to investigate. The only initials given for the listing were 'CG'.

At this point, Lucien heard Chante come upstairs with Melodia and take her to their room for Melodia's nap. Gervais was right behind her with the paper tucked under his arm, and he came into their makeshift office in Gervais' room.

"How's it going? Find out anything helpful yet?"

"Yeah, I think I have a lead. I know that at least the attorneys are communicating."

"If there is anything I can do, just let me know." Gervais laid back against his bed's headboard and was going to reopen his newspaper, but Lucien had other ideas.

"I believe I do have something for you to do. I need you to search for news articles published in 1945 and 1946 with any mention of the E.P.E. organization. I have a feeling that it wasn't particularly kept a secret when it was established. In fact, I think it might have made the news. Any places that were attacked during the war and then consequently cleared of debris, especially any archaeological sites, would have been newsworthy. I realize those articles might be in Greek, so first do a world news search, and then use an online translator to search for published articles in Greek. If you need assistance, I'm sure Gala or Nils would help. I'm looking for a name with the initials CG."

Gervais had already opened his computer. "Will do."

Then Chante entered the room. "Anything turn up?"

"Come look at this." Chante looked over his shoulder. "This entry in the agent's phone book has only symbols instead of phone numbers. It must be some kind of substitution cipher. Do you think you could see what you can come up with?"

"Sure, that looks like fun. Send me the list of symbols." Then she got on her laptop to tackle the challenge.

Chapter Twenty-Eight

While Chante and Gervais proceeded with their tasks, Lucien continued to go through the agent's phone listings, and when he completed that he began to read through the agent's texts and emails. On the surface, it seemed the agent led a fairly boring life, working long hours with few outside entertainments, while under the surface it appeared that he was acting in the interests of a secretive organization. He tried to keep fit, as his calendar showed irregular visits with a trainer at an Athens gym, and now and then he booked a handball court. He appeared to be single and preferred it, as no women's names for evening dates were listed. There were several businesses that Lucien cross-checked with the Rhodes' online phone book, but they turned out to be a barber and retail stores.

An hour went by so Lucien decided to check in with Chante and Gervais.

"You two have been very quiet and studious. Anything turn up?"

Gervais nodded slightly and began. "Yes, I have a couple of things, though I'm not sure they will help us. First, I looked at major archaeology magazines. Some are focused only on their own country or region, such as Britain, Mexico, Egypt and the Near East. I ran through the archives of World Archaeology magazine, but their issues only go back to 2003, and Archaeology Magazine only goes back to 1996. National Geographic is the oldest magazine for archaeological articles, as they were first published in

1888. I searched their 1946 and 1947 issues, but all I could see were the front covers and none of the listed articles mentioned Greece. Then I focused on magazines on archaeology specifically based in Greece and found the Journal of Hellenic Studies in English, which had a very interesting article on work from 1945 to 1947. Greece was going through a tough time after the war, and barely able to restore its museums and monuments. Also, the Dodecanese Islands were newly acquired, and it was only just beginning to set up ephorate positions to oversee archaeological sites.

"However, I found two sentences that caught my eye. I quote: 'During this stringent financial period, Greek archaeology was not without a major contributor. Had it not been for a philanthropic organization founded by the Greek shipping magnate Chrysanthos Galanis, work on the Rhodes acropolis could not have continued so quickly after the Italians left the island.'"

This got Lucien to react. "Chrysanthos Galanis — C.G. Did you by any chance do a search on the name?"

"I did, and here is what I found, but I don't think he is going to fit your timeline." Gervais continued to read from his notes. "Chrysanthos Nikator Galanis was born to Yolanda Jacinta and John Latsis Galanis on January 23, 1915. Having learned about ships from his father, who was a captain in the Greek Navy, Chrysanthos, also known as Cy to his associates, began working on several Mediterranean shipping vessels to learn the shipping trade. When his mother died in 1932, he inherited money which allowed him to purchase a small cargo vessel the following year at the age of 25. By the time he was 35, he owned three ships and was a millionaire. He had no brothers or sisters and he never married. He died in 1984 at the age of sixty-nine, leaving his entire fortune to his long-time friend and protégé.' But no name is mentioned."

"We have to find out who that friend and protégé was."

"I could pretend I'm writing a book on the early cargo shipping industry of Rhodes, and walk around the docks asking the oldest people I can find who the big shipping players were during the last fifty years."

"Papa, that's an excellent idea. Would you be willing to do that?"

"Yes, but before I do, I think it might be just as good, if not easier, to ask a local newspaper that's been around for a while if one of their reporters already did that research. This reads like a eulogy, but there could be others that tell more."

"Yes, that would work, too."

Gervais was back to his computer to look for a list of Greek newspapers.

"There are only two newspapers that publish in Rhodes, but their websites don't say when they were established. However, there are half a dozen greater Greek newspapers that have been around since before 1984. It may take me a while to get that information. I'll have to call them and see if I can speak with their historians."

"Sounds good. Thank you." Then Lucien turned his attention to Chante. "Chante, I know I didn't give you much time, but have you come up with anything?"

"You've presented me with a big challenge. First of all, normal encryption uses letters that stand for other letters, known as a transposition cipher. I found out that the Classical Greeks used a scytale transposer where a piece of parchment was wound around a short rod to read a hidden message. But of course, that's not what we have here. Basic code breaking depends upon frequency analysis. But all encryptions take a key to decipher them — the one thing that opens the door to breaking the code. If I was looking for letters then I would base the work on the twenty-four letters of the Greek alphabet. When one has at least a sentence to begin with, one can generally start with a single standalone letter, usually 'a,' and from there look at repeated letter pairs or double letters. Looking at a line of symbols that represent numbers may also start out that way. One would think that only dealing with ten digits, zero through nine, might make it easier, but numbers have their own set of challenges. The most used number in a line of numbers, 9.7 percent of the time, is the number '7'. The second most used number in a line of numbers is the number '3'. The third is '8'. So you can see they don't follow in order. Number '2', for instance, is listed in ninth place.

"We know that a phone number has an area code, followed by a three-digit prefix, and then the line number of four digits, also called a subscriber number. Greek landlines have ten-digit phone numbers that begin with a '2'. Let's set aside those last seven digits for a moment and look at the area codes. Because Greece is so spread out in land mass and has so many islands, no matter where one calls, the area code needs to be used in front of the number being called. There is one place that has only two digits and that is Athens with the number '21'. Also for the Athens area, since it is only two digits, an additional number from zero to six is added after the area code. Some areas of Greece have a three-digit area code, which is used in Heraklion, Kavala, Larissa, Patras, Thessaloniki, and Tripoli. All others have a four-digit area code.

"That might sound like the full number might have more than ten digits, but it doesn't. Athens, with its two-digit area code, is used with an eight-digit number, a three-digit area code is used with a seven-digit number, and the four-digit area code is followed by a six-digit number. So they are always 10 digits. To complicate matters, if one is calling a cell phone, the prefix is always '69'. If we assume this number you gave me is a cell phone, then we know the first two numbers are "69'. I looked for the same symbol in the line of numbers, but a '6' was used only one other time, and after that, it is pure guesswork. So that is as far as we can get."

"Well, you gave it a good try. We'll just have to find out that person's number some other way."

All three continued their work, but then Melodia woke from her nap and wanted some attention, so they took a break.

Just after dinner, Lucien got a notification on his phone that the attorney Axios Milas was making a call. But Lucien was confused because the symbols that displayed were for the individual with the initials C.G., who they thought was Chrysanthos Galanis. But Cy Galanis was dead. He had to be, or he would have been over one-hundred years old! The conversation was in Greek. Lucien raced upstairs to translate the conversation. It was short and instructive. *"The next dig report is in,"* Attorney Milas said. The reply was, *"Need to meet. Bring that and usual package to me tomorrow at usual place and time."*

Lucien's heart began to beat a little faster with anticipation. That had to be the new owner of E.P.E., but it wasn't Cy Galanis. Could that person still be using Cy's same cell number? Was that even possible? Were there cell phones back in 1984? He looked it up. Apparently so. Motorola had produced a mobile phone and it began selling in 1984. They had been extremely expensive though, at $4,000 apiece, which would be a minor amount for a millionaire. But the phone system had changed twice in Greece since that time, so having the same number was impossible. What was more likely is that the new owner must have told Milas not to use his real name in his phone, but to identify him with Cy Galanis' initials. That was pretty smart if he wanted to stay hidden. What was much more promising was the prospect of finding out where they were meeting. Now that Lucien could track the location of the cell phone through Milas' GPS, Lucien felt that he was getting much closer to the mystery man, for now he had a strong feeling that it was not a woman but a man. That night he would sleep with his cell phone on, next to their bed.

Early on Thursday morning, Lucien woke and turned on his computer while Chante and Melodia still slept. Attorney Milas was already on the move in Athens, heading northeast, and then shifting to the southeast. Lucien pulled up a map. It looked like Milas was headed for the Athens airport. If he had made a reservation, he had done it from his laptop or a landline and not his cell. Lucien got dressed and took his phone and laptop downstairs to the living room. Gala was also up early and was surprised to see him. Lucien was happy to receive a cup of coffee as he sat and waited. Then the phone connection broke off. That confirmed it, as he knew that the GPS would not work while Milas' phone was on airplane mode. All Lucien had to do was wait to see where the signal picked up again. Lucien looked up what flights had departed that morning, but there were too many heading in too many destinations to tell. It could be more than a dozen places in Greece.

A little over an hour went by when the connection finally returned. Lucien quickly checked the GPS location. He was shocked when he saw that it was on the island of Rhodes! He nearly knocked his computer off his lap when he jumped up with excitement. He nervously paced the small living room.

What should he do? This was totally unexpected. Would Axios Milas rent a car at the airport? Should Lucien call Inspector Nomikos and have one of her officers make calls to every car rental agency to see if he had rented a car? Could they get the car plate number in time, anyway?

And even if they got to the vehicle and found the place and man he was meeting with, there was no proof that either of them had done anything illegal. Taking the man in for questioning would be fruitless, as he had his attorney with him, who would no doubt instruct his client not to say a word. And then what? Both would be on high alert to lay low, and the chances of catching them doing something illegal would be greatly reduced.

What if Milas just took a taxi? He could certainly afford it, no matter where he was headed on the island. That's what Lucien would do in his place, deliver the report and head right back to Athens. But the short conversation had intimated a discussion. Would they meet at a restaurant, a bar, a park, or maybe at the boss's home? That last possibility seemed unlikely. It was someplace where they had met before. Regardless, Lucien was wasting time. He ran to the kitchen where Gala was preparing breakfast for the family. He quickly asked if he could borrow her car for the morning. She was rather surprised at his hurried manner but she said yes, handed him her keys and told him where the car was parked. He knew he shouldn't go alone, but there just wasn't time to wait for his father, who had not yet come down from his room. Lucien ran out the door and to the lot where many of the residents parked. There he saw Officer Tavoularis and told him he had to run an errand, and asked him to remain and guard his family. The officer could sense his haste and asked if Lucien was sure, but Lucien assured him that he was.

When Lucien got in the car, he checked his phone to see where the GPS was indicating that Milas was headed. He was surprised again when Milas did not head south on Highway 95, but went south along the coastal road. Lucien took off as fast as he could to leave the city. He figured he was about fifteen minutes behind the agent. Just as Lucien was clearing the city, his cell rang. It was Chante.

"What's happened?" she asked.

"The agent took an early flight to Rhodes and is headed south. I'm following him."

"Lucien, you know you should have waited for one of us to go with you. What are you going to do when you catch up to him?"

"Nothing, I am only observing. I don't want him to know that I'm following. This is only to see where he's going. Then I promise I'll be right back."

"I don't like this, Lucien. You're usually more careful."

"Don't worry. I will not engage. I promise I will be *very* careful."

"All right. Please do. I love you."

"I love you too. Now let me concentrate on my driving." And they hung up.

Half an hour later he saw that Milas had turned off the coast road at Kalavarda and headed south on the Apollona Road. When he got to the turnoff, Lucien did the same.

Chapter Twenty-Nine

Lucien continued to follow Milas' GPS signal. The next turn went southwest to the town of Embonas. The Reynards had not come inland on this road, so it was new territory. He'd read about the area were Mount Attavyros rose to the highest point on Rhodes. He saw it looming up in front of him as he got closer to the town. An ancient Greek named Althaemenes, the son of Catreus, the king of Crete, had built a temple at its peak and dedicated it to Zeus, but it was now in ruins.

The GPS movement stopped. Milas had obviously arrived at his destination. Lucien had driven fast, so he had made up five minutes in the last hour, making him only ten minutes behind the attorney. He slowly made his way through the small streets of Embonas to the center of town. The GPS indicated that Milas was nearby. There was a small square where cars were parked under some large trees, so Lucien pulled in. The stores around the lot seemed to be closed, except for a market across the street and a restaurant near the parking lot. He had his doubts that a millionaire would be meeting Milas in a supermarket, so he opted to go into the restaurant. Lucien could detect the smell of good food from his car.

When he entered the restaurant, it was packed. The town had looked nearly deserted, but apparently a bus full of tourists had unloaded and they were all having breakfast. The room was large, with high ceilings of wooden beams, rows of tables, and some with large booths against one wall. There was a bar to one side, and the kitchen was partially open to view. It was noisy and waiters rushed back and forth. It was impossible to tell who Milas was and who he might have met. The place was just too packed with people of all ages. Had there been seating for just two people it might have been easier to spot two men seated together, but everyone ate family style, eight to a table, regardless of the size of their party. He turned around and walked out.

The only thing he could think to do was wait until two men walked out of the restaurant together, or the bus returned to pick up the tourists and cleared most of the room. There was a bench in the shade near his car, so he decided to sit and wait. A few minutes later, an old man with a cane walked gingerly toward him and sat down on the bench with his newspaper. The man nodded hello then opened his paper and began reading. Lucien got an idea and turned toward the man.

"Excuse me. Do you speak English?"

The man shook his head apologetically, but his grin was friendly.

Lucien brought up the translator app on his phone and typed a sentence in English to appear in Greek. *"Do you know of a very wealthy person who lives in or near the village?"*

The man nodded, and pointed up toward the mountain.

Lucien was confused and typed again. *"They live above the village?"*

The man again nodded.

Lucien continued. *"Do you know what the person looks like?"*

The man shook his head no.

"Do you know their name?" Lucien persisted.

The man replied, *"To όνομά του είναι To Liontári."*

This translated to: "His name is the lion."

The man's response confirmed that the person in question was a man, but the name puzzled Lucien, so he repeated the word in Greek, *"To Liontári?"*

Then the old man nodded several times and smiled widely.

Lucien couldn't resist asking and typed. *"Why is he called that?"*

The man just raised his shoulders and shook his head. He didn't know. At least Lucien now had a name. It was obviously not the name the man was born with, but it was a name nonetheless. The old man waited to see if there were more questions, but Lucien just thanked him, *"Sas efcharistó."* At least Lucien knew how to say thank you in Greek. The man nodded in acknowledgment, opened his newspaper and continued reading.

Inside the restaurant, in a back corner, there was a seat for two people that Lucien had not seen as it was behind a wall. Normally it was used only by employees taking their breaks, but today it was being used by a special guest. Axios Milas handed over the report from Professor Ekonomos, which had been passed on to him by the Council's secretary. The Lion picked up the small blue folder, opened it and read it. The report did not contain what he was hoping for. He pulled out the printed pages, folded them in half, and put them into an inside pocket of his jacket. Then he handed the folder back to Axios.

Axios then handed over a briefcase full of cash for the man to use for the next month. Then he leaned forward. "There's something I need to tell you, sir, but I didn't want to say so on the phone. That detective I told you about who was working on the theft from the acropolis with the Rhodes police, showed up at the council meeting two days ago wanting to know who was funding the E.P.E. The council did not tell him."

The lion leaned forward with a smirk. "Good." Then he sat back and squinted with thought. "There is something I want you to do for me. Dump the remaining items taken from the site someplace outside of Athens. I don't care where. Then submit another application for a third dig this season, and make sure it gets accepted."

Axios nodded. "Yes, sir."

The Lion finished the last bite of ham on his plate and pushed the plate away. Then he stood, took the briefcase, and walked out the back door, where his chef and sometime driver was waiting. As soon as he left, Axios breathed a heavy sigh. He would be glad to be rid of the stolen items. He finished his eggs, laid money on the table to pay for both meals, and then he also went out the back door.

While waiting outside the restaurant, Lucien watched several middle-aged and elderly women and two older couples come out, but not two men or a single older man. A few minutes later the tour bus pulled up right in front of the restaurant to pick up all the tourists it had deposited earlier and completely blocked Lucien's view. He patiently waited ten minutes while all the passengers got in, and then watched it leave with a trail of gray exhaust behind it.

Lucien now focused on the front door of the restaurant, but when no one exited after a few minutes, he couldn't wait any longer and crossed the street. He tried to look through a window, but couldn't see anything. He went in to look around, but the place was completely empty of anyone sitting and eating. There was no one but three waiters rushing around clearing tables. Lucien silently cursed and went back to his car. He opened his laptop and watched the GPS slowly move a street away from the square, stop, and then move more quickly toward him. Lucien looked up just in time to see the back of a taxi go around the corner. He thought about quickly following after the taxi, but changed his mind. He would explore the mountain instead. A millionaire's home should be fairly easy to spot.

He drove to the east side of the village, traversing several dirt roads that went up the hillside. There were groves of olive trees and lots of terraced vineyards, some ranch-like buildings and a few small farmhouses, but nothing that struck him as being a place where a millionaire would reside. He finally decided to drive south of town and stopped at a café to get directions to other roads that went up the hillside. The hostess understood only a small amount of English. She assumed he was looking for the road up to the temple like most who came to the area, so she showed him on a map at the hostess stand used for this precise reason. She pointed to the road he should take.

He followed her directions, though not intent on driving to the top. As he wound back and forth on the steep and narrow paved road, partway up the mountain he saw a glimmer against the hillside and wondered what it was. As he continued to climb, he realized that it was sunlight reflecting off a large window. After a turn of the road, suddenly he came to a large closed gate to his left. He drove a little higher to get a better view of the house. The road narrowed and became gravel, so he slowed. On one turn higher on the hill, he was able to look down and get a glimpse of a fairly modern building, built on three levels, with vineyards draping down the hill around it. Now *that*, he thought to himself, is a wealthy man's home. He briefly stopped to take a picture of it with his phone and note the GPS coordinates. Then he checked Milas' GPS and saw that the taxi was headed north back to the city.

Lucien decided to do the same, but first he called Chante.

"Did you find him?" she asked.

"I was able to follow Milas to a restaurant. But it was so crowded with tourists that I couldn't tell one person from another. I waited out front on a bench to see if two men would come out, but a bus blocked my view so I must have missed them. While I waited, I had the company of a local old man who sat next to me. From him I was able to find out that the wealthiest man in the area lives part way up Mount Attavyros. I've been driving around the hillside and I think I found the house. And the old man furnished me with a name of sorts, 'the Lion'."

"The Lion? That's an odd nickname. What now?"

"Tell Gala I'm on my way back with her car."

"Okay, see you soon."

When Lucien returned to the B&B, he saw the GPS indicate that Milas had flown back to Athens.

That afternoon while Melodia was napping, Chante, Lucien and Gervais met in Gervais' room to discuss their situation.

"It was a good day, despite not seeing what Milas or 'the Lion' look like. At least I think I now know where the man lives and the name he uses."

"Well, I was busy while you were gone," said Gervais. "This morning I called each of the six Greek newspapers that have been around since prior to 1984, before Cy Galanis died. I told them I was writing a book on the Greek cargo shipping business for the last fifty years and wanted to know about the key industry players. I had to have Gala's help with some Greek to clarify what I wanted, but I was able to connect with one man who just happens to be coming to Rhodes in two days. He said he would check in his archives tonight and agreed to meet with me."

"Good, now you can ask him about a man called 'the Lion'."

"What else can we do?" asked Chante.

"I'm going to keep an eye on the attorney and follow up on any new intel from his texts, emails and GPS, but there isn't anything else to do for now aside from that." Then Lucien got an idea when he saw their fallen faces. "I've had you three cooped up at the B&B for a few days. What do you say we have Chloe take us out for another bit of island touring? I'm not sure what's left to visit. We've seen most of what the island has to offer. But maybe we can have Gala pack us a picnic lunch and we'll take a drive. There is a large lake in the middle of the island. It might be a good place to get away and perhaps see some Rhodian deer."

Gervais thought that would make for a nice break. Chante beamed with the idea of getting away for the day. Besides, Melodia was getting tired of her toys and needed some distraction. Chante called Chloe immediately and asked if she was available to take them on a day tour. Chloe was glad to hear from them and had wondered if everything was okay. Chante explained that they had taken a couple of days to relax and remain at the B&B because of the heat, but now they were ready to venture out again. Chloe explained that it was the last weekend she would be free, as she was leaving Rhodes and going to England on vacation for a couple of weeks before school started again in September.

When the Lion returned to his house, he went into his private chamber and put the cash he had received in his vault. He also could not resist once again looking at his two gold chain pieces. Compulsively, he picked one up and ran his fingers over the fine snake chain. Then he picked up the second piece and did the same. He had hoped that more of the chain would have been unearthed by now. He was not getting any younger. He needed more time, along with some luck. The gold sparkled enticingly under the desk lamp. With a sudden impulse, he grasped both pieces and put them into his pocket. Just feeling his fingers rub over the two pieces elated him.

That night, the Lion decided to celebrate. An overwhelming sense of wellbeing came over him. Touching the chain pieces had brought on a sense of euphoria. The chef announced that he had purchased a fresh baby goat that morning and would roast it, just like his boss preferred. An hour later, the Lion nodded with satisfaction while he sat on his terrace. He was enjoying glass after glass of his own Mandilaria wine, while inhaling the scent of the goat roasting over the coals on a spit. By the time the roasting was done, the Lion was ravenous. Instead of having the goat sliced, he insisted on having the entire thing set on a large platter in front of him so he could break off what he wanted and chew on it to his heart's content. Finally, after gorging himself, he pushed the platter aside and ordered a bottle of Souma. He drank until he could barely make it to his bed, and there he collapsed, still dressed.

Chapter Thirty

That evening, Lucien kept a close eye on the attorney's communications, but nothing significant showed. He let Officer Tavoularis know that he would not be needed the following day to watch the B&B, as they would all be going on a drive and having a picnic.

The next morning Chloe arrived and sat with a cup of coffee while Gala finished packing a picnic lunch which Chloe was sure contained more food than they needed. Melodia insisted on taking her stuffed donkey so it could drink from the lake, and her bathing suit so she could play in the water.

Just before they were to leave, Lucien went upstairs to check on the attorney's communications. He saw that Milas had sent a text to an unknown person. The text read, *"Meet me at the following address in one hour. I need you to deliver a package for me."*

The person who was sent the address replied: *"Will be there."*

Chante stood at the base of the stairs and called up to Lucien that they were packed and ready to leave.

Lucien quickly looked up the address the attorney had sent and saw that it was a public storage facility. This more than intrigued Lucien. He immediately suspected that the attorney had received the stolen goods. As soon as he realized this, a flutter hit his stomach and a chill ran up his back. This was it! He saw that Milas was on the move and heading toward that address. Lucien went down stairs and spoke to Chante.

"Chante, something has come up. I have to stay here and follow this lead."

A frown appeared on her face. "Lucien, you promised we would have the day together."

"I know, but I can't. You, Melodia and Gervais go. I'll keep in touch by phone."

Chante took a deep breath and agreed. She knew that when Lucien got that look on his face and that sound in his voice, it meant he had a hot lead and couldn't let it go. Disappointed by not having his company, she wished him luck and said she would see him later.

Lucien went back to his computer and five minutes later, he saw another text from the person Milas had contacted.

"*Running behind. My car wouldn't start. Getting a charge from my neighbor. Will be there as soon as I can.*"

Fifteen minutes later, Lucien saw another text from Milas: "*Where are you?*"

The man replied: "*On my way, be there in twenty minutes.*"

Milas responded: "*Can't wait that long. Have to be in court in half an hour. Leaving box behind large trash bin at the back of the storage yard.*"

The man replied: "*Fine. To what address should I deliver the package? And when do I get paid?*"

Milas texted back: "*Sending address. DO NOT break the seal on the box. Will send payment when job is done.*"

Lucien looked up the address and saw it was outside the city limits, at a city dump. He had to act quickly and make a call. Luckily, the phone was answered.

"Inspector Nomikos. I've got a strong lead on where the stolen items have been taken."

"You do? Where?"

"I believe they are at a public storage facility in Athens. I need you to make contact with the local police and have them go to the address I'm sending you. Have them watch for a man picking up a box at the back of the building in the alley. But hurry, the officers only have twenty minutes to get there."

"Will do," and she hung up.

A rusted 2002 Toyota Camry slowly rolled down the dirt alley behind the Thanpoulos Public Storage Company. Ahead was a large blue waste container, and just behind one of the rear wheels on the ground was a brown cardboard box. The driver pulled to a stop and got out. He bent over, reached for the box and slid it out. It was heavy and his curiosity was aroused. Milas would never know if he opened it, so he decided to take a look. He pulled out a knife from his back pocket and slid it across the taped box top. Then he closed the knife and put it back into his pocket. When he opened the box and lifted the scrunched up newspaper on top, he saw a series of bundles wrapped in more newsprint. When he opened the first bundle he saw some old coins. His eyes grew wide with excitement.

But the man was puzzled. Why was he supposed to take these things to the dump? He had a much better plan. He would take them to a pawn shop and get money for them, plus get the money for the job. And he knew just the pawn shop to take them to—a place where he had taken things for years, where no questions were asked and money was readily handed over. He unwrapped another package and saw an old metal bracelet which had turned green with age. He reckoned he could clean it up nicely. When he unwrapped a third item and it was the head of a spear, he was elated. Yeah, he thought, he'd make really good money with this box. He quickly wrapped the items back up and closed the box. He opened the trunk of his car and carefully lifted the box and put it in. Then he got into the car and slowly drove away down the dirt alley back toward town.

As the man turned out of the alley and on to the main street, a police car pulled in front of him so suddenly that he almost hit it. A police officer told the man to get out of the car, while a second officer reached in, turned off the car, took the keys and opened the trunk. He opened the box and nodded to his partner with a grin. The man was handcuffed while the other officer radioed in that the suspect had been apprehended and they were coming in with the box of goods.

Half an hour later, the man sat in a holding cell, and Inspector Nomikos was informed that the stolen items had been retrieved and a man was being held. They had already obtained the list of stolen items from her. They quickly went through the list and let her know that everything was there except for one item, the snake chain. Inspector Nomikos called Lucien to let him know. When Lucien heard the news, he loudly yelled "Oui!" The inspector told him to come into the station to make a statement concerning his involvement. Lucien's heart skipped a small beat, but he was prepared for this. Nomikos said the Athens police were running tests for fingerprints on the items, which would take a few hours. And the man who was picked up had yet to be interviewed. But she expected Lucien in her office the following morning, and he readily agreed to be there.

After his burst of excitement he sat exhausted, but he had one more thing to do before he could call Chante. Lucien went online to close out the app he had used to track Milas. The cloud site was wiped clean. Then he called Chante to tell her the good news.

"Hello, my love."

"Lucien, is everything okay?"

"Better than okay. The stolen items have been retrieved outside a storage facility in Athens, and a man is being held for questioning."

"Lucien, that's wonderful! Including the gold chain?"

"No, but I think I know where it is."

"The man who was picked up, was he the Lion?"

"No, but it won't be too much longer before he is caught, too."

"Oh, my love, that is excellent news!"

"Where are you, Chante?"

"We're at that lake you mentioned, the—let me see if I can get this right—the Limni Fragmatos Gadoura. And it is beautiful here. I wish you could see it. We spotted a small herd of Rhodian deer as soon as we arrived. Now Gervais has rolled up his pant legs and is getting his feet wet walking with Melodia along the shoreline, while Chloe and I are getting ready to lay out a feast for lunch."

"It sounds wonderful, but don't hurry back on my account. Enjoy your day and I'll see you when you return." They said goodbye and hung up.

Then Lucien lay back on the bed and closed his eyes. He hadn't slept much in the last couple of days.

The next morning, Lucien was at the Rhodes police station by nine o'clock and was escorted to Inspector Nomikos office. She stood and smiled widely at him when he entered. They shook hands and were seated.

"What's the news from Athens, Inspector Nomikos?"

"Not surprisingly, the fingerprints of the man we picked up were found on the outside of the cardboard box and on three of the items inside. Additional prints were found on the items and we are running a trace on them. Even after a couple hours of hard questioning, the man is not talking and refuses a lawyer. The Athens police retrieved his phone and after examining all of his communications, they determined that he had been instructed to pick up the box by an Athens attorney named Axios Milas. Two officers went to the attorney's home bright and early this morning. He has been arrested for the theft, and information on his phone is being analyzed."

"All of that is excellent news," replied Lucien.

"Detective Reynard, I have to ask, how did you know that box would be there at that time?"

Lucien was ready. "Remember when I told you I went to Athens last Tuesday and found out the name of the Agent of Service? Well, I had to act on that information somehow." All this was the truth. "After that, inspector, I cannot divulge my sources."

"So you hired someone to follow him?"

Lucien paused and raised his eyebrows. It was as good an answer as any. "I cannot say."

"But the call to the Athens police came from me. How am I going to explain how I got that information?"

"You could say that you were acting on information from an informant, whose identity you cannot disclose."

Inspector Nomikos looked at Lucien askew. "But *you* are the one who informed me."

"Exactly, inspector."

She sat back in her chair and thought about that.

"Then I have to assume you used means that were not exactly permitted."

"On the contrary. As an officer of the law, I used what I have permission to use and it seems it has paid off, much to the relief of our side of the law."

"You realize, of course, that there is still one piece missing from the list of items that were taken?"

"Yes, I do. And I have a feeling it will be turning up fairly soon."

"And how do you know that? Wait, don't tell me. I suppose I will be receiving a call from the same informant."

"Perhaps you will."

"Well, I'm not sure I completely approve of your methodology, but whatever it is, it seems to be working."

"There is one thing I would ask, inspector."

"And what is that, Reynard?"

"It might be wise to keep the attorney's apprehension out of the press for now. The person with the gold chain might go into hiding and that would spoil our chances of getting it back."

"What about reporting the box of goods that was retrieved and the man found with it?"

"That should be all right, but nothing else, for now."

"Well, how long is this to be kept quiet?"

"Not long. Maybe twenty-four hours."

"I'll do what I can, but then I expect some answers."

"Yes, inspector. I promise."

"Okay, but write out your statement before you leave."

Lucien agreed and they both stood.

"And Detective Reynard, good work."

Chapter Thirty-One

The next day, Lucien's plan was to borrow the car again and drive directly to the Lion's home and confront him. Because Gervais had his meeting with the newspaper historian at a nearby restaurant, Lucien dropped him off and then headed south. Lucien wanted to meet the Lion for himself. He wasn't even sure he would be able to get past the driveway gate, but he had seen an intercom there and thought he might be able to talk his way in. He would say that Axios Milas had sent him to deliver some important papers to sign, and that the attorney could not come on his own as he had to be in court. If the man tried to reach his attorney, he would not be able to. If there was a problem getting in, he would call Inspector Nomikos and a search could be conducted.

However, when Lucien reached the town of Embonas and turned onto the narrow paved road that wound up the hillside to the Lion's house, an ambulance roared toward him down the hill, blaring its siren. He had to quickly pull over onto the dirt shoulder in order for the large vehicle to go by. He thought that some hiker going to the Temple of Zeus must have been hurt. When he got to the gate to the Lion's property, it was wide open and a police vehicle with its blue light on was just coming out. Not wanting to be a part of that situation, he slowly cruised past the gate and continued up the hill to the same place he had parked before to look down on the house. Another police vehicle was parked in front of the house and an officer was speaking to a man wearing a dark blue striped apron. Lucien sat there watching, wondering what to do. A few minutes later, the officer left. Lucien was tempted to drive in and find out what was going on, but he decided that might not be a good idea. Instead, he made a call.

"Hello, Inspector Nomikos. It's Reynard. I'm near the home of the man whom I am certain has the gold chain, but several police cars are here and someone was just rushed off in an ambulance. Can you find out who was just taken away, where he went and what has happened?"

"Why were you approaching a subject without backup?"

"I was not approaching. I was simply watching his house."

"All right. I'll find out what's up and let you know. What's the address?"

Lucien didn't have the address, as none was listed at the gate, but he gave her the exact GPS coordinates and told her it was located on the hillside above the village of Embonas. There was nothing he could do now but drive back to the city.

Half an hour later, while Lucien was still on the road, he got a call back from the inspector.

"Yes, inspector. What did you find out?"

"It seems the occupant of the home was discovered unresponsive this morning in his bedroom by his personal chef. By the time the ambulance arrived, he was pronounced dead. His body has been taken to Rhodes General Hospital."

"How strange, I wonder what happened."

"I don't know, but I'm heading there myself. We can meet there."

"Will do. I should be there in about half an hour."

Now Lucien was more than perplexed. What could have happened so suddenly to the man? Had someone gotten to him for some unknown reason? Was it someone after the gold chain? Could Inspector Nomikos conduct a search in the home for the gold chain now? He hoped the answers would soon be known.

Lucien arrived at the hospital and made his way to where Inspector Nomikos was waiting to speak to the pathologist. After half an hour, a female doctor came out to speak with them.

"Doctor, what happened?" asked Inspector Nomikos.

"We don't know yet. We are prepared to perform an autopsy, but we need to wait until his next of kin can be notified and can come to identify the body. Do you know the man's name? There was no identifying information on him. An officer interviewed the man's personal chef, but even he didn't know the man's real name. The chef was instructed only to call him 'sir,' but he didn't know the man's real name. Do you?"

"No, we don't know his real name." Nomikos answered, then looked at Lucien. "But he has been under surveillance in connection with an archaeological theft."

The doctor nodded. "Then follow me."

The doctor led them down the hall and into an examination room where items were laid out on a table.

"These are the clothes he came in with. He was found fully clothed in pants and a shirt, and these two items were found in his pocket."

The two pieces of gold chain were on the table.

"Those two pieces of chain were stolen."

"You will be able to take possession of them as soon as the paperwork has been completed."

"Well, be very careful with them. They may have a high value."

At that moment Lucien's phone vibrated. It was Gervais. Lucien excused himself and stepped into the hallway.

"Papa, what's up?"

"I've got news for you. The man I met from the Athens paper was very helpful. He said that it took some doing, but he had a list of all the big names in the cargo vessel business for the last fifty years, including Chrysanthos Galanis. Of course, besides that name, I wouldn't know one name from another, but when I said I had heard of a man simply called 'the Lion,' and that he inherited the shipping business from the man named Galanis, he pointed to a name on the list. The man's real name is Adrian Pancas Rosi."

"Papa, you're a wonder! Do you know anything more about him? Did he ever marry or have children? Any living relatives?"

"No. None of those. He was a loner who was known for his reclusiveness."

"Thank you, Papa. Thank you very much. I've got to run, but I'll meet you at the B&B soon."

Lucien returned to the room.

"We have just found out the man's real name. It is Adrian Pancas Rosi, he never married and he has no known relatives."

"Can we see the body?" asked Nomikos. "I would like to see exactly who has caused us so much trouble."

"Yes, of course. If you just stand over here at this window, I will go into the next room and open the curtains so you can see him."

Finally, after all this time, they would be able to see this elusive man. When the curtains opened, they stepped forward and saw the man on his back with a white cloth covering most of his body. Only his head was showing. He was at least seventy years old, with short white hair, a white chevron moustache, and gray eyebrows. The doctor returned.

"If the police department can confirm there are no relatives, then we can conduct the autopsy.

Nomikos nodded. "Go ahead. We need to know what happened to him."

"The autopsy will take a couple of hours."

Nomikos gave the doctor her card and thanked her. The inspector promised to call Lucien as soon as she had heard the results of the autopsy.

Lucien returned to the B&B after picking up Gervais from the restaurant. He sincerely thanked Nils for the loan of the car, once again. Nils was relieved, as he had to pick up new customers arriving at the airport who were booked to stay at the B&B that weekend.

Now that the case was coming to a close, Inspector Nomikos dismissed Officer Tavoularis, who came to the B&B door to say goodbye. The Reynards sincerely thanked him for his work, and the officer wished them well.

Four hours after Lucien left the hospital, at 4:20 that afternoon, he got a call from Inspector Nomikos.

"I've got the results from the autopsy, but you're not going to believe it."

The Reynards were in Gervais' room talking while Melodia was playing in the garden. Lucien put the phone on speaker so Chante and Gervais could also hear the results.

"Go ahead, inspector."

"The man had high blood pressure and a deteriorating liver brought on by too much alcohol over his lifetime. He had a very high amount of alcohol in his blood at the time of his death. But it wasn't the alcohol that did him in. It took the doctors additional time to find out the cause of death. It seems the man had a voracious appetite and had consumed a great amount of goat meat the night before, which was found in his stomach. But it wasn't overeating that killed him. It seems that while eating so much goat the night before, he also swallowed a sharp sliver of bone. It's surprising that it didn't lacerate his throat. The bone sliver punctured his stomach lining and caused him to die slowly from internal bleeding. He might have awakened due to the pain, but because he had passed out from the alcohol, he never did. If he had, he could have been rushed to a hospital and possibly been saved."

"Whoa, I've never heard of such a thing."

"Well, you have now. The coroner said it was extremely rare and it was the first case he had come across. The man's chef said he very often ate roasted goat. It was his favorite meat.

"I have more news. The prints on the other items in the box were found to belong to a man whose phone number happened to be on the attorney's phone. We believe that man was working for the attorney and acted as a middleman between the attorney and Bouras. It was most likely he who killed Bouras. He has been arrested, and it looks like he made calls from a building across from the hotel that overlooked the acropolis."

"Well, that ties things up nicely."

"And, by the way, all the stolen items arrived from Athens this morning, and I delivered them with the gold chains to the curator of the archaeological museum. Because they were the stolen items that got so much press, the curator has decided they will go on display. The official opening of the display will be held tomorrow at 3:00. The press will be there, and I've been asked to deliver a statement summarizing the crime and the recovery of the items. But if you want to be there for the placement of the items in the display, the curator asked that you and your team be there an hour before so he can personally thank you."

"Thank you, inspector. We'll be there."

That night, the Reynards decided to take a walk and go out to dinner to celebrate, finally feeling safe. They all agreed that it was time to go back home to France as soon as possible. Now that the case had been solved, Lucien gave Monsieur Teniet a call and told him the entire story of the search for the truth and how the mystery had been solved. Teniet could only be amazed once again at Detective Reynard's determination and perseverance in solving another case.

The next day they were at the museum, along with Inspector Nomikos, and the historian Eugene Manikas. They watched as the curator opened the glass case. All of the stolen pieces had been put on display in the case, and the two pieces of gold chain had been carefully pinned together to hang from an abbreviated model of a neckline so they could be best exhibited. When all of the items were properly placed and the glass display case was locked, the curator expressed his thanks for the return of all the items which had been stolen. But the necklace, sparkling under a special small light, took center stage. Small cards listed what the pieces were, their approximate age, and where they had been unearthed. But nothing of the necklace's possible mythical connection was included, for only the Reynards had looked into its fabled history.

After Manikas, the curator, and Nomikos stepped aside to discuss the preparations for the official opening, Chante, Gervais, and Lucien, who now held Melodia in his arms, all stared at the items in the case.

"Odd don't you think?" commented Gervais. "That the man's last name was Rosi, meaning 'rose'? Rhodes means 'where roses grow,' because of the unique Rhodian rose, but no other person on the island had that last name."

Lucien agreed. "So, he was unique unto himself. He was the rose of Rhodes."

"What do you think, my love?" asked Chante. "Do you think it was the curse of the necklace that caused the man to die, or do you think it was a goat that finally got back at a lion?"

Lucien shrugged his shoulders, not knowing. "He was so desperate to believe what his mentor had told him about the necklace that he lived his life believing something that most likely wasn't true."

Chante looked up at him. "Or was it? Look at what happened to him."

Lucien shook his head. "I guess we will never know. He had money and power but it only took one prick to cause his death."

Melodia turned to her father. "Everyone knows that roses have thorns. He should have been more careful."

Author's Note

The Greek Dodecanese island of Rhodes, located in the south Aegean Sea, is known for its ancient Colossus of Rhodes and as the historic home of the Knights of Saint John of Jerusalem from the early 1300s to the mid-1500s. The island has a long history, spanning the Minoan, Mycenaean, Archaic and Classical eras and the Hellenic, Roman and Byzantine periods. It was ruled by Crusaders from eight different countries and Turkish Ottomans, it was occupied by the Italians and Germans, and was under British administration for two years before finally becoming part of Greece in 1947. The island is an archaeological treasure chest of discoveries from all periods, with Greek Orthodox, Latin Catholic, Ottoman Turkish and Judaic contributions which have added to Rhodes' culture and architecture. There are only forty-three towns and villages housing its approximately 115,000 inhabitants. Rhodes greatly depends upon tourism, and to a lesser extent, on stockbreeding, fishing, and agricultural produce including olives, wine grapes, and citrus fruits.

I visited Rhodes in 2005 and remember especially the narrow streets of the old city, its extensive and rich cuisine, its archaeological wonders and its exquisite panoramas. It was easy to feel the deep scars that the island had endured, but also equally stimulating to appreciate how the island had persevered and thrived. With a land so full of contrasts, placing a mystery within its shores was a pleasurable undertaking.

How could I not take the Reynards on another amazing adventure? The research talents of Chante and Gervais are as sharp as ever. Lucien's additional training for the last six years proves advantageous in tracking down archaeological thieves, and the most elusive criminal of all. And for the first time, Chante and Lucien are joined by their six-year-old daughter, Melodia. When I first wrote *The Rose of Rhodes*, the world's pandemic was only beginning, and because Lucien would not have risked his family's lives, Melodia got older as we all waited for a time when the Reynards could continue their adventures. At last, in 2022, it became possible for them to do just that.

There are many places that the Reynards visit in the story, and each of them really exists on the island — at least they did at the time I wrote this book. There are five ports around Rhodes, so it seemed natural to have the villain's wealth come from a long successful cargo shipping enterprise. The two older archaeological digs of 1912 and in 1946 did take place, so it was easy to add a new dig at the Acropolis of Rhodes. The B&B within the old city where the Reynards stayed was much like the one I stayed in when I visited.

Greek mythology plays a major role in this story. It begins with how the island got its name from the nymph Rhodos, who had seven sons with the sun god Helios. Helios is named several times when Chloe guides them around the old city. The name Rhodes is believed to be derived from the Greek word "rhodon" which translates to "rose." The rose is also a symbol of the island. Because of the island's name, it seemed even more appropriate to give the mystery man the last name of Rosi, also meaning "rose."

At the heart of the mystery is the story of the Necklace of Harmonia. The tale of the necklace revealed by Lucien, describes the long story of how it was handed down, family by family, all the way to the tyrant Phayllus, who did historically exist. The Greek god Hephaestus was reputed to have fashioned the necklace. If the great poet Hesiod believed that the so-called "Golden Age" of the Olympian gods was approximately around 1710 BCE, and we now know that humans roamed the earth well before that period of time, those gods may have been simply embellishments of a real group of ancient people who lived in the foothills of Mount Olympus. And if fine metal-working of gold chains was documented to have occurred in Egypt in 2500 BCE, who's to say that serpentine gold chains couldn't have been produced during the Golden Age, eight hundred years later?

Where does the fable end and the truth begin? Could remnants of the original necklace still be found? Could such a curse still be attached to it, as the character Adrian Pancas Rosi experienced? Various archaeological digs and rescue excavations continued on Rhodes between 1970 and 1990, and more began in 2000. Most of the discoveries have been Hellenistic, but others have widened the understanding of the island's long history in more detail, and will continue to do so. Who knows what future treasures the archaeologists on Rhodes might dig up?

Other Books by the Author

Poetry
From the Mundane to the Magical
Poetic Emanations of Light, Life, Love & Liberty
The Town with the Feather Crest

Cookbook
The Thelemic Cookbook: Cooking with Correspondences

International Mystery and Crime
The Collioure Concealment
Murder of the Mystras Nun
The Cypriot Secret
Hiding in Paradise
The Blythewood Curse
The Sylvan Woods of Lake Nemi

Social Commentary
Sticks and Balls: A Sexologist Pokes Fun at Sports

Fantasy
Pearl and Garridan: A Roma Love Story

Forthcoming Books

International Crime and Murder
Isis' Secret Treasure
(An archaeological mystery set in Egypt)

Panic in Patpong
(A spy story set in Thailand)

About the Author

Lita-Luise Chappell writes poetry, short stories, mysteries, plays, lyrics, rituals, cookbooks, investigative articles, social commentary, reviews, and travelogues. With her background in psychology, half a dozen careers, many world travels, and a magical perspective, her broad experiences and opinions are reflected in everything she writes. Her works have been published in books, magazines, journals, and online. She lives in Southern California with her husband, Vere Chappell, and their cat, Lily. Visit her online at litachappell.com, and find her works on amazon.com.

www.ingramcontent.com/pod-product-compliance
Lightning Source LLC
Chambersburg PA
CBHW060417260626
47161CB00013B/718